Beasts *of* Burden

Imayam

Translated from Tamil by
Lakshmi Holmström

THORNBIRD
NIYOGI
BOOKS

Published by
NIYOGI BOOKS
Block D, Building No. 77,
Okhla Industrial Area, Phase-I,
New Delhi-110 020, INDIA
Tel: 91-11-26816301, 26818960
Email: niyogibooks@gmail.com
Website: www.niyogibooksindia.com

Jacket image: Painting by Perumal
Coordination courtesy: Apparao Galleries, Chennai

Editor: Mini Krishnan
Design: Shraboni Roy

ISBN: 978-93-86906-62-5
Publication: 2019

Printed at: Niyogi Offset Pvt. Ltd., New Delhi, India

Contents

A Note from the Publisher

Niyogi Books is happy to publish this revised edition of Lakshmi Holmstrom's translation of Imayam's first novel. In a sense it was her last work. The first edition of *Beasts of Burden* was published by Manas, an imprint of East West Books (Chennai) and edited by Subashree Krishnaswamy (2001).

This second edition has been made possible by Mini Krishnan who completed the revision of those sections Lakshmi Holmstrom was unable to finish.

Author's Note

Koveru Kazhuthaigal is my first novel. I wrote it in 1987 when I was 20 and while studying for my bachelor's degree. The work, however, appeared in print only in 1994. Soon after its release, the novel faced serious criticisms and opened up debates on Dalit identity and Dalit literature in multiple spheres including the political.

Twenty-four years have passed since then. Debates on this novel continue even today. No dip in sales either! After that I wrote four novels: *Arumugam* (1999), *Sedal* (2006), *En Kathe* (2015), *Sellatha Pananam* (2018); and five short story collections: *Man Baram* (2002), *Video Marimman* (2008), *Kolai Seval* (2013), *Saavu Soru* (2014), *Narumanam* (2016). Even today people introduce me in public forums as 'the author of *Koveru Kazhuthaigal*'. Anyone who approaches me says: 'I have read your novel *Koveru Kazhuthaigal*'. All these years it was *Koveru Kazhuthaigal* that defined both me and my writing.

When I read the novel now as its English translation is being prepared for a reprint, I do not get the feeling that it could have been written this or that way. Nor do I get a feeling that a line may be added or removed. I can confidently say that I wrote it well.

I will not say that the novels and the short stories that I have written so far, have been written intelligently, intellectually and sensibly. Neither did I write in order to marked out as a writer, nor do I continue writing to remain so. It was the fire of everyday life that forced me to write and keeps driving me to write. I do not see society with any likes or dislikes. Never did I view society through a lens of theory, say Marxist or Feminist, realist or existentialist, modernist or postmodernist. Nor will I ever, in future. In the creative universe, maintaining a disinterested vision is more important than assuming an ideological position. My writing helps me understand both society and the world I live in. To me, writing and literature are cultural activities. I am very particular that I should not use my writing to shoot down rats.

The world is an ocean, in which concepts and theories are like ships which appear and disappear. My works were not composed with the comfort offered by these ships, but written from within the sea and by looking at its vastness. My writings try to draw a map of the time, place and culture of the geographical space in which I live. That was how *Koveru Kazhuthaigal* came into being. From the time of creation itself, from the time humans began to think, speak, write and preach, the most widely preached and written message is: 'Learn to love and how to love fellow humans'. But the only thing that the human animal did not want to learn and did not like to follow is this love. 'Learn to love and how to love' is what I have been saying in my writings. That too in the most direct way possible, and with the utmost simplicity.

I would like to convey my sincere thanks to S. Ramakrishnan who published *Koveru Kazhuthaigal* in Tamil in Cre-A publications; Lakshmi Holmström who translated it into English; Manas publishers who brought out its first edition. I also thank Nirmal Kanti of Niyogi Books the publisher of this second edition, and Dr Mark Holmström who permitted us to do so. I thank Prof. R. Azhagarasan, (who never campaigns for my writing), for his candid foreword to this second edition and for his translation of this note.

Ms. Mini Krishnan was the one who kept saying that *Koveru Kazhuthaigal* has to get visibility in the English world. She cares not only for my works but for all good writing. I cannot just thank her. In the *Ramayana*, while introducing Gugan to Raman, his brother Lakshman says: "(He is) greater than a mother!" I am now reminded of those words. We do not have the culture of thanking mothers!

Imayam

Foreword

I have certain questions about the beliefs and behaviours of the society I live in. I have disagreements with its values and its pronouncement of justice. This forms the core of my writing.

– Imayam

Next year we are going to celebrate the 25th anniversary of Imayam's epoch-making novel, *Koveru Kazhuthaigal*. Imayam has now become a celebrated Tamil writer with three more novels. His short stories have appeared both in literary journals as well as in popular magazines, winning the attention of a wide range of readers. Niyogi's reprint of the English translation of *Koveru Kazhuthaigal – Beasts of Burden –* by the acclaimed translator, Lakshmi Holmström, is coming to us sixteen years after its first appearance in 2001. Notwithstanding Imayam's critical remarks on Dalit literature and his continual resistance to his works being read within the framework of Dalit literature, *Koveru Kazhuthaigal* has acquired a unique place in the history of Tamil Dalit literature.

Today we may find it easy to read *Koveru Kazhuthaigal* as a Dalit novel with the received knowledge of the Dalit uprising of the 1990s, of our acquaintance with a range of Dalit literature that have appeared in Indian languages and been made accessible through their English or vernacular translations. We may also like to locate the novel today within the dialectics of Dr. Ambedkar's 125th birth anniversary, the visibility of Dalit movements in the electoral politics and the renewed violence against Dalits as reported in the mainstream media. But Imayam's visibility among the Tamil readers does not have any direct link with these celebrations and debates. He has been continually challenging such attempts to invoke an ideology out of his fictional universe.

Imayam's stories represent the moments that go beyond our narrow understanding of social relations limited to caste. His stories continue to warn us against our desire for easy solutions and oppositions. Naturally, he is scorned by different circles with varied ideologies. While a few regard *Koveru Kazhuthaigal* as an anti-Dalit text for representing the function of caste among Dalits, some (especially the academic readers) like to read it simply as a Dalit text. For example, the abusive dialogues between characters – which are part of the narrative and are rooted in everyday situations – cannot be regarded as an attack on a particular social class nor can be classified as 'dalit language'. However, those who seek diversity praise Imayam's ability to vouch for the truth of caste, not just Dalit oppression. He stands for love, but is read only as a Dalit writer who launches a protest against the dominant. This is similar to the reception of writers like Mahmoud Darwish, the Palestinian poet. The 'love' these writers try to represent is not just a humanistic one. It suggests the recognition of love that would serve as an answer to despair. For Imayam, caste, along with gender, is an institution that establishes a strict binary between love and hate, and one against which everyone should protest. Caste thus becomes a significant social factor that obstructs the language of love and destabilizes social well-being. It is this view on caste as the lack of love in human relations – that has secured him the status of a celebrity writer among the Tamil readers.

We may justify our reading of Imayam's fiction merely as Dalit fiction, citing his participation in the Dalit panel in regional, national and international conferences. But, we choose not to lend our ears to his vocal condemnation of any identity-based readings of literature and production of a literature guided by an ideology. During the post-90s, the autobiographical and testimonial narratives insist on the return of the author (against the notion of the death of the author). It is significant to note that Imayam (and a few other Tamil 'Dalit' writers) refuses to claim that identity and this demands our serious attention. The question is not just about their denial of identity but also about the need to respect their anonymity.

Expressing doubts about the popularity of Dalit autobiographies, in a conference organised in April 2017 by Sahitya Akademi in New Delhi, he said: "When academicians and media persons interview a writer, they ask them to comment on the role and function of literature, and the writer's vision of life and literature. But in the case of a Dalit writer, questions are asked about their primary education, family and the suffering they've faced in their life. This forces the Dalit writers to adopt the autobiographical mode of narration. The concern for Dalit literature arises not out of ethical responsibility but out of mere sympathy for their sufferings." The narrative of *Koveru Kazhuthaigal* resists such a reading. The narrator remains a witness (as against the participatory voice that we find in the Dalit autobiographical narratives) to the struggle of Arokiyam and her husband Savuri, the Christian-convert dhobis who serve the Dalits. Their hand-to-mouth existence and their sufferings at the hands of the villagers (which include Dalits as well) threaten to subvert the ideological claims of Dalit subjugation at the hands of the dominant castes. This has led to a counter-reading of *Koveru Kazhuthaigal*. It is apt to recollect the repeated insistence of Dr. Ambedkar here: it is not untouchability but caste that is the problem. But what we fail to see are the moments that display the complexity of human relationships, which cannot be reduced to subjugation and oppression on the one hand (for example, Savuri's relationship with the landlord Periyaan), and the power and impact of the modern social life (children's neglect of parents to suit the urban demands) on the other. It is a world devoid of ideologies as it foregrounds the complexities of the everyday. What characterises Imayam's fictional world in *Koveru Kazhuthaigal* is the nature of human relationships that border on love and hate, subjugation and subservience.

His commitment to the letter and his writing forced the Dalit ideologues, who once scorned him, to later celebrate his writing. Feminists who heard a male voice in his writings later showed interest in the voices of women in his fiction. Replying to a question on the function of women in his fiction in the *Hindu Literary Festival* on 16.1.2018, he said: "When I think of women the first thing that comes to my mind is the 'food' that they are deprived of. The very idea of family and house represents not men, but women. It is this kind of women who appear in my stories." It is in this way that *Koveru Kazhuthaigal* has become an iconic text that represents the complex social matrix and intricate human relations. That is why the Tamil modernist writer, Sundara Ramasamy, says:

There is no other novel in Tamil that can be compared to *Koveru Kazhuthaigal* in artistically presenting the divisions and hierarchies created by the humans among themselves, in containing the depth of human suffering, and in successfully transferring the experience into writing. (*Kalachuvadu*, October 1994, p.4)

The literary-critical circles which opt for an ideological reading conclude that Su.Ra's praise testifies the novel as elitist and pro-brahmanical. But Su.Ra's celebration of the novel rests not on the object of representation but on the manner of representation, i.e., the brilliant intermixture of characterisation with the nature of narrative.

There are two important aspects which pull the readers into the narrative of *Koveru Kazhuthaigal*: first, his characterisation and second, the nature of narrative. Anyone who reads the novel would at once look at Arokiyam as the central character as she is placed within the tension between the past and present, the old and new social order, the Dalit and non-Dalit. She is the one who handles the difficulties at home, gets food from houses, manages the master, worries about their son's future and daughter's sexual exploitation. We ignore Sauvri who remains a voiceless individual and almost functions as an absent character. We can find this aspect of absent character in many of Imayam's stories — Danabakiyam's son, Arumugam, in the novel *Arumugam*; the nameless Dalit boy in his novella *Pethavan*; the dead girl in "Satyakattu" and Revathi, the victim of bride-burning case in his recent novel, *Sellatha Panam* (2017). This absent character, who is in collusion with the witnessing narrator, functions as the central principle of Imayam's fictional universe and gives the narrative the impact of a narrative painting. This may also be read in connection with his preference of anonymity over identity. In *Koveru Kazhuthaigal*, Arokiyam's suffering is as important as Sauvri's invisible resistance against various moments/agents of oppression. It is this resistance of the absent characters – which is central to Imayam's verbal art – that thwarts any attempt to frame his stories merely as narratives of Dalit oppression. In this sense, Imayam's fiction seeks to extend our limited understanding of the realist mode of writing.

The function of the narrator as a witness seeks to offer a different perspective of the represented life of the characters. Let us not forget that Imayam always chooses to call them not 'paathirankal' (characters) but 'kathai maantharkal' (persons in the stories). By way of looking at individuals as carriers of stories, Imayam presents his characters as humans with stories to tell. The narrator facilitates this relation between the characters and the readers by inviting them into the fictionality of the life represented. The boundary between truth and fiction disappears. Such an erasure happens at the level of language, particularly in his stylisation of folklore. It shows the way people's language and values are shaped through the castelore and sometimes the castelect. It is not the language that is called to serve the plot but it is the plot that is conceived from people's expressions, which presuppose stories. Imayam told me in a personal conversation that the story of *Pethavan* emerged when he heard a person in a tea-shop swear, 'He pimped his daughter', referring to someone. "I kept thinking about the rudeness of that expression, its caste connotation and then developed the plot of *Pethavan*," Imayam recalled. The story of *En Katha* came out of the expression of a small boy who casually said, 'The river you have gotten into does not have the other shore'. The story of *Koveru Kazhuthaigal* also materialized out of his rumination over the cry of a woman in the neighbourhood. "The cry made me see the life around me, and the nature of the society and the geography in which I live," he had told on several occasions. In his interview to the January 2018 issue of the literary magazine, *Thadam*, he said: "I write only about those I see in my everyday life and about the events that happen around me." For him, words are not just words but carriers of people's history and stories.

Failing to notice such intricacies of the narrative, we may look for references to Dalits and trace a Dalit way of life in his fiction. In his novel *Arumugam*, the backward Naidu caste Vasantha is caught up in prostitution along with the Dalit woman Dhanabakiyam. But we disregard Vasantha as an insignificant, minor character and miss the moments that cross over ideological perspectives. Imayam continues to develop this complex matrix of social relations in his later writing in a much more effective manner. For example, the reference to a Dalit boy (who never appears in the story) in *Pethavan* may force us to read it as a story 'about' Dalits. But it remains a story 'about' the dominant caste girl's family members, who are trapped within their own vainglorious notions of caste.

Imayam's fiction wins our attention to the life beyond the ethnographic data at a time when we see new forms of history-writing that challenge the dominant modes of history by using local data. The anthropologist Clifford Geertz insists on the need to 'convert the entire culture into folklore and collect it' for a proper ethnographic study. Similarly, Imayam's stories like "Thiruttu Pona Ponnu" (the abducted girl) and *Sedal* demand us not to be trapped within the data, and urge us to listen to the voice of the subjugated who do not raise any claims of victimisation. Imayam's fiction seems to tell us that while we are equipped with the ability to identify the caste-ridden human and social relations, we should also try to find the people's capacity to surprise themselves as well as others and move beyond the boundaries of caste. Imayam's *Koveru Kazhuthaigal* offers that 'capacity to move beyond' as a possibility in the form of a fictional narrative.

R. Azhagarasan

Introduction

Koveru Kazhuthaigal was published in 1994. It is the first novel of Imayam, a school teacher in South Arcot district, near Chennai. The title means 'mules', but carries the sense here of 'beasts of burden'. It has a particular significance because the story is that of a vannaan (washerman) family, who traditionally carried their bundles of washing either on donkeys or mules. The 'mules' of the title, though, refers ironically to the vannaan and vannaatti themselves.

The story is that of decline and change in the village, seen through the perspective of the vannaatti, Arokkyam, who serves a Dalit community of agricultural labourers, attached individually as bonded labourers to Gounder families. It is located in the early seventies, a time when ritual status and payment in kind were giving way to a contract based solely on cash wages.

Arokkyam and her husband Savuri serve only the dalit streets, always known as 'the colony', which also has its own lower caste priest; a separate washerman serves the upper caste village or uur. The harijan or dalit washerman is not even allowed into the houses of the other dalits he works for, and they pay him partly in cooked rice and leftovers every evening, and in grain, foodstuffs, clothes, etc., at other fixed times of the year.

Although they play an important role in all Hindu rites of passage, it is striking that Arokkyam and Savuri are Catholics. This means—besides personal devotion to Christ and to Saint Anthony—going to the Church of Saint Anthony as and when they can, particularly on Feast days. As the church is some distance from the village, and their services in the village are needed constantly, it is not often that they can find time to attend. Most importantly, they defer to the authority of the priest there, and seek his blessing at all Catholic Church services, and on important occasions like weddings.

Koveru Kazhuthaigal gives us an extraordinarily detailed picture of a lifestyle that has now passed; a lifestyle that is reclaimed and told with pride, without any attempt to 'Sanskritize' it. That is, there is no supposition that the lifestyles of the upper castes (vegetarianism, brahminic rituals, etc.) are, or ought to be, the norm. Yet it is not even the rich ethnographic detail that makes the book so valuable, but the insight it gives us into the life of the woman, Arokkyam, literally in the margins of society (her house is outside the colony, while the colony itself is outside the caste village) and poised between Hindu ritual and Christian devotion. The names, incidentally, have a ringing poignancy: Arokkyam means 'good health', 'well-being'; Savuri is the Tamil version of Xavier.

The novel is constructed on two journeys: a pilgrimage of hope at the beginning; a routine trip to the washing pool in drudgery and despair at the end. Between these, it is signposted by rites of passage which give a sense of cyclical time, but also by landmarks of historial, linear time. This climate of time and change is important to the novel whose primary theme is Arokkyam's dilemma within changing systems of belief about the self and society. First, there is the gradual commercialization of traditionally caste-linked functions. The village acquires a regular tailor and a laundryman with a box-iron, both of whom serve not only the village people, but the colony dwellers too, taking away the custom from the traditional washerman. Changing styles of dress contribute to this too, as men begin to wear shirts and trousers that need pressing rather than the traditional veshti wrapped about the waist. Both Arokkyam's sons move into more liberated worlds: her elder son, Josep, is persuaded by his wife to leave home and go into partnership with his brother-in-law to start a laundry business in town, while the younger, Peter, cannot understand why they do not go in for coolie work that would be paid in daily cash wages. At the same time as this loss in main livelihood, there is a steady decline and breakdown in the old caste prerogatives: the amount of grain that Arokkyam and Savuri were allocated by right at each household where they winnowed, dwindles to no more than a single scant tray; the head and intestines of the sacrificial goat which was traditionally the vannaan's by right begins to be auctioned. And the payment for all ritual services grows less and less; is often no more than a token.

Arokkyam has one main hope in coping with change: that the church will intervene in support of the old order, and appeal to the elders of the colony to keep up their caste obligations to their vannaan. The novel begins with a pilgrimage to the Church of Saint Anthony, which is a journey of hope. In fact when the church intervenes much later, it is with an offer which is totally unexpected: to take the youngest son Peter away, and train him to become a priest. In a beautifully developed central chapter, Arokkyam struggles with the anguish of her choices. The novel turns on this central dilemma.

The indomitable but suffering mother figure is a repeated image in Marathi dalit writing. She is often the sole breadwinner, sacrificing everything for the family. Namdeo Dhasal, Vaman Nimbalkar and Jyoti Lanjeswar have all written poems entitled, 'Mother'. Gail Omvedt in her article in *Nirappirikai* (Nov. 1994) points to the mother figure in the poetry of dalit men as a continuing symbol of oppression, and also of struggle, sacrifice and sense of duty. But she adds that in all such portraits, 'These women did not challenge nor change greatly the nature of the functions and duties that were traditionally theirs.' The portrait of Arokkyam is in that tradition, but at the same time different from the symbolic archetype. She is not described objectively, but from within; from the perspective of her own dilemma, within the terms of her own anguish.

The worst oppression of the caste system, Imayam suggests, is that his protagonists become totally dependent upon it for their living. Thus he presents Arokkyam as trapped within the dilemma of her changing times. She has neither the skills nor the economic independence which would enable her to take risks, and to take the responsibility for change. All the same it is she who fights consistently for what she understands as her rights within the old order, she fights continually for the happiness of her children. It is she who provides a model of strength for her daughter Mary, to whom she addresses her final words in the novel: 'Lock the doors behind you and come out with me.'

Koveru Knzhuthaigal can be read both as the individual stories of Arokkyam and Savuri, and as part of the story of the dalit struggle as a whole. This theme of struggle can also be seen reflected in the use of a prose style which in many ways subverts and challenges the reader of modern Tamil fiction. In the first place, although Imayam retains a more formal style for his narration, he reports with a complete lack of inhibition the colloquial conversational styles of the protagonists, both in their reference to their work, and in their exchange of banter between themselves.

The vannaan and vannaatti of Koveru Kazhuthaigal own certain aspects of dalit culture and make constant references to it in their conversation. It is a conversational style full of proverbs, sayings and analogies as the protagonists are emphasizing a life of hardship with few rewards:

'If you chase a dog, it is not only the dog whose legs will hurt.'

'Even though the rain falls from the heavens, the water has to flow along the earth.'

'In a house where there is nothing, what does it matter, who rules?'

'He hoped to belch after feasting, but his stomach will only rumble from fasting.'

A more formal reference throughout the book is to the repertoire of oppari (mourning songs and laments) which is the cultural heritage of the vannaatti, and a necessary part of her role at funerals, a heritage that is being rapidly lost in changing times. (The tensions suggested here are of course part of the central themes of the book. Mary, Arokkyam's daughter, was brought up to know this repertoire; it is a large part of Arokkyam's frustration and sorrow that Sahayam, her daughter-in-law, wishes to have nothing to do with the traditional role of the vannaatti.)

The novel actually ends with a cycle of oppari songs, with its own poetic system based on punning, playing on symbols of marriage and death, and with internal as well as initial rhymes. And, as well as oppari, Imayam makes use of a Malayali astrologer's chants, a chakkili elder's sexually suggestive ballads, and the songs of the kuutthu performers and drummers as they precede the funeral procession. All this creates a very rich and special cultural background, almost with a classicism of its own. And finally, Imayam invents for Arokkyam a particular spoken style, which is not quite formal lament, but is very similar, often depending on a string of related exclamations. It is a style that draws very strongly and confidently upon this oral tradition of songs, ballads and chants based on punning, balance and repetitions, and where the distinction between prose and poetry becomes a very fine one. This powerful and persuasive voice is Imayam's finest achievement.

Lakshmi Holmström

Beasts *of* Burden

Yes, they had all liked the idea. And so it was agreed. Arokkyam had spoken out her mind first. At once, Sahayam had declared that she certainly was not staying behind. It was only in this matter, by the way, that Arokkyam and Sahayam happened to be at one, and not at each other's throats. Then Mary and Peter began to torment Arokkyam like little insects. Of course, Josep was also in favour, but as always, he kept quiet about it. And as always, Sahayam was annoyed with Josep because of that.

Savuri alone kept on grumbling incessantly. He complained and complained about Arokkyam and the rest. Throughout that particular week he talked a great deal to Periyaan, the Elder of the leather-workers. If ever Savuri was troubled or uneasy, he could only abide the company of Periyaan. But it was extremely rare for him to be in such an unsettled frame of mind.

It had been Sahayam, really, who stirred up the whole business. She had been longing to go on an outing somewhere. One ought to go to church every Sunday, she claimed. Should one only attend for the festival, and on special days? When she said, this is the reason why the Lord is testing us, Arokkyam immediately latched on to the idea.

But Savuri still grumbled.

'It's just about the end of the month of Thai. It's the season for work. At such a time she wants to make a trip to the church. How will people stand for it? What sense does it make? At a time when it's a struggle to fill one's belly with a little gruel!'

'There's a church and a God only for those who have rice to eat and a place to rest. Or even kith and kin. Where's all that for those of us who can't even cover their crotch?'

'Doesn't realise we have to tread on the earth. Seems to think she can walk on air.'

Savuri finally shut up after Arokkyam scolded him roundly, saying, 'Stop your drivelling, big mouth.' All the same, he was anxious about what the elders of the village, the *karaikkaarar* and *kothukkaarar* would say.

Throughout the next week, Arokkyam flew about in distress. She went and asked the elders to give her permission to go. Savuri of course went with her just for the looks of it. They refused at first. Then, at last they agreed. But she really had to suffer for it at the hands of the kothukkaarar and the karaikkaarar. Ramasaami and Chadayan were the ones most prone to leap at her in anger.

'What need is there for you to go to the church at an ordinary time like this?'

'And who's to wash our clothes meanwhile?'

'If anything happens in the village, good or bad, who's to deal with it?'

'Are there four vannaans in the village or what? Thieving rogues!'

'Exactly what I say.'

'If you push off with your entire family on some sudden whim, who's going to put up with it?'

The way you are carrying on just isn't right. There's nothing else for it but for us to bring another vannaan here instead of you.'

'We don't need all this showing off.'

By the time she had got everyone to agree, Arokkyam felt she had aged ten years in a single week. At last she had finished everything, and late at night she had prepared the koottaanchoru which they would eat on their journey. How long it was since she had last cooked koottaanchoru!

She made the koottaanchoru with all kinds of lentils in a base of millet. Tying it up in a piece of cloth, she woke up everyone in the middle of the night and led them out. She was not even conscious of it, but an enthusiasm had awakened in her. She was in a rare state of excitement, as if an important event were just about to take place.

Arokkyam had been to the church with her family to attend the festival last year. At that time they were just thinking about Sahayam as a prospective bride for Josep. This would be their only visit to the church since that time.

When they reached Melnariappanur, the sun was shimmering high in the sky. The priest was not at the church. Apparently he would only come there in the afternoon.

They all knelt before the sorupam, the holy image. Then Sahayam rose to her feet, joined the others under the shade of the neem tree outside, sitting down amongst them. Arokkyam alone was prostrating there, her hands pressed firmly into the floor. She lay there as if she were attempting to burrow into the earth.

The first thought that came to her was the way she had gone to the kothukkaarar and karaikkaarar, wandering from house to house, so that it would be possible for her to come here this day. Then she thought of her own family, of Mary, Josep and Peter, in a sequence that went on lengthening. She really wanted to worship the Lord. But only thoughts of her community and family would keep surfacing in her mind, one after another.

When Arokkyam came out at last, to join the others under the shade of the neem tree, in front of the church, she was exhausted from weeping. Savuri teased her. Poor God, he said. But Sahayam could not stop smiling.

Then they all began to eat. The aroma of the koottaanchoru spread everywhere, but Arokkyam refused to eat. Her heart was heavy. It always turned out like this when she came to this church. As soon as she had heard that the priest was not there, her hopes had wilted away. She took it as an ill omen. She blamed Savuri most of all, and was furious with him. It was he, after all, who had said they should not go to the church at this particular time. How can there be someone who forbade you to go into the presence of God? Really, Savuri's attitude was steadily worsening with time.

They sat by the well and ate, receiving the koottaanchoru which Mary rolled into balls and placed into each outstretched palm in turn. Tears came into Arokkyam's eyes as she watched Mary, the vessel in front of her, shaping handfuls like a grand old woman. She said nothing. Pretending to blow her nose, she wiped her eyes with the edge of her sari.

Yes, Mary had been a worry to her from the moment of her birth. In those days, Josep listened to her at home, the whole day long. Mary alone had caught all the diseases which had never, otherwise, come to Arokkyam's house. Every morning,

Arokkyam would go off to the thorappaadu, a water-hole dug into the riverbed where they did their washing. Josep it was, who was everything to Mary. For Peter, too, Josep was the mainstay and support. But Peter was more of a devil.

Josep too began to go to the thorappaadu while Peter was still a baby. Then it was Mary's turn to mind Peter at home. From that very time, Mary learnt how to do the household chores. As Mary grew older, Arokkyam's duties began to lessen gradually. Now Arokkyam had ceased to go anywhere near the cooking hearth. Although she gained some good because of this, she was also beginning to be concerned for Mary. And as if in tune with her anxieties, Mary herself had said something. One morning, when she had gone down the main street to collect the washing from the houses, a quarrel had broken out between her and Chadayan. He had provoked and teased her. Mary had reported this to Arokkyam and wept. For the rest of the day, she could not do anything. Nor could she stop weeping.

'Don't you even care about me?'

'What's the matter, now?'

'Why don't you just hand me over to some fellow?'

'Why, di?'

'I don't know why my body is like this.'

'What's the matter with it now?'

'It's all because of this rolling-pin body of mine that I get into fights with all these people. They want to take a nip at me, not even caring that I am low-born.'

'Has anyone said anything to you?'

Arokkyam's heart missed a beat. Had anyone spoken out of turn, or had anything bad happened? Chadayan was a kothukkaaran, after all. Times had changed to such an extent that these fellows were tormenting low-caste girls. First she was angry. Then her anger changed to tears.

'In our town, even old men with white moustaches make suggestive remarks to me. I can't stand any of the men here. They make me so angry. They are always staring at my lower belly.'

'Where are you going to find a town where there are no men?'

'We have to get away somewhere, to a place that's a bit better than this, that's all. We have to live out our lives somehow.'

'But wherever we go, we'll still be beneath someone else. They'll always treat us like that, because we do the lowest duties to the lowest communities.'

'Then whatever am I to do?'

'We just have to carry on somehow, in the same way that our people and our community always managed, even before our time. You have to have strength of mind and heart. Don't ever let that go. It's like your life-breath. If the breath goes, then the life goes. If we lose heart, then that's it; we're finished. So make your heart as hard as stone.'

'O God! O Saint Anthony!'

Mary had gone out, sighing deeply. Arokkyam sobbed and wept all that night. She repeated the conversation to herself and wept in anguish. She was filled with concern for Mary who needed a man. Then she wept for that unknown man as well.

The next day, no sooner had it dawned than Peter arrived, having been beaten up in a fight with the other street lads. Although Mary had scolded him before this, and even hit him for mixing with the town boys, he would not obey her. As the boy grew older and bigger, he was refusing to heed anyone.

It had rained recently. The boys had patted out the wet mud, packed it firmly into empty coconut shells, and then tipped these out to make a pile of round mud cakes. Then they divided the entire pile into rice, curry, and so on. It was when they all sat down to eat, each boy mixing his portion and relishing it, that Peter started the fight by kicking away what they had put to one side for the crow, the dog and the vannaan's boy. It really came to blows and bloodshed. Peter got soundly thrashed. He spoke to Arokkyam that night.

'Amma, why do we have to call at houses for our evening meal? Why can't we cook at home every day?'

'Why, da?'

'Why don't you cook at home, like everyone else?'

'Till I twist your arms and legs for you, son of a donkey!'

'All the boys torment me, calling out "raachoru, raachoru".'

'What shame is there in that, let them say what they like.'

'They keep on calling me "the vannaan lad" and shoving me away.'

'All right. Shut up now.'

'Why can't we go for coolie work?'

'Is it likely we'll be given it? It will be the case of losing the chicken first, and the monkey after it.'

'Everybody else does.'

'Everybody else has a bit of a garden or a piece of land.'

'And why haven't we got any?'

'O yes, you think your father comes from a raja's house, do you? He's got acres and acres of land, does he? Useless son of a bigmouth! Asking questions, are you?'

'Hereafter I won't go to the thorappaadu with you.'

'So you are going to feed off what grows in your father's garden, then, are you? I'll peel off your skin and fling you to the dogs, son of a donkey.'

'Even if I come to collect the washing, I won't come to fetch food.'

'Just come here, I'll twist off your leg and thrust it into the fire, idiot!'

Peter had run off into the street. After a while, Arokkyam had wailed, 'Saint Anthony! O God!' and begun to weep. Her tears moved no one. But she continued to weep throughout the night.

There was nothing in all this that was new to Arokkyam. It had been the same in her own town; it was the same here. It had always been the same since the day that she had arrived in these parts. Some folk had tried to tease and provoke her too, even though one of Savuri's sisters had always been beside her. And even though she, at that time, never went to the thorappaadu, nor to the street to fetch food in the evenings. But all the same, those times were not quite like this, nor did people at that time behave as they did today.

Nowadays, even small children would call out to her, 'vannaati woman!' Arokkyam would smile and ask, 'What's the news?' She would think to herself. Nowadays, our children get cross over any old thing. We are a humble community. What's the use of getting angry? She would forget about the incident immediately. It was important for her to put it right out of her mind. Otherwise she would have gone mad. It was only by forgetting that she survived.

***

Sitting outside the church, silently, Arokkyam was almost in a trance. Josep was the first to finish eating, and to come and sit by her side. She looked intently at his face, as if she were seeing him for the very first time. She did not weep, but the tears kept gathering in her eyes. In a little while, Josep put his upper cloth under his head and lay down, curling himself up.

'Why haven't you eaten?'

'I don't want anything, Thambi. Did you eat properly?'

'O, I'm full up. Look at my stomach. It's as tight as a drum.'

'O God, have you got any sense? Will anyone lie down on the earth with their shirt on? Do you think it's enough just to grow as big as a bull? And what about you, I ask you, is it enough just to bear a son and let him be?'

Both Josep and Arokkyam were startled out of their wits. Sahayam was hastening towards them, calling out loudly. Once again he rolled his cloth into a ball and placed it under his head. But she made him remove his shirt and took it from him. Arokkyam's temper rose. Sahayam now stopped Josep from lying down once more, and shouted at him again, 'Why have you gone and put so much oil on, as if you had thrust your head into an oil-press? It's streaking down behind your ears. Wipe your ears first. It's going to be all over the cloth if you lie down like that. And why couldn't you have washed your legs?'

There were layers of dust plastered over all their legs—Arokkyam's, Josep's, Peter's, Savuri's—right up to their knees. Arokkyam only just realized that they had forgotten to wash themselves. She wiped Josep's neck where the oil was dripping. She wiped her own neck. Then she wiped the street dust away from his legs. His skin showed black where her hands touched it; elsewhere it was stained clay-red.

Arokkyam would often say, 'It's like the story of the man who went out to hunt an elephant, but caught a cat instead.' She felt sorry for Josep who always kept quiet, however much Sahayam shouted at him. Nor would he ever quarrel with Arokkyam herself. She would often get angry at the thought that her sweet-natured son had gained such a termagant of a wife. Always Sahayam and Arokkyam were at loggerheads.

One day Mary had come and reported something to her. It was the one thing that Arokkyam had not brought up in a quarrel. But since that day, she was fearful for her son's future. That fear struck at her heart to this day.

'Why don't we just finish with this business once and for all?'

'Now what's the matter?'

'We'll ask people to give us our wages properly, in money.'

'Is that likely to happen?'

'And why not?'

'Do you think this is something that was set up yesterday or today?'

'Then why can't we keep a shop like my brother does?'

'They say that even a dream should be appropriate to the eyes of a dreamer. But you—you say the most outrageous things. And at a time when you don't even have a change of clothes what if the cloth around your waist should fly off.'

'Then what if we should take off for Chinnasalem?'

'That's not going to happen either. Do you think we come from a line of rajas to act out our wishes? We are people who can't so much as change our loincloths.'

'Then what is to happen to us? The people here don't even call me by name. It's always "vannaati woman, vannaati woman".'

'Look, it's not that I don't like your idea. But Amma won't come with us. Nor will she let us go.'

'When is your mother likely to come away. No, she'll always stay here, always standing in front of each and every person, scratching away at her backside.'

'Well, it seems it is the only way to fill one's belly.'

'What is this, belly, belly, all the time? O Jesus!'

'It's the belly that's Jesus, God, Lord and devil. Everything.' Mary had laughed.

Was it likely that a woman who was always talking about going away to Chinnasalem would consider this family's well-being seriously? When Mary reported this conversation between herself and Sahayam, Arokkyam thought, town bitch, but she said nothing out loud. She asked herself bitterly how such words could be spoken by one who had just come into the family. Into this family of hers, which she herself had held close in her protective care all these years.

But Sahayam's great anxiety seemed to be that the family's present troubles should not destroy her as an individual.

As for Josep, he always walked off without retorting, whatever anyone said to him. Peter was not like that. It was imperative that they should arrange a marriage for Mary immediately. Meanwhile, here was Sahayam, always hostile towards everyone, always finding fault with the family. And Savuri who never heard anything that was said. Above all, the townsfolk; what about them? Everything they gave had diminished and dwindled; the cooked food every evening, the amount of grain doled out at harvest time, the small change that was distributed at rituals.

***

The priest appeared at a distance. Without even being aware of it, in an instant Arokkyam had stood up. She had a feeling as of flying in the air. She was aware of a lightening and disburdening of heart. A few tears came to her eyes. But, truly, she had no wish to weep at the time.

They all rose to their feet. As soon as the priest approached them, they fell to the earth and prostrated themselves. Removing his outer robe, he asked about all of them.

'Are you keeping well?'

'Yes, aandavare,' answered Arokkyam.

'Be seated.'

'Very well, saami,' Sahayam spoke up.

'Your permission, aandavare.'

'O Jesus, O God.'

To the last, Arokkyam kept her hands folded together, palm to palm. The priest went inside. In a little while, his cook came out to speak to them. 'Saami is eating now. After that, he'll have a nap, and then come and see to you.'

Once more, they all went and sat under the shade of the tree. Sahayam did not like this priest one little bit. Peter agreed with her wholeheartedly. Savuri was worrying because it was time to return home. Even though he had no pressing business, his thoughts kept returning there.

Arokkyam decided to speak out her heart to the priest. She ought not to hide anything from him. She might keep things from anyone else, even from Savuri. But if she hid anything from the saamiyaar, God would not forgive her. So she decided to speak to him about all her grievances and troubles. He would show her a way. She must surrender her heart to the saamiyaar.

She assured herself that he seemed a very good priest. It was he who had conducted the wedding of Sahayam and Josep. Arokkyam had liked the way he had answered all her questions without grimacing, and the way he had conducted the puja. She made up her mind that they should finish with Mary's marriage too, while this priest was still holding office.

Josep's wedding was celebrated at this very church, on an auspicious day at the end of the month of Thai, last year. They had also come here for the festival of Saint Anthony. They had arrived early one morning, and returned home the following day, late in the evening. It had been a time when they had a lot of work at home. Even though a huge, unruly crowd had gathered at the church, the priest had still found the time to speak to her. She had let those kind enquiries wash away all her sorrows, until she had no troubles left in her mind. At that instant, she had gained a new hope.

So many people round about these parts came to this church of Saint Anthony. There were huge jostling crowds here from the first day of the festival, until well after it was all over. Lights shone as if it were always daytime. Priests came here even from abroad. Numerous cars and buses gathered here at festival time. In the days when Arokkyam first came here, soon after she was married, the crowds were never so big as this. Neither was the church itself so big at that time. There were not so many trees. Now, though, you couldn't begin to describe the crowds. New buildings, lights, and a road had all appeared recently.

Arokkyam's idea was to invite the priest to the town and to ask him to speak to the members of the panchayat. When she had first entered Savuri's house as a bride, the priest of that time had come to bless the family and to ask all the townsfolk who had gathered there to be good to them and to treat them well. Since then, no other priest had said anything to the townsfolk on their behalf. If this saamiyaar were to come, then the people would certainly listen to him. No one would argue against him. Arokkyam thought that her family would surely prosper in that case. Her heart grew hopeful. She would speak to the saamiyaar very soon. Her saamiyaar.

A peal of laughter came from Sahayam, breaking into Arokkyam's thoughts. Peter was laughing with her. Arokkyam had not even been aware of their conversation so far. Now she saw that Sahayam would not leave Peter alone. She kept on pestering him, 'What did you say in your prayer to Anthonyaar, da?'

'I didn't say a single thing.'

'O Anthonyaare! Truly, Peteru?'

'Truly.'

'So you just knelt there in pretence! I saw you prostrating yourself, so why couldn't you say just a little prayer to God?'

'All this about God is rubbish. Jesus was an ordinary man, just like us. There are lots of men in our town, but we don't worship them, do we?'

'You empty-head, you'll go to hell.' Arokkyam came furiously towards Peter. He rose and fled. Arokkyam kept on pursuing him. Except for her, though, the rest could not contain their laughter. It was Sahayam who finally caught Peter, brought him back, seated him on her lap and questioned him. Peter seemed to treat only Sahayam with respect. And she, for her part, seemed to like only Peter in this family. Arokkyam was enraged as she listened to them chatting.

'And then?'

'First tell her to say she won't hit me.'

'Leave that to me. Go on, tell me. Who taught you all this?'

'Arumugam told me.'

'And what else did he say?'

'You know when our boys take clay from the bottom of the lake to make holy images in play and take them out in procession as a game, and some elders kick them. Why doesn't God pull their eyes out then? We make the images with clay, they do them with wood. Those people cheat us properly, he says.'

'Only Arumugam?'

'No.'

'Who else, then?'

'Lots of people talk when they are squatting in our church.'

'What do they say?'

They'll say, look we're smoking bidis and blowing smoke at God's back, why isn't he tearing our mouths apart?'

'Just you come here, I'll fill your mouth with fire,' shouted Arokkyam, grabbing hold of Peter and pulling him away from Sahayam. He wriggled out of her grasp and ran away. Sahayam fell about with laughter. Josep lay there, silent. Mary laughed too. Savuri drew lines upon the earth.

The cook came and told them that the saamiyaar had sent for them. They all trooped inside.

'We bow to you, aandavare.'

'Hanh. Come in, come in.'

'Aandavare,' began Arokkyam.

'How's everyone in town? Keeping well?'

'By the Lord's grace.'

'Mm. Very well.'

'Saami,' said Sahayam.

'What is it, amma?'

'That place is dreadful, saami. Nothing goes right.'

'Is that so?'

'Yes, Father.'

'Very well, Father.'

'No, Father.'

'Father...'

'Your wish, Father.'

'Very well, Father.'

Except for Sahayam, all the rest of them were in a state of trembling fear until they made their final obeisance and went outside. The saamiyaar was continually swinging from one side to another in his swivel chair. Arokkyam had not expected this. She was surprised and shocked to see Sahayam speaking to the saamiyaar in that casual manner. But neither did the saamiyaar seem to resent her speech. He is a good priest, she thought. Mentally she bowed to him.

Arokkyam had thought to tell him all her troubles, one after the other, starting from the very beginning. But she actually forgot it all. It was as if everything had suddenly come out all right. At that instant, it seemed to her that within her lifetime, her family would lack for nothing. All the same, she thought that she ought perhaps to say something along with Sahayam.

'People are not what they used to be, aandavare.'

'Is that so?'

'Durai,' said Savuri.

'Yes sir. They pick a quarrel over the least thing. They don't give us the *tavasam* as they used to in the old days. The *padi* from each house is miserable. And in the rituals they forget all about their vannaan. Everything is lost, aandavare. In the evenings, our bowls are not filled. I have children, yet I am destitute. I might as well have gone into the forest to do penance, Lord.'

'Is that what they are up to?' he asked with some indifference, at the same time drawing on his cigarette and blowing out the smoke with relish. Before the rings which surrounded them could quite vanish away, the next set of rings issued from his mouth.

'Yes, Lord.'

'Truly, saami.'

'Durai.'

'It's true, times are changing.'

'If you should...' Sahayam began. He had turned his face away, so she did not pursue what she wanted to say.

The priest was deep in his thoughts, contemplating the image of Christ behind him and above his head. Arokkyam thought that he might be praying on their behalf. After a long time, the saamiyaar asked, 'What can we do?'

'Your wish, saami.'

'Durai.'

'If you come to our town and get the panchayat together, and open your mouth and speak a word to them, that will be enough, aandavare.'

'Is that what you think?'

'Yes, saami.'

'And will they listen to me?'

'Just one word from you will be enough, saami.'

'Right, maybe I'll come one day.'

'By your leave, aandavare.'

'And what else?'

'That's all saami.'

'Very well, goodbye then. You ought to come often to this church. You ought to participate in the puja. Only then will God show his mercy towards you. You've come now for the first time since the festival. Mm.'

'We'll go then, saami.'

'Very well, goodbye.'

'Give us permission, aandavare.'

Instantly the saamiyaar turned and went inside. Except for Arokkyam, everybody else prostrated themselves in the direction in which he had gone, and then left the house.

Arokkyam alone remained in prayer for a long time while the others stood outside waiting for her. As much as she had prayed for her own family earlier, she now prayed that the crops should grow plentifully in the lands owned by the townsfolk. In her heart she also praised and thanked the dark sturdy form of the priest.

Sahayam was pointing at Arokkyam, at prayer for such a long time, and ridiculing her to Mary. Everyone burst into laughter, listening to her.

By the time Arokkyam joined the others, the bright yellow sunlight fell from a westerly direction and lay glittering upon the earth. Arokkyam walked swiftly ahead of the rest. Next came in order, Mary, then Sahayam, Josep, Peter. The evening darkened, spreading like smoke everywhere between earth and sky.

They made haste in the knowledge that they must reach home before dead of night. All the same, walking along the narrow footpath which ran through fields, and surveying the crops that were nearly ready for harvesting, Arokkyam almost forgot her weariness. She thought, This year all the villages are going to have a good harvest. Her heart filled with happiness and peace. There was a scent of smoke in the breeze. A stillness at the start of the night. Then the sound of wild insects and tiny bees. The smell of maturing grain, carried by the wind.

She was sure that the saamiyaar would come very soon and speak to the members of the panchayat. Her own family's difficulties and distresses would all dissolve away. And then they should finish off Mary's marriage too. Arokkyam walked on, reflecting on a variety of things. She made a number of resolutions.

As they drew nearer and nearer home, though, her anxieties returned. The evening meal would need to be collected. It would be near impossible to answer all the questions people would put to her at that time. Yet she had to answer all of them.

'Where have you been, di, Arokkyam?'

'It seems you went to the church, Arokkyam.'

'So you went off on a whim, did you, fancying a visit to the temple and the tank? You are a lucky one, you are.'

They would question her as if she had gone for a whole month. It was because of this that Arokkyam hardly ever went anywhere. A journey out of town was something extraordinary for her; it happened as seldom as the occurrence of the Mahamaham festival at Kumbakonam.

By the time they entered the town, it was dinner time. Dogs were barking in the street. Mary lit the lamps. Josep and Arokkyam took the vessels in which they received food and raced towards the colony. Nobody could run faster than those two along the narrow footpath. Now they dissolved into the darkness and disappeared.

It was only then that Mary would speak to Sahayam. Josep had quarrelled with Sahayam on the way back, for talking too much and too familiarly to the saamiyaar. None of them had approved of the way she had behaved towards the priest. They had all thought it wrong of her. Nobody spoke to her along the road home. As for Sahayam, her very walk suggested that she preferred it that way. She had been really annoyed with the saamiyaar.

As they walked home through the fields, Arokkyam had broken off a few ears of cholam and given them to Mary. Arokkyam had looked at the hanging ears of cholam heavy with milk, the growing millet and pigeon peas, the coriander, and had forgotten her anxieties. She had bent a few ears of cholam, wondering when they would be harvested, and then plucked some off to roast and eat. She pulled off a handful of coriander to grind into a chutney with a touch of tamarind.

Although there were many different kinds of cholam that were cultivated in these fields, it was the red cholam that Arokkyam liked best. As soon as they reached home, Mary and Sahayam lit the kitchen hearth and began to roast the cholam. They made haste to have it ready by the time Arokkyam came home with the food she had been given in the colony.

At first, two roosters had called out the hour. Following upon them, many others continued to crow. In the darkness, though, one could not make out where they actually were. Arokkyam and Savuri lay curled up asleep, upon outspread pieces of worn sacking. Except for really cold nights, at all other times they preferred to sleep on the pathway in front of their house. Fast asleep, they were never bothered by mosquito bites, however severe. Arokkyam had slept inside the house only until Josep and Mary were born. Savuri always slept on the pathway.

'Ei, Savuri...Savuri.'

'Arokkyam, Arokkyam.'

'Savuri!'

'Hanh!'

Arokkyam looked up first, startled awake by the sound of that voice. It was earlier than the first light of dawn. She was still half asleep. In the darkness she could not recognize the person who was calling. She shook Savuri awake.

'Wake up, da, useless fool,' shouted Ramasaami. Savuri woke up, in shock. Sleep fled from both of them. Savuri was deeply troubled. For an instant his mind raced. What could have brought this man here? He never, ever, came this way. He was joint head of the panchayat, and leader of the colony.

He was an important man, besides. And here he was, at such an hour. Savuri was full of confusion. Arokkyam rose and stood up with him. Savuri shivered. Even if a small boy raised his voice to him in broad daylight, he tended to start.

Ramasaami began to shout the louder, assuming that Savuri's confusion was because he was still half asleep.

'Blockhead, are you still asleep, or what? Shouldn't you be up and ready the minute you hear a single call? How can you sleep so heavily at your age, da?'

'I was dog-tired, saami. Don't get me wrong, saami.'

'Saami?' said Arokkyam.

'Why are you waiting, da?'

'Saami?'

'The old lady's gone. We must send her on her way. There's all the rites and rituals to be done. Couldn't even find a fellow to come and fetch you. So I had to come myself.'

'Saami,' said Arokkyam. She looked eastward. The darkness was clearing.

'Come on then, Savuri.'

'By your leave, saami.'

'A funeral the very next day after we return from church. Whatever next,' exclaimed Arokkyam, sitting down in a state of shock.

Undoing his vetti from his waist and wrapping it about him, Savuri ran. Ahead of him, Ramasaami walked on rapidly, pulling at his cigarette and making it glow. He had a reputation in town for an unequalled swiftness of stride.

Ramasaami himself was nearing the age when he might die at any time. But it was only now that his mother was ready for her last resting place. This old woman, Ramaayi, was the oldest person in the town. Ramaayi's death would bring no sorrow to Ramasaami, nor to his wife and children. Nor would the townsfolk mourn her passing. There would not be a single tear in anyone's eyes. A death that caused no grief; a good death. A death that would not disturb a single soul.

Ramaayi too had tired of living. She was well known in the town as 'that scorpion'. People said of her, 'Ayyo, that woman.' Savuri had seen her often when he was a small boy, holding his father's hand as he went to collect the evening meal. She was in her prime then, glowing with health. She had two daughters as well as Ramasaami. But nobody would have said that she had borne children, leave alone that she was the mother of three. Such a firm body she had. And she owned four kaani of wet land, together with a lift-well device. To the end of her life she seemed to think that there was no reason why she should not own all the wealth of the town.

Already the women from the neighbouring houses had arrived and were weeping loudly, holding on to each other. Their loud wailing seemed to echo round the entire town. They had laid Ramaayi in the middle of the room, and sat or stood about her, raising loud laments which seemed to demand how on earth they were going to survive her. Their wailing woke up the townsfolk and broke into the quiet of the early morning. Even the dogs which were just about to fall asleep at last had gathered together in corners and were howling in chorus.

Ramasaami ran to the chettiyaar's shop to buy coconut, camphor and incense sticks. Even as he ran past, he did not forget to shout, 'Blockhead, be ready. I'll be back before you can draw breath, you'll see.'

Savuri laughed quietly. It was not an open, loud laugh, but something throttled back. He stood there, gazing at the way Ramasaami walked off into the dark. Suddenly he felt a great weariness of spirit.

At a leisurely pace, Savuri brought some cowdung, tipped it on to the ground, kneaded it and rolled it to the thickness of a coconut and formed it into a ball. He went off, found a beanstalk, broke off a piece of it, the length of his arm and of the thickness of his thumb. He then went to Ramasaami's wife, Kullammaal and asked for some white cloth, and tore it up to make a wick which he twisted about the beanstalk. Then he fetched some oil from Kullammaal for the wick. He drenched the wick in oil and then planted the stick in the middle of the cowdung ball.

'Shall we go now, da?'

'It's done, saami. Everything is ready, sir.'

Ramasaami summoned Kullammaal who was weeping with the women, and spoke to her. 'Ei, little one! These females who have come here for the wake are quite likely to make off with whatever they can lay their hands on. There now, I've warned you. Watch out. Otherwise you won't be able to move a limb.'

Ramasaami and Savuri came to the corner of the street. The street ran from east to west. Savuri placed the cowdung ball with its attached beanstalk and wick upon the earth. He tucked an incense stick to one side of the cowdung.

'It would be better if there were a couple of men with you, sir.'

'Why, da?'

'There should be a couple of men there when you send her on her way. They must be pangali, co-inheritors, sir. That's the tradition sir.'

'Idiot, how does a friend or foe matter to a dead woman, da? Finish the rite quickly, now.'

'Then you must not complain about me later on.'

Ramasaami lit the wick, the camphor and the incense stick. He broke the coconut and then prostrated himself in front of the cowdung, facing westward. Savuri prostrated himself as well. Then Savuri took one half of the coconut, poured in a little sacred ash, tied the other half into his waist cloth and ran after Ramasaami.

Dawn had broken, bright and clear.

'Go and cut down four bamboo canes from the Gaunder's garden to make the processional bier. I'll explain to Gaunder later on. If anyone asks you anything, just mention my name.'

'Very good, saami.'

Savuri continued to stand there, blinking in confusion.

'Idiot, be off with you, then.'

'It would be better if I had someone with me, sir.'

'Where's your son got to?'

'...'

'What are you saying, da?'

'He has to go to the thorappaadu, sir.'

'If the washing is left for this one day, nobody is going to be ruined for ever. Drag him along with you and run! You must be back before I draw a single breath.'

'Your leave, saamiyov.'

Ramasaami walked off in haste, in search of the men who would announce the funeral. Savuri stood stock-still where he was for a while and then went towards the Gaunder's house and grove to cut down the bamboos.

By the time Savuri had cut down the third bamboo and dragged it to the house of mourning, it was long past the time for the colony's customary frugal meal of leftover rice. Cutting the bamboo had tired him out and made him very hungry. Nowadays, he wasn't able to work as before. Since the loss of his donkey, his back had grown even more bent. He would always walk staring at the ground. Not that he ever cared about that. If anyone asked him, 'Are you hunchbacked,' he would not know how to answer. He'd just stand there, scratching his head.

Women and men had crowded into the house of mourning. A pandal had been put up, filling half the street. Small boys were fighting each other to find places to sit on the benches and bedsteads surrounding the pandal. Amplifiers and speakers had been arranged, into which women were singing laments and weeping. Before this, Savuri had only seen loudspeaker sets in the higher caste streets.

The actors were all getting ready for the street theatre performance. They were discussing what play they should put on. But the man with the harmonium had already begun playing on it. Now and then the drummer would give a flourish upon his melam. Savuri did not care for the way he did that. A drummer worth his name should play with a bit more verve.

When she saw her husband approaching, Arokkyam came out of the house, wiping her face; but Savuri was thoroughly fed up. She went and fetched the vessel of rice which she had left in the house opposite, and placed it beside him. He pretended to take no notice and kept on stripping the nodes from the bamboos.

'Why can't you pour some kanji into your mouth first and then carry on with your work?'

'Get out of my sight, di.'

'Why is he pouncing on me, now?'

'Call yourself a family woman? Did you give a toss about what happened to a man after he left in the morning? It's past noon now.'

'Just see where this fellow's tongue is taking him.'

'I said, get out.'

Arokkyam was shaken by the look that Savuri gave her. He had taken off his vetti and tied it as a turban around his head. A twig was stuck behind his ear. The crucifix which was around his neck was swinging about. He wore only a loincloth.

He split each bamboo into two, then four, then eight. Then he cut each length into smaller pieces. Savuri placed his sickle right in the centre of the bamboo, and held it firm. As Arokkyam tapped the sickle hard with a stick, the sickle moved, splitting the bamboo neatly in half as it went. Nobody else could split bamboo into canes with the same speed as Savuri. He had a special skill in this.

Now he put a whole chilli into his mouth and chewed on it to release its fire. Then he raised the drinking vessel in which Arokkyam had poured the thinned out cholam rice and tipped it right into his mouth. With a loud gurgling sound, he emptied the vessel in an instant. At the end of that, he put another whole chilli into his empty mouth and chewed it with relish.

'Are you done, de, Savuri? Finished?'

'Here we are, nearly done, sir.'

'Finish it now, da, finish it you idiot. Is this the time to be eating and drinking?'

'It felt as if my guts were gnawing at me, saami.'

'What is rice, after all, da? Can it be more important than we are?'

'If you give us a bedstead now, we'll have it ready in an instant.'

'Why couldn't you have said, you blockhead? Very well, go and collect one from Kattayyan's house; say I sent you.' Ramasaami was about to rush off from there in an instant.

'Are they likely to give it to us if we people ask them? You are a big man; you should send one of your men.'

'O, very well then.'

Two different kinds of drums called out loudly alongside the women's wailing. Relatives from the towns nearby began to foregather.

He didn't know where the thamru-melam drummers came from. They were playing at a terrific rate. They must be from Vilangkatur. They were beating away at their drums, leaping about, crossing their feet forwards and backwards, then sideways. Seeing their dance, Savuri felt a sudden spurt of joy. The women's weeping voices were utterly defeated by the thamru drummers. Savuri thought they played brilliantly.

'Beat the hell out of it! Strike it, saamiyov, strike it loudly!'

Kattayyan brought the bedstead and left it with them. It was a rope bed. There were two bundles of straw besides. Arokkyam went home swiftly, to bring the cloths which would be tied on to the processional bier. Savuri took the straw and twisted it into ropes. Leaving one of the bundles to one side, he turned the bed upside down, and began to build the bier with the split bamboo canes. When Arokkyam came with the cloths, he asked, 'Did he take the clothes round?'

'Mm.'

'Why are you grunting, di?'

'Yes, appa, your son has gone to deliver the clothes.'

'So why are you braying as loud as a donkey? Daughter of a nobody.'

'You vile creature! How dare you look at me and say such a word!'

'I'll peel the hide off your back in strips.'

'O yes, it's been flayed enough already.'

Arokkyam pulled a clown's face at Savuri. He brandished the bamboo sticks as if he was going to beat her. Then he went back to building the bier, laughing. Arokkyam handed him the bamboo pieces, cane by cane. The sweat ran down Savuri's neck and armpit. The bier was one and a half times a man's height, and shaped conically, like a gopuram. Once the pieces of cloth were tied on, it would look exactly like a processional temple-cart.

***

In great haste, the town dwellers began to drag the dancers and drummers to the street corner. Arokkyam ran quickly to join them, calling to Savuri. Now Arokkyam and Savuri lifted on to their heads the *vaaykkarisi*, the uncooked rice which would be ritually sprinkled on to the dead woman's mouth, donated by the local townsfolk. People donating vaaykkarisi from elsewhere had brought their own vannaans. Those who had no vannaan with them asked Arokkyam to carry their rice for them. Every time an outsider asked Arokkyam to do this, she would say, 'Saami, how could I refuse you.' They commented that she was a more respectful vannaati than their own.

Arokkyam carried five large brass vessels, usually used for rinsing rice, on her head, stacked one on top of the other. Savuri carried four. The paddy was heavy and weighed them down. Now as the street players danced and sang to the rousing beat of the drums, Arokkyam and Savuri walked ahead with the outsider vannaans, all of them carrying paddy containers. Behind the dancers and the drummers came those who donated the vaaykkarisi, and all the other mourners. The dancers sang songs to the vaaykkarisi donors, praising them and asking for money. Both kinds of drummers beat out a variety of rhythms, while they too danced and called out, 'Give us some money, saamiyov!'

Ramasaami's younger sister's husband arrived. He was an extremely shy man. But the dancers would not let him get away.

With money, elelo, the bow is bent
(chorus) The bow is bent
Amma, this man is of Kama's vamsam
(chorus) Of his vamsam

With cash, elelo, the bow is bent
The bow is bent
Amma, this man is of Duryodhana's vamsam
Of his vamsam

With coins, elelo, the bow is bent
The bow is bent
Amma, this man is of the Pandavas' vamsam
Of their vamsam

Good money, elelo, he must give us
He must give us
All his bad deeds will come to an end
Elelo...

Ramaayi's younger brothers had brought the material for the shroud. They praised him, dancing and singing, demanding money. Now the solo singer came and stood in the middle, while drummers, harmonium player and accompanists surrounded him, breaking into the singing every now and then with 'O, yes!'

'Sing me a couple of songs, good and loud; I'll loosen my purse then,' said an outsider. They had begun to get a little tired with all that singing and dancing. But still they kept on, in expectation of more money. The smell of arrack was beginning to be all pervasive.

Savuri gave a sudden yell, 'Beat it hard, brother! Beat it good and loud; louder still!' Arokkyam struck him with the back of her hand, signalling to him to shut up.

Where will we search for him
where will we see him
the most generous one in this country
and the wealthiest?
I saw him at the dark koil's concert
I saw him at the pandal in the morning.

All the accompanists had stopped, and the singer alone gave a solo chant. The man with the moustache handed him a five rupee note. The singer leapt with joy and called out, 'If anyone present should ask who gives us this award, let them know that it is given by one who is most royally generous, most honourable; the lion of virtue, the emblem of duty, our chief, lord and master presents us with these five hundred gold coins.'

They leapt a great leap together, enough to make the whole earth shake, and raised their voices in a shout of praise. The melam vibrated. The thunderous sound of laughter battled with the sound of the drums, reaching the very skies. No, it was not like a funeral, at all.

So far, the vaaykkarisi procession had only gone half way. Savuri was shouting joyously, along with the drummers and dancers. Arokkyam had to keep signalling to him not to be carried away. As for her, her neck was cutting deep into her shoulders. The top of her head had lost all sensation. Her feet could barely tread on the earth. They felt as if they were touching fire.

The dancers were singing again, directing their ridicule at a man who would not part with his money. He was a co-inheritor of Ramasaami's. It was his donation of vaaykkarisi that Savuri was carrying on his head. As for Arokkyam, she was wondering whether Josep had delivered the clothes, forgetting for a moment her painful neck, the afternoon heat and the dust.

The dancers sang:

Handsome, O handsome man, resplendent in your Vaikasi chariot.
What festival, what chariot? We seek you out with empty hands
Are you really a man? Is it in vain that we believed in you?

The smell of country arrack came out of every mouth, filling the whole street with its stench. The dancers and drummers began to look as if they had not slept for all of four days. Froth gathered in the corners of their mouths. Even so, they neither lost the rhythm nor missed a single beat. They knew exactly what they were singing, and to whom. When the guests and onlookers and children applauded them, roaring their appreciation, they forgot their weariness and sang with renewed strength. They whirled about as they danced in a great circle. The one in woman's guise was particularly good. His voice was exactly like a woman's.

As the crowds grew and grew, the dancers and drummers were even more enthused. They went through enough songs and dances to fill two whole plays. They leapt up and down and the drummers never let up.

When they returned to the house of mourning, the thamru and thappattai drummers rested for a while to chew betel. They smoked cigarettes and bidis. In a little while, some of them lit varagu straw to warm and stretch the skins of the drums. Others ran towards the store of arrack. It was impossible to distinguish between the stench of arrack and the stench of sweat.

Now the dancers resumed the performance from the point at which they had stopped. Groups of men and women watched, sitting at the entrances of their houses, and even on the street. This performance was from the story of Prahalada. When they had stopped the play in order to take out the vaaykkarisi procession, women had taken turns to sing funeral songs into the loudspeaker, and to weep out aloud. Some sat together in groups, weeping quietly. There were a few censorious remarks about the loudspeaker system. A minor scuffle followed, led by those who countered, 'They have them in the main streets of the town, don't they? Have we become so worthless, or what? Are you saying a paraya funeral mustn't have a speaker set?'

Now Arokkyam, Savuri and all the vannaans from out of town set down their pots at the front entrance of the house. As each vessel was set down, Ramasaami's wife, Kullammaal, scooped out a measure of grain with her cupped hands and gave it to the person who had carried the vessel. The vannaans received the grain either by holding out the fold of cloth at their waists, or by spreading out their upper cloths. But Kullammaal's hands had become a shrunken, narrow cone when she doled out the rice. In the normal course of affairs, a good scoop of rice should measure three quarters of a maakaani. But at the rate at which Kullammaal's hands were going, she would not give away a maakaani in total, Arokkyam thought. Her whole body grew warm. She was incensed. She wiped away the sweat that was pouring down her neck, with the end of her sari.

Whatever the community, when a death happened, it was never the inmates of the house who distributed the rice. Always it was relatives or neighbours who did it. Scared, perhaps, that if a third person did it, they might be too generous to the vannaans, Ramasaami had been cautious enough to insist that Kullammaal do it herself. As soon as Arokkyam had heard the news of the death, that morning, she had hoped that for once she might cook a meal of rice alone, without having to mix it with other grains.

Savuri loosened the vetti that he had tied around his head and received four scoops of rice for the four vessels he had carried. The vannaans from out of town stared for some time at the way Kullammaal shaped her hands, then went silently away to watch the street theatre. Something about their gait declared, 'If this were my town, would I let her get away with this?' But it was Arokkyam alone who actually opened her mouth and asked the burning question.

'What is this, saami? Why this pretence of generosity?'

'What are you asking me to do? Do you want me to pick up the whole vessel and tip it all out to you?'

'Why would I want so much?'

'Then how dare you say I am making a pretence? Who is there in this town who is more generous to you than I? Give me an example.'

'What would happen if you were to give me just that bit more? What would you lose? We people fill our bellies only by depending on you, saami.'

'So who can do anything about that?'

'Hanh...'

'Come on, di.' Savuri came and dragged Arokkyam away to the place where the bier was kept ready. Arokkyam poured out all the resentment she felt against Kullammaal. 'I hope she puts her hand into a snake pit. I hope a snake or a scorpion bites her hand. This day next year, she'll not have the use of her hands.' Scolding and cursing, she tipped the rice from her lap into Savuri's portion and bundled it all together. Since that morning, the thought was uppermost in her mind that they would eat rice that day. Rice on its own, unmixed with other grains! How long was it since they had feasted on that!

Listening to Arokkyam's angry words, a woman from out of town remarked, 'The vannaati of our town isn't like this, she listens to what she is told. This one seems to behave like a rakshasi.'

Arokkyam immediately went on the attack and began to quarrel with the woman. Savuri intervened, asked her to hand him the bamboo pieces and went on to weave the rest of the bier. But Arokkyam was not to be restrained so easily. She kept on reviling and abusing Kullammaal and the other woman together.

Savuri began to tie on the banners, he wrapped the cloths around the bier. She handed him some sharp kattanji thorns so that he could tack the edges together. He finished binding the entire bier with the strip of cloth. Arokkyam hung it about with festoons of plaited coconut palm decorations.

Once again they carried the vaaykkarisi to the end of the street. They went in a great celebratory procession, surrounded by a resounding troupe of dancers, drummers and young people. Arokkyam, though, was thoroughly fed up with all of it. Every time the paddy was distributed, a wrangle broke out between her and Kullammaal.

Four or five times, Arokkyam took the vaaykkarisi in procession. Even so, it won't even make up a marakkaal's worth, she said. She spoke up in outrage against Kullammaal. 'She cuts down our lives at a time when we are already starved, the wretch.' Her temper rose steadily. The sun was really hot. One could scarcely place one's feet flat against the earth. Then there was the loud sound of the drums. Savuri, for his part, was merrily dancing. He had been on an arrack drinking session with the street performers. At every funeral, Savuri somehow managed to get some drink. He would acquire some, one way or the other. His very stance invited the offer of arrack. If ever a death was announced, Savuri had reason to feel happy.

Fireworks and drums mingled to produce deafening sounds. Because it was a funeral in an important family, the crowd that had gathered was huge. The relations and kinsmen in the colony, as well as the karaikkaarar, stood or sat in front of the house of mourning. In between singing the funeral dirges, women chatted about kinship links, about their joys and sorrows, about the state of their crops, about rainfall, about their cows and calves, about weddings and celebrations.

Peter tied an umbrella to the apex of the bier. Savuri held him up meanwhile. Peter had run away and come straight to Arokkyam without first going to the thorappaadu. Savuri was irritated by the very sight of him. Because of Arokkyam's presence, though, he didn't say anything. Besides, he was well lubricated with arrack. That made him suddenly compassionate towards everyone.

Savuri had prepared the processional bier with banners and back cloth, exactly like a temple car which takes out the gods in procession. He brought out these cloths only when he had to deck out processional biers, or wedding pandals. At other times, Arokkyam bundled them up carefully and put them away in a storage jar. Now Arokkyam laid out the straw upon the upturned bedstead, put in place the two straw-filled bolsters where the head and feet would rest, and spread out an old sari over everything. It was all ready.

Savuri, well intoxicated by now, was drivelling away to himself. It was enough for him to sniff at a tumbler of arrack. He got drunk so easily. He kept calling Peter his beloved son. Every now and then he went towards Arokkyam, threatening her and raising his hand. He had never so far hit Arokkyam, though. It was she who struck him now, with the back of her hand. But she also laughed, saying, 'Worthless fellow!'

If ever there was a funeral in town, or if ever he was called upon to carry vaaykkarisi elsewhere, Savuri was sure to be treated to arrack that day. That day he would make trouble at home. He'd go off to Periyaan and complain about Arokkyam. Then he'd pour out his whole biography, starting with the words, 'In those days...' It was only when he was full of arrack that Savuri wept, remembering his past years. As soon as he was sober again, he would return to his usual taciturn self. He would not argue with Arokkyam. He'd wait, ready and anxious, to do as she directed him.

'Whores and donkeys, where's the rice? What's the curry?'

'There are three females in this house, but not even gruel at meal times. Why do I have to struggle so hard, all for the sake of this hand-span sized belly?'

'O the stench! Can't you smell the stench of shit! They are cooking food the likes of which you can't get anywhere else in the world! No flavour, not even salt. No fire in the curry. Nothing but cow's piss, that's what it is.'

'My whole life is ruined!'

'I'm not going to leave off until I've chopped the three of you to pieces. Josep! Hand me the axe.'

So long as he was drunk, Savuri would curse and bluster in this manner. In normal times, one scarcely noticed his presence in town. He spoke in such a way that he was scarcely audible to the man standing next to him. He was a mild man.

'Is the bier ready?'

'Is the bier ready yet, you fool?'

'It's ready saami.'

'It's all done, sir.'

Ramasaami hurried to the side of the corpse. Everyone from out of town claimed that the bier looked fantastic. They admired the bolsters made out of straw and placed in readiness for the head and feet. This was all Arokkyam's work. If she put her mind to it she'd do things really beautifully.

'The vannaan of our town thinks no end of himself.'

'This one is not so bad.'

'Vannaans just don't do things properly any more. Those days are lost forever.'

'Do they know what it means to be a vannaan? These people seem to think they are landlords and mirasdars.'

'In the past...'

The spectators of the street theatre were chatting amongst themselves as they pleased. Kullammaal wept loudly, hugging the newly arrived women. She spoke of Ramaayi's fine attributes and described how well she had always treated her. At the same time, she didn't forget to castigate Ramasaami whenever she got the opportunity.

'What possessed this man to burn up money like this?'

At last, Ramaayi's two daughters arrived. At that moment, a great lament burst out from the house of mourning. After that, the women sat about in small groups, talking together.

'She wouldn't reach out her hand even to an innocent child in need, the scorpion.'

'Didn't I say it? I said she would die alone, cleaning out her own shit, right to the end.'

The day was descending. Arokkyam's thoughts were at the thorappaadu. At the same time, the knowledge that Josep was working there brought her some comfort.

They placed the corpse upon a bench and bathed it. They rubbed it with oil, shikakai and other things. Had Ramaayi been alive, she would have said, 'Why all this fuss?' Ramaayi's body had shrunken and grown pale. To the end, her mouth gaped open.

'Savuri'

'Savuri'

'Savuri'

'Savuri'

The women's cries seemed to echo throughout the whole town. As Savuri pushed his way past them, to the side of the corpse, all mouths were screaming, 'Savuri'. Sons, grandchildren and relatives had poured pot upon pot of water over themselves. Everyone stood about with wet bodies, and with bands of sacred ash all over themselves. Datchinamurti Aiyar had smeared them all liberally with sacred ash.

Savuri shouted out, 'Those who wish to throw the vaaykkarisi, please do it now.' His voice rang out with fervour because of the arrack he had drunk. He took off his waist cloth and spread it over the corpse to receive the vaaykkarisi.

Savuri took up a small brass vessel, usually used for cooked rice, but now holding paddy, hulled rice, a sprig of neem leaves, turmeric, and small coins; he showed it around to everyone there. He had shrouded the corpse entirely, except for the face; he was allowed to handle the corpse as he thought fit. Then everyone waved a handful of rice towards the mouth of the dead woman and dropped it on her chest. A few small coins already lay there. Arokkyam called out loudly to the grandchildren who were to carry the torches soaked in ghee, 'Distant and close kinsmen, if you haven't done so yet, throw on your rice.' Arokkyam called this out again and again.

Tying together the rice that had fallen on his vetti into a single hasty knot, without even binding it properly, Savuri hoisted the bundle on to his head; at the same time he covered the corpse and tied it on to the bier. He tore off the rest of the shroud cloth which hung away from the feet and handed it to Arokkyam. She gathered up any rice and coins left upon the corpse, and tied them all up at her waist. At last, the crowds who had come to pay their respects to the dead began to move. It was only then that Savuri and Arokkyam could breathe freely.

'He's torn off half the entire cloth!'

'This is a fine thing, helping themselves to what belongs to the dead!'

'How dare they tear off the shroud!'

'It was not like that, saami.'

'What do you mean, "not like this, saami, not like that saami"?'

The person who was last to throw the rice rounded upon Arokkyam. This set off all the rest who surrounded the corpse. She repeated the same thing again and again, 'It was not at all like that.' She thought to herself that the extra piece of material was not even the length of her arm. But out loud, she attempted to answer all of them at the same time.

Earlier in the day, Arokkyam and Peter had laid out ten to twenty saris to cover the street. The drummers finished their sequence with a great flourish. The bier set out in procession. A great sound arose, as if from a battlefield.

Row upon row of men, women and children knelt down upon the saris which were spread out upon the street, and then rose to their feet. Women laid babies down on the ground and then lifted them up. Other women rolled on the ground and wept, then ran all the way towards the boundary of the town. A single drummer went ahead, beating his drum between long intervals, dong...dong...dong...dong. Behind him everyone followed along what was by now an old, well-worn path.

Arokkyam and Peter rolled up the muddied saris, picked up the scattered coins and walked home.

Voices called out at the cemetery:

To reach Kailasam
To reach Kailasam
To reach heaven
To reach heaven
To reach Sivalokam
To reach Kasi Visvanatham
To reach Sivalokam
To reach Vaikundam
To reach Vaikundam
To reach Govindam
To reach Govindam

Everyone bustled about. There wasn't, actually, very much more to be done now. All the same, there was an air of importance and activity.

Ramasaami and his children walked three times in a circle around the raised ground which held the grave pit, from left to right. They repeated together, loudly, Savuri's chant. Ramasaami walked in front, carrying a mud pot of water. As soon as they finished the first circle, Savuri made a slit in the water pot. At the end of each circle, he made a slit with the edge of his axe.

The pot was held on Ramasaami's shoulder. The others sprayed the water that was trickling from the pot on to the corpse, using mango leaves, as they walked round it. Savuri, who had left only the face exposed, called out, 'Check if there are any bits and bobs of jewellery, saamiyov!'

'There's nothing, da.'

'Do it as a matter of routine, saami.'

'Idiot, finish it soon now, da.'

'Quickly.'

'My stomach is pinching with hunger.'

'I haven't so much as had a gulp of cold water since I heard the news. I came flying like the wind.'

'My insides are screaming with hunger.'

'Hurry up.'

'Hurry up.'

Ramasaami's eldest son-in-law kept urging him on. An outsider kept talking to him incessantly. Savuri gave each of Ramasaami's children a stick, about the length of a finger, asked them to prostrate themselves facing the north, and then to place the sticks upon the ground. Some of the other relations, too, prostrated themselves. Everyone did as Savuri instructed them.

Now there were only a few people left, surrounding the grave pit. The dancers, the drummers and the visitors had all gone off to bathe. Those who were left were scolding and haranguing Savuri.

'What next?'

'Come on, blockhead. What do we do next?'

'Hurry up and finish your job.'

'Go on, tell us. Tell us, da.'

'Finish it. Wind it up. Enough now.'

'Hurry up, da.'

'Hurry.'

They lowered the body into the grave. From Ramasaami came a loud, lament. Three times with the back of his hand he pushed earth into the grave as Savuri instructed him, then he went off to his bath without looking back. Some of the visitors went with him. After Ramasaami's children sprinkled earth on the grave, the rest did so.

Josep arrived just then, having collected all the bundles of washing and left them at home. Savuri gave him an intense stare. Josep stood there awhile, silently, then he began to untie the cloths attached to the bier and to bundle them up.

At some distance from the grave mound, and in the direction where the head of the corpse lay, Savuri made another hole. Then he mixed tender coconut water and cow's milk, and poured the mixture over the hands of Ramasaami's children, outstretched over the grave. After this, he closed the hole that he had made a little while earlier, placed the coconut shell upon it and lit incense sticks.

'Fall down and prostrate yourselves in a northerly direction, and then leave without turning around. Hurry, hurry.'

'Yes. Now that's the end, saamiyov.'

Kattayyan cut through the knots binding the bier and took away the bedstead as well as the bent bamboo canes.

Savuri mixed kumkumam and sandal paste and poured it over the grave mound. With his axe he split the broken water pot into tiny shards. He prostrated himself in a northerly direction and set off homewards. Josep followed him.

He untied the bundle in which he had gathered together the vaaykkarisi that had been scattered in the house and in the burial ground. He picked out a piece of coconut which lay mixed together with the rice, and flung it into his mouth. He thought, If only I had a glass of arrack, the pain in my body would disappear like the wind.

Arokkyam had already laid out a sari where the fee money would be handed out, following the funeral. All the elders, the kothukkaarar and the karaikkaarar sat round in a circle. The visitors who had come for the funeral were sitting there too, having had their bath. Those who stood held out their wet clothes, letting them dry in the wind. In the middle of the circle lay a pile of small coins. They were of many sorts and dominations.

Savuri arrived, having had a bath, drying his vetti upon his body as he came. Josep came and stood at a little distance from the crowd, the banners from the bier tied together in a bundle which he carried upon his head. A little while later, Mary, Peter and Sahayam arrived together and stood to one side.

'Why are you wasting time, friends?'

'Here, we are ready now, Ramasaami anne.'

Chadaya called out, 'Thamru drummer, come forward, appa.'

The lead thamru drummer tied his cloth about his waist, bowed to the ground and stood up. Mottayyan gave him a fistful of coins. The drummer untied the cloth from his waist, received the coins, and left.

'Who's next?'

'The players and dancers.'

'Come, appa.'

'Next?'

'Thaathan.'

'Here I am, saami.'

'And then?'

'Chakkiliyan.'

'Here I am, saamiyov.'

Periyaan came and made a low obeisance. His eldest son Ambaayiram came. After that, his wife and his daughter Kosalai received their money and left.

'Come on, de, vannaan.'

Arokkyam and Savuri fell to the ground, bowed deeply and rose. Mottayyan gave Savuri his due. Then Arokkyam held out her sari and received her portion. Her heart missed a beat. She dared to ask out loud, 'What is this, saami, it won't even come to two rupees, it seems.'

'That's quite enough. Off you go, ma,' laughed Chadayan.

'These are the funeral rites in a big house, saami. We wouldn't beg you if you didn't have enough. We are people who spend our lives under your shelter, saami.'

'Have you gone that far? Shut your trap, you donkey!' admonished Mottayyan.

Savuri dragged Arokkyam away, scolding her, 'How dare you speak out in such a gathering!' Dancers, drummers and visitors had all left by that time.

Josep, Mary, Peter and Sahayam, all of them fell to the ground and rose up. But Sahayam alone knelt briefly as she did at church, without prostrating, and rose quickly to her feet to stand erect. It was Chadayan this time who distributed handfuls of coins to them, not Mottayyan. Mary's portion was heavy. Peter's was somewhat generous too. Mary was startled and surprised.

'De, Josep, what town does your wife come from?'

'Chinnasalem, saami.'

'That's what I thought.'

'A fine chick, that.'

'O yes, a town lass.'

Arokkyam walked ahead in disgust. Mary, Sahayam and Peter followed her. Josep waited in the darkness to take up the outspread cloth.

Arokkyam prayed unceasingly to Saint Anthony. Throughout the month following their visit, she was filled with thoughts about the church. She was usually in this frame of mind after they had attended the festival. Savuri would at times tease her about this, too. But she didn't take much account of what Savuri said. She remained in a reverie about her family, the church and the priest.

After each visit, as they were busy about their chores, the townsfolk would ask Arokkyam to repeat the story of her journey. Without wearying of it, she would give a complete account to each and every person. At last, she would heave a great sigh and go on her way, saying, 'Was it just to witness all this that God made me? So many people live in so many different ways in this world. How can I hope to be so fortunate!'

But this time, very few people asked her to relate the story of her journey. Even that was hurriedly, in passing, in a single word tossed towards her, 'By the way, what happened when you went to church?'

'It's not even worth asking about, akka. Even before the mouthful you spat was dry, we were back, I tell you; as quickly as if a bomb had gone off behind us. What pilgrimage has brought us any good anyway?'

It was also true that Arokkyam did not have the leisure to tell the tale in full. The very next day after their return from the church, work began on the dry lands. So she didn't make a big issue of it. Neither did she have the time.

Ramasaami's mother had died the day after their return from the church. That very week the harvesting began in right earnest in the fields, and so Arokkyam was very busy winnowing grain on different threshing floors. If this had not been the case, she would have gone to each house with her story. Even if she had not done so, the townsfolk would have most certainly questionned her themselves. Every household in the colony was made aware of everything that happened to Arokkyam, and immediately. In many ways she had a special relationship with each household there.

***

At harvest time, all of them, women, children and old people as well, worked at full stretch. As soon as the harvest season arrived, it was always like this. From daybreak until nightfall they were as hard at work as they were at seed-time. Those who were unable to work in the fields, the very old and the very young, chased away pigs and chickens right through the day, each clutching either a stone or a stick. They were perpetually shouting at and abusing the pigs and chickens. Without so much as leaving to eat a meal, they kept guard over the grain spread out to dry in the streets and on threshing floors. Rooted to the same place throughout the day, they became bored and tired, and so they vented their frustration upon the animals.

Peas, beans and various grains lay spread out, drying. They were spread about in the streets and pathways, in fields and on threshing floors. The livelihood of the whole year to come depended on the grain gathered at this time. Even in the house of one who was perpetuallv destitute there would be a pot which held four measures of grain.

They all gathered up and winnowed the grain: the men in hope of betel leaves and areca nuts, bidis and cigarettes; the women in hope of salt, tamarind, chillies and garlic; the children in sure expectation of sweets, puffed-rice balls and ices. During the harvest season, everyone behaved as if they were rich, and suddenly acquired the generous attribute of giving as soon as they were asked. Even the tenant farmer walked with the gait of an overlord.

The chettiyaar merchant bought varagu, cholam and other grains with which he filled different tins. The ice-candy man carried different kinds of bags and sacks. Nowadays he had given up bartering ice for old iron, broken plastic chappals and such things. The nomadic kuravar exchanged sacking needles, beads, hairpins, ribbons, eye make-up and face-powder for grain. Wherever street dogs gathered and barked in unison, kuratti women plied their trade. Throughout the day, the howling of dogs reverberated about the town. The kuravar who made baskets and winnowing trays, bottles and plates, colanders and fences, kept circling the town. They brought large mortars and pestles of wood and stone, as well as grindstones, on mule-back. Dancers and street performers went from house to house singing their songs. Thombans sharpened the horns of cattle and held games and performances at night. Kaavadi-bearers set out in their saffron-coloured clothes, carrying sacks. They went to all the villages nearby, collecting grain for the feast which would start the ten days of street theatre in honour of the goddess Amman. From the very beginning of the month of Thai, the thaathan blew his conch from street to street every morning, never minding the dew or mist. And everyone came out, competing with each other for their share of the grain.

All sorts of people arrived in the town: Naidu girls selling bangles, gypsy women who roughened up the surfaces of grindstones, kurattis who wove baskets and winnowing trays, women skilled at tattooing, people who read palms or foretold the future with the help of parrots who picked out cards, sorcerers and spellbinders, the boom-boom maattukkaaran with his cow which would nod or shake its head in answer to any question, troupes dancing to gramophone records. Traders of mud-pots or utensils made of aluminium and stainless steel and sellers of saris, jackets and underskirts rang their bells and called out their wares as they cycled the streets. Aasaari women selling ropes, pads to set under heavy vessels, ladles, ladle-holders and churn-sticks; the thomban who sharpened bulls' horns; men who fixed brass tips to the horns; men who shod horses and bullocks; sellers of ankle-bells, of herbs and medicines, of salt-fish; men driving salt carts; men who leaded the insides of brass-vessels; and yet others selling weeding-hooks, sickles, curved spades, pestles, mats, bedsteads and shovelling-baskets made of reeds—all these entered the town, endlessly following each other like a procession at festival times, when all the world sets out to sell its wares.

And there was not a soul in town who was idle. The notion didn't even strike anyone. The jobs awaited, appropriate to each person. Even those who were considered utterly useless—the crippled and the lame—kept guard over the drying grain.

Yes, every single person had their work cut out. Even those who had a reputation for laziness made it a point to spend the entire day out in the fields. People were constantly walking between field and home, as if it were a festival. Where was there the time to eat?

Arokkyam felt as if her head was bursting. She found it difficult even to snatch enough time to relieve herself. There was so much work, the whole time. There was grain to be winnowed at each house. This was the season during which Arokkyam earned her yearly income. She must use what she got now to run her household until the next harvest season. There were not less than two hundred families living in the colony. And there were only Savuri and Arokkyam to serve all of them. Arokkyam went from one house to the next without even catching up on sleep.

Winnowing was not something that was all that easy to do. You had to scoop up the grain in the winnowing tray and then stand erect to judge the direction of the wind exactly. If there was no wind at all, then it was really tricky. You had to winnow the grain by sifting it down in the same direction all the time, standing in the same position. At such a time there was no way of gauging exactly where the grain would fall, or how fast to throw it in the air. Because all of a sudden the wind could blow up strongly, beating against the grain and scattering it everywhere. If one tried to winnow at such a time, the strong wind might blow the grain right into the fences surrounding the threshing floor. The owners were not likely to be quiet if the wind carried away their grain like that. They'd fall upon Savuri in a fury. They'd shout at him and say that he had wasted their entire harvest.

Depending on the status and worth of each family, the grain would vary from two bundles to as many as thirty. Mostly it tended to be varagu or cholam. At night time some would yoke bullocks to tread the grain out, and then heap up the grain and chaff separately. But Arokkyam and Savuri were the ones who did the winnowing the next day. They could manage only one house each day. Because of this, every year, inevitably, there were violent quarrels. Neither those who had a little land, nor those who had a great deal were prepared to give in, and so there were a lot of conflicts. It was Arokkyam who pulled them all together somehow, and made peace. She'd claim kinship towards all of them, addressing them familiarly as maama, appa, anna, amma, akka, athai; she'd stop their bickering one way or another. After all, they too had to make sure of their incomes at this time.

Often it was the fear of losing their income that made them irritable and ready to fight. Each of these families had a traditional employer or aande whom they served, and who belonged to the wealthy communities of Gaunder, Udaiyaar, Servai or Pillai. The families in the colony had to winnow the granaries of all these landowning families. They could not be tardy in going to them; the masters would be too ready to pick a fight. If they stayed at home minding their own work, and did not turn up at the winnowing, it was quite likely that the master would choose other bonded labourers. Then they would no longer be eligible for the privileges which fell to the labourer on special days. That is why they turned on Savuri. Harassed him.

But nowadays people no longer waited patiently for Savuri to arrive, covering the grain with a sack or matting. Those who only had a little had begun to do their own winnowing. If there was too much, they had begun to engage hired labourers. If this happened, Arokkyam could not receive her own extra harvest time award of a tray's worth from the threshing floor. She would only receive her obligatory annual allowance of grain from each family. From the month of Thai last year, Josep had also joined them at the winnowing. This lightened Arokkyam's burden somewhat. It was now possible to winnow at two houses simultaneously. The arguments in the colony lessened. Then complaints began to arrive that it was not right for Josep to be winnowing.

***

Chadayan came to summon them early in the morning. But Azhagan had been after them for the past two days. Arokkyam was in a turmoil. Both families were important ones in the colony. Of course one had to serve the important families first. But then the extra tray's worth was the same at each house.

Savuri arrived at Azhagan's house just as the sheep and cows were being untied and taken out to graze. Josep was winnowing at Chadayan's place. Mary was working with him. Arokkyam made haste to fetch some food from home. By the time she had stored away the extra trays of cholam which she had received at the previous two houses, and helped herself to some gruel, Mary too returned. The dirty washing that Peter and Mary had collected that morning lay about in bundles. Sahayam was lying down, stretched out. Peter had taken Mary's little goat out to graze, the goat she had bought out of her little savings.

They set off again, Mary with Josep's meal and Arokkyam with Savuri's. Arokkyam shouted instructions after Mary until she crossed over at the street corner and disappeared, 'Tell him to watch how he is winnowing. I'll just hand over this food, and I'll be there myself in one stride.' Mary, for her part, went on her way, shouting, 'All right, all right.' Savuri might even be sitting there idly, without saying a word, thinking to himself that he would only begin after Arokkyam arrived Arokkyam made haste. She was even more driven by the anger and repulsion she felt towards Sahayam than by her anxiety to take the food to Savuri. She normally winnowed in equal partnership with him. Without her help, Savuri could scarcely complete the winnowing of a single granary each day.

Well before Savuri's arrival at his house, Azhagan had spread out the varagu to dry, using his feet as well as the winnowing muram. The moment Savuri arrived there, he began to tread and plough the dry grain with his feet. The sun was high in the sky and there was a hot wind blowing. Around the threshing floor, pigs and chicken circled about like a processional fan. But none of their cunning tricks and devices made any headway with Azhagan. He was using the cart peg to threaten them and chase them away. They rested in the shade momentarily, then returned to circle the threshing floor.

Silently, Savuri examined the drying grain as it lay spread out. Using the muram, he spread it out more thinly. It lay there, entirely mingled with dust and insects. After a while, he scooped up a muram-full, threw it up to test it. The grain and the rest separated easily, falling into different heaps. Deciding that it was the appropriate moment to start winnowing, he worked out exactly where the grain would fall, and began to work. Suddenly he grew anxious that Arokkyam might be annoyed when she arrived, and began to work fast. He wanted to scold her severely.

The varagu kept rising up into the air and falling back to the ground. The dust and chaff flew in the wind and fell away, separately. Every now and then, giving weight to his left hand with his right, he fanned the heap of grain vigorously; he blew away the surrounding dust and chaff. Then he threw the grain into the air, muram by muram.

To the east of the threshing floor, the straw had been heaped up like a hill. The sun began to descend. Azhagan incessantly chased the pigs and drove them away. Then Azhagan's wife, Karuppaayi turned up. At once she began to sweep up the chaff which lay about the threshing floor. A little while later Arokkyam joined them.

Savuri stared hard at Arokkyam. Then he hurried on with his winnowing, without a word. Arokkyam picked up a muram silently, took up position directly opposite him. Each facing a different direction, they flung the grain into the air alternately, muram by muram. As for the varagu, it flew into the air like a pile of feathers, and came to rest in a heap upon the ground.

'What have you been up to all this time?'

'Making pots and pans, what else?'

'What did I ask you di, and why are you answering back in that jeering tone, you beggar's daughter!'

'Who asked you to drag in my father? Yes, turn your face away. Who do you think you are looking at when you say such things!'

'So you've become Kubera's daughter then, have you?'

'Did I ever open my mouth and tell you that I am Kubera's daughter?'

'What is it, di, Arokkyam, why are you both snarling at each other?' asked Karuppaayi.

'What's the point in asking, the man just torments the life out of me.'

Azhagan had fallen asleep as he sat under the shade of the puvarasam tree. The wind had dropped for a while. Karuppaayi went on chatting to Savuri. His entire body was wet with sweat and covered with varagu chaff.

Arokkyam went to sit under the shade of the trees surrounding the threshing floor, waiting for the wind to rise once more. Savuri seemed even to have changed colour. Arokkyam thought his hunch looked even more pronounced. He had become completely black. He no longer had his former energy. He looked a different person altogether. After all, he was growing old.

'Get a move on, it's late.'

'Wait for the wind.'

'Are you looking to squatting here forever instead of finishing it off quickly, two murams at a go?'

'Shut up di, are you my daughter-in-law?'

'She's the one who will ruin you.'

'It's you she'll ruin. Get out, get lost.'

'Right, you carry on shouting here. I'll go and see how that boy is getting on.'

'Go on. Go. I'll twist your legs off you.'

Arokkyam went on to Chadayan's threshing floor where Josep was winnowing. As Mary kept filling up Josep's muram, Josep was throwing the grain up into the air. Arokkyam asked Josep to move aside in order to winnow in his place. Josep refused to give way. So then they stood opposite each other and began to winnow alternately. Mary continued to keep filling up Josep's tray.

'What need was there for you to come running here?'

'I came to see what you are getting up to, and how you are managing. Why don't you just sit down for a while, son?'

'No fear. You sit down if you like.'

'No, I'd better go back now. Just get on without scratching and fighting. I'll return.'

Arokkyam left Chadayan's threshing floor and hurried back to Azhagan's. Savuri was hard at work. Azhagan kept walking round the heap of grain. Pigs waited at the holes in the surrounding fences, grunting, and ready to grab what they could. Chickens were tormenting him in a variety of ways. Azhagan wasn't for letting them off lightly. He kept up a constant stream of abuse. One moment he'd say, 'Don't know which whorehouse this hen is from. It looks as if it's quite capable of swallowing up a man.'

Next minute he'd say, 'Look at these pigs coming out of a brothel, like a procession.'

'You won't see such monstrous fowl anywhere else in this whole country except in this village.'

He flung the stick he had in his hand at a hen with a brood of twenty, thirty chicks. Arokkyam could not stand the way he was tormenting the pigs and chickens. She asked straight out, 'They are harmless creatures, saami. Is the whole granary going to diminish if they eat a little?'

'Whose grain is it? Do you think all this grew on your father's land?'

'It's good that what grows in your fields should fill the mouths of four different kinds of living creatures, saamiyov.'

At that moment, Azhagan's daughter Bhakiyam and five or six other children flung themselves upon the mountain of straw that had been piled up, and began to leap about there. Some hid themselves completely in the straw and called out to be discovered. Some thrust the thicker pieces of straw into their mouths, pretending to be smoking cigarettes. Others stuck pieces of straw into their hair, playing at evil spirits and trying to scare the rest. When the pandemonium increased, Azhagan chased them off the premises.

'Useless vagabond children! Is this the place for you to come and play? Just come near me and I'll break your legs for you.'

He laid hold of Bhakiyam. Karuppaayi gave the child four hard slaps. The other children went outside the fence and lurked there, feeling ill-used. They kept provoking Azhagan deliberately, laughing and giggling. They began walking around the fence, still eager to climb back on to the straw heap.

They determined to bring away the straw in heaps and bundles for the early morning fires of the next day. Some loitered on deliberately, with the pretence of catching the dragonflies which were darting above the hedge. Yet others were chucking stones at the fence in an attempt to catch the lizards there. But Azhagan abused them nonstop.

'Just you come here, I'll show you. You'll come to your senses soon enough when I give you a couple of fine ones on your backsides. How carefully I'd built up the stack. They've gone and tilted the whole thing and ruined it. Children of bitches!'

'But what has happened to the wind? It was blowing perfectly well, and now it's stopped as if the devil has got into it.'

> Drrov drrov
> drrov drrov
> drrov drrov
> drrov drrov
> oo oo oo

Arokkyam and Savuri whistled and called out 'drrov' in an attempt to call back and encourage the wind. But it would not return. Always, at the end of the day, the wind tended to drop. All the same, Arokkyam kept sifting the grain ceaselessly. Karuppaayi swept it back into the varagu heap. Azhagan was probing his ears with a chicken feather. His face was tight and inscrutable.

After some rime, the wind blew up strongly once more. In a single movement Arokkyam bent forward, scooped up the grain, straightened up and tossed it into the air. For a while both of them bent, scooped, straightened up and winnowed. They vied with each other as they tossed the grain up as high as the sky.

Karuppaayi continued to make small talk with Savuri. Arokkyam did not like this one bit. She kept quiet about it, all the same. It wasn't easy for her to start a fight unnecessarily. She did not wish to make an enemy of anyone.

'Stop a second, now. You can carry on after a while, da, Savuri.'

'Let it be, saami. Here, we'll finish it any moment now.'

'You've lost a lot of weight, da, Savuri.'

'I'm getting on in years, saami. How can one help it?'

'But you were so well, always! You were in a fine shape.'

'Those days have gone, saamiyov.'

Having finished the winnowing at last, Arokkyam undid the top end of her sari and dusted off the chaff from her head and body. Savuri had tied his vetti round his head, like a turban. He always preferred to be in his loincloth alone. The dust and chaff had covered him so completely that he was hardly recognizable. In one go, he gulped down the cooked cholam gruel that Karuppaayi mixed and gave him. Then Arokkyam drank a tumbler of it. After that she chewed on a whole chilli. Savuri tossed an entire handful of chillies into his mouth.

'Make the Pillayaar, da, Savuri.'

'Here, it's done, saami.'

Shaping a makeshift Pillayaar out of cowdung, Savuri placed it in the northern corner of the courtyard. Arokkyam went and plucked some arukam grass which she planted on the head of the Pillayaar. She was anxious to go to Josep. Supposing those people had said anything to him...

***

Everybody in town knew of Azhagan as something of a bully. But all his bravado and show of anger was directed solely at the townsfolk. None of his brave words had any effect on Karuppaayi. Everything in the house was actually done according to her command. He never spoke so much as a single word in opposition to her. There was also a lot of gossip about Karuppaayi in the town. Arokkyam was perfectly aware of all this; for what indeed could go on in this town without her knowledge?

It was said that from the time Subbu Gaunder had gained enough strength as a child to enable him to take a few steps, Azhagan had worked for him as an adimai parayan or a bonded labourer. And it was in the same gaunder household that both his grandfather and his father had worked as bonded labourers.

In due course, gaunder had arranged for Azhagan to marry, saying that he was getting on in years. And gaunder had spent more money on this marriage than other landowners usually did for their labourers. Gaunder's daughter's house was in Niramani. Karuppaayi used to work there as a household servant. After she married Azhagan, came with him to this town, and started working with him in the gaunder's house, a 'certain' relationship developed between gaunder and Karuppaayi.

Karuppaayi was certainly pretty. She had a light skin. Her look, her laughter, her conversation, the tilt of her face, the way she walked—everything about her was seductive.

At one point, gaunder became seriously ill. Afraid that he might die at any moment, somehow or the other, Karuppaayi got him to gift her in writing a field by the stream, and this very threshing floor. The whole town knew; and Azhagan knew. The townsfolk gossiped about the way Karuppaayi and Azhagan came by the land. But Azhagan never said a word.

Because he had written away the field, gaunder had been chased out of his own house by his son, and had gone off to live in his daughter's house in Niramani. When his son-in-law came to know of the affair, he asked his wife, gaunder's daughter, to make sure gaunder left the house. Even though Karuppaayi had married and gone, if ever she returned to her own village, she always went straight to gaunder's son-in-law's house. To that day her father and mother were adimai labourers in that house.

***

It was said that long ago, the Nawab of Arcot had returned from a tour once, by way of the site of the present town. Acceding to the plea of one of his followers, a certain Muhammad Hussain, he had made him a generous grant of this very land.

Apparently Muhammad Hussainbhai knew nothing about land or agriculture. Soon the fields were covered with thickets, and developed quickly into a dark and dense jungle.

Those who stood high among the upper castes gave Hussainbhai sheep, chickens, cows and calculated amounts of arrack; and in return, they were given permission to cut down the trees in the jungle. At the same time, they dared to keep some of the land for themselves. Later, there were others who gave Hussainbhai's son, Muhammad Bashir, jewels and grain, receiving pieces of land in return. Some who could commandeer numbers of men under them, obtained further bits of land by intimidation. Whatever was left, they gradually encroached upon during the sowing season, and appropriated.

Muhammad Bashir died, and was followed by Abdullah and Nasir. Now their descendants were traders of poultry, with their lanterns at night, their cycles and their cages, and their cry of 'Chicken, have you got a chicken?'.

It was Venkatachala Servai who first wrested this land from Hussainbhai. He was followed by Arumuga Servai,

Ramanatha Pillai, Kannusaami Udaiyaar and then Subbu Gaunder who gave the land into Karuppaayi's hands.

What did this town not contain? What did not happen here? Whatever the upper castes and those who possessed fields and land did, the townsfolk became accustomed to, and finally accepted.

***

'Ei, Savuri, scoop up your grain with your winnowing tray, and go now.'

Arokkyam pushed forward and gave Savuri the muram that she still held in her hands. Savuri was just about to scoop the grain with it. Azhagan stopped him summarily, and gave him an old, threadbare, partly split muram instead. It was with this muram that Karuppaayi had been gathering up the rubbish from the threshing floor and throwing it out.

'Scoop it with this, da.'

'I can't measure it with that, saami.'

'If you can't, then just go.'

'Why are you speaking so sharply, saami? Where can we go if we just leave you?'

Arokkyam stood there, stunned and unnerved. She never expected that Azhagan would speak to her like this. Savuri, though, behaved as if nothing had happened. Arokkyam thought for a moment that she would weep. She realized that the sugared words that Azhagan and Karuppaayi had spoken to them since the morning had only been a means to get work out of them. Now she didn't even know what to say. Azhagan kept staring at Arokkyam. Finding it unendurable, Arokkyam broke out, 'We are people who depend upon you, saami, in order to work and make a living.'

'You shut up, you bold female.'

'Just ask a few of the other elders, like you, what is right.'

'Ei, donkey of a washerwoman, are you trying to tell me about justice, mongrel bitch?'

'Because we have worked for you until our waists are broken and our joints ache, you could give us a couple of measures worth, out of the generosity of your hearts. After all, am I going to build myself a mansion out of this much?'

'If you had even a small piece of land you would know the pain and the anxiety of it, vannaati woman. What do you care? Ei, Savuri, are you going to use this to scoop the grain or what?'

'When you big men say something, is there any way that we can go against your word?'

'No, you keep it yourself, saami.'

Arokkyam picked up the empty rice vessel and started off. Karuppaayi stood in her way, stopping her.

'Ei, vannaati woman, come here, di. We won't lose anything by letting you take a couple of murams' worth. Why do we need all this argument and fuss just at the time when Lakshmi, the goddess, enters the house?'

Arokkyam took the vetti that Savuri had tied into a turban and spread it out just by the heap of grain. Savuri took the new muram which he had used to winnow the grain earlier, and took two scoops, pouring the grain on to the vetti. As he reached out the third time, Azhagan plucked the muram from his hands and flung it away.

'Get out now.'

'But it's the custom to take three scoops, isn't it?'

'That was all in the past. For all the work you've done, two scoops are more than enough. Now go.'

'In this whole town, it is only you who can claim a harvest of forty or fifty kalams. If you yourself do this, then what will the others do, saami?'

'What do I care what they do? Do you want me to heap up the entire harvest for you?'

'Please don't start a new custom in this town. Give us our three murams worth, saami.'

'Hereafter it is to be two murams worth. If you like it, you can winnow for us; otherwise you don't have to come next year.'

'If you say that, then where are we to go?'

'What does that matter to me?'

'Saami, we are humble people.'

'There is no place here for a female who talks about justice and the law.'

Savuri was still silent. Arokkyam stood still, not knowing what she should do. She could not understand why Azhagan spoke to her in such a curt, sharp way. Then she tied up the varagu into a bundle and made to go, thinking, Let it be, whatever is bound to happen will happen; she didn't even pause to say goodbye. But Karuppaayi interrupted, as if anxious to make her peace with Arokkyam, 'What is it, di, why do you talk as if it is all going to be lost this very day? Where will it go? Think that it is all your own. When the cholam is ready for reaping, I will give you two extra scoops myself. Go quietly past the place where Lakshmi stands. I will send Savuri after you.'

Arokkyam made no reply, but left the threshing floor hurriedly and came outside. She could hardly contain her frustration and anger. She went home directly, put away her bundle and sped towards Chadayan's granary. Josep and Mary were coming towards her.

Arokkyam took the bundle away from Mary and put it on her head. Mary stopped awhile, wanting to relieve herself.

'What is it, da, Thambi, it feels less than usual.'

'That's all.'

'What do you mean, that's all?'

'They would only allow us to take two murams worth.'

'And why was that?'

'Why don't you go and ask them? If you ask me, how can I say?'

'And how do they suppose we are to survive if they keep on decreasing our share by a muram every year?'

'I'll go and pour some water over myself and come back.'

Darkness had descended entirely. Sahayam was cooking rice. Peter had gone off to play with the street children. Arokkyam thought at first she should ask Sahayam whether she had given the goat its water. But thinking to herself, everyone else held on to the roller stone; but I just put my hands around a fart, she silently handed Mary the bundle, and went to sit at the threshold. She didn't even wish to look at Sahayam.

She asked Mary to bring her some water in the rice container, and, removing the top part of her sari and winding it about her waist, she washed her hands, back and chest. Then she gathered up the vessels and set off towards the street to collect the evening's cooked meal. Josep was just on his way home. She took him along with her.

She collected the food street by street. To each person who asked for her services the next day she said yes, she would winnow their granary. At last she gave the vessels to

Josep to take home, and set off herself towards Azhagan's threshing floor.

Azhagan came along the street with a cart full of bundles of grain. Arokkyam stepped to one side. No signs of Savuri.

'The vannaati woman is coming opposite us. It's certainly an auspicious sign. Next year the crops should be good.' A man walking behind the cart said that. In the darkness, Arokkyam could not make out who it was.

Arokkyam glanced about the threshing floor and was just about to leave when she saw two dark shadows emerging from behind the straw heap. She walked home swiftly without saying a word.

She said to herself, though, let him come, today I shan't allow him inside the house. Immediately after that, she thought of the priest who had promised to come to them, and who had not appeared so far.

Arokkyam thought that unless the priest came and spoke to the panchayat, there was nothing she could achieve. Full of anxiety she walked homeward in the darkness, asking herself why he had not come as yet.

'You must turn round immediately and come back. I don't have the heart to let you go at this time when there's so much urgent work. But that girl stands there as if she's pouring hot water all over her feet, ready to go. Well then, go and come back soon. Come back before your footprints have disappeared. I want to see you standing before me before the spittle I have spat out has dried.'

'Very well.'

Arokkyam had said the same thing over and over again. But Sahayam had been obstinate. Arokkyam, caught up in the urgency of winnowing at different granaries, had not taken much notice of her. It was only when Mary reported that Sahayam had not touched her food for two days, that Arokkyam, seeing no other way out, had agreed to let them go.

A messenger had come from Chinnasalem with the news that Sahayam's elder brother was not well. From that moment, Sahayam had dug her heels in, insisting she must go to Chinnasalem, come what may. She would listen to nobody. She seemed utterly unaware of anything that anyone said to her.

After Josep and she were married a year ago, Sahayam had come here directly from the church. On the one hand, Arokkyam did think a whole year had gone by, after all, she should go home for a while. On the other hand, Sahayam's arrogant words rankled.

Josep had left in the middle of the month of Thai, this year. The months of Maasi and Panguni had already gone by, and it was Chittirai. Josep had still not returned. Arokkyam could not think why. She badgered Savuri to go and find out what had happened. He refused to budge. All Thai and Maasi they had been busy with the granaries. After that there was the town festival. Arokkyam could not have gone anywhere out of town. Besides, she would not leave Mary on her own. Because Josep was not there to help out with the winnowing, their income from the harvest dropped sharply. That was a great blow. They should, by rights, have received at least two or three more kalams of grain.

Arokkyam had decided that she would sell the grain that they would accumulate in total that year, both from the padi, owed to them by custom from each family, and the extra harvest income. But the total amount this year was very much less than their income last year. For whatever reason, the villagers had lessened the amount allocated for the winnowing by a muram's worth. You could never be sure what the village people would get up to, all of a sudden. They'd pick on something new and turn it into a tradition.

Arokkyam had set off for the street early in the morning one day, and was startled to find, on her return, that Susai Manikkam of Nariappanur was sitting at the entrance of her house. She sat down beside him and asked for news of the family. She wanted to know all about the members of the family at Nariappanur, about the state of their crops, the amount of rains that had fallen. But all the time a single question tormented her innermost mind: Why had he come? Arokkyam could not even bring herself to look at his face properly.

It was only after Susai Manikkam had explained that he had brought the betel-nuts as invitation for Anthoniamma's wedding that Arokkyam was at peace. He then told her that when he had gone to Chinnasalem with the wedding betel-nut, he had seen and talked with Josep and Sahaya Mary. He talked a great deal about those two. Sahayam had served him a meal. Then, at last, he left, insisting that the whole family should come to the wedding.

This same Susai Manikkam was Sahaya Mary's younger uncle's son. Before Josep's wedding, he used to visit them often. But it was the first time he had come to see them since that occasion.

They had all assumed at one time that Josep would marry Anthoniamma. It was Arokkyam, though, who would not consider the match. Obstinately she had insisted that she would only accept Sahaya Mary. Even after all that, Susai Manikkam had come to Josep's wedding.

Now she thought, perhaps it might have been better for Josep to have married Anthoniamma after all. Susai Manikkam had two donkeys; he possessed his own house. Sahayam had an only brother, Albert. He too had left the village after his parents died, and worked for daily wages at a laundry business at Chinnasalem. Sahayam had been to school for a short while, that was all. The rumour went out that she had even learnt a little English.

Savuri had not liked the idea at all. A city girl will never suit us, Savuri had said. But Sahaya Mary's parents were more closely related to Arokkyam than Anthoniamma's were. So

Arokkyam said that they should arrange the marriage with Sahayam in memory of her parents who were dead. Neither girl was lacking in wit, yet Sahayam at least could read and write a little, she thought to herself.

Arokkyam had celebrated the wedding in style, saying, 'One's own kith and kin after all; in times to come it is they who will take pity on one and make sure of one's daily gruel.' Yet when the townsfolk asked her about the wedding, she changed her tune. 'I just had them exchange garlands, and brought them away before you could say ara-gara Govinda, saami.'

During the month of Thai that year, there had been the regular winnowing on the one hand, preparations for the wedding on the other. She spent the entire year's accumulated income on the wedding. She asked permission of the elders and had two trees felled for the cooking hearth. From each family she collected different items: chillies, lentils, tamarind, vegetables, until she had gathered together all she needed. She told everyone that it was to be her eldest child's wedding. She made a big performance of it.

She went to the kothukkaarar and karaikkaarar of the town and managed to buy a tali worth a quarter of a sovereign, out of the common funds. She cooked and served a grand dinner for the relations, and held the wedding ceremony at Saint Anthony's church at Melnariappanur. When Sahayam came home, she grieved that the bride did not bring with her even a set of ladles. She wept over it to herself.

In the days immediately after the wedding, she never sent Sahayam to collect the evening's cooked meal. Only very occasionally was she sent to the thorappaadu. And for the first few days, Sahayam too had seemed cheerful enough. But after that, when she always seemed to turn her face away, aloof as a cobra, Arokkyam didn't like it one bit. Then Sahayam began to sit in one place the whole day long, without moving. She didn't even pay any heed to Josep.

In that first month that Sahayam came to them, Arokkyam took salt and chillies, circled them three times about the bride's head, then threw these things into a burning hearth. Watching the salt splutter and the chillies emanate their pungency, Arokkyam scolded the townsfolk for their jealousy, and hoped to get rid of the effects of the evil eye of envy. In a strange way, her heart was full of happiness for having acquired a daughter-in-law with such looks. But she never said a word about it to anyone.

Arokkyam had once described Sahayam approvingly as 'a well-proportioned little one, pleasing to the eye'. Sahayam was a good looker, all right. But then, what did Josep lack? He was robust and strong. He was well muscled. There was a small image of Jesus about his neck, on a red string. He was somewhat dark, like Arokkyam. What good did it do, having a light skin?

Josep began to wear a shirt on Sahayam's insistence. Her brother Albert had one tailored, and brought it himself. When Josep walked along the street with Sahayam, people would tease him. Josep would smile shyly.

'De, Josep, you've caught yourself a fine one.'

'What does he lack? He's got a bride like a paappaati.'

'Where did you find her, Josep, with that skin like a glowing fire?'

'He's a lucky old fellow.'

Arokkyam often thought to herself that she had been charmed by looks alone. She blamed herself for not having looked for a girl from a family which could claim at least a padi or two in privileges. Surely she had been at fault in this one thing.

***

Although Arokkyam's own wedding had not been held before a priest, it had been grand enough. All the relations, kith and kin, had turned up. They had slaughtered a pig. Arokkyam brought with her a baby donkey, eight kalams of varagu and three kalams of cholam, besides forty rupees in cash. Also a few necessary household goods: a set of ladles, bottles, baskets, woven rests for utensils. In those days, such things were the mark of a grand wedding. People who were the same age as Arokkyam spoke of all the goings-on at her wedding to this day. Arokkyam's father belonged to a large family, and they came from a big town. The colony there was made up of eight hundred households. In fact it was the one town in the entire region that had the largest number of colony dwellers. There were only two hundred families belonging to what might be called upper castes. But the hearths of the eight hundred colony dwellers would come to life only through the good offices of those two hundred families.

Arokkyam was just twelve years old when she first got married and came away here. And it was all of four years later that she came of age. Two years after that Josep was born. When Arokkyam first came here, what a crowd there had been in Savuri's house! They had all lived together in this one hut: Savuri's four younger sisters, three younger brothers, her mother-in-law, her father-in-law, Savuri. Arokkyam, as a young girl, had to cook for and serve all these individuals. After her arrival, Savuri's sisters refused to do any of the household chores. Only the eldest, Theresa, would help her a little. And it was Theresa whom Arokkyam liked the best. A girl with a tender heart. She always wept readily. She was easily teased by everyone.

In those days, they were given food by the kundaan full. All the same, the food that they collected would go round only once. She had to cook more rice in the large earthen pot. Everyone ate their fill. Arokkyam would be exhausted by the end of the day. She'd always be cooking something or the other at the hearth. She hardly ever got a chance to leave the fireside, or to go out.

On festival days such as Pongal or Deepavali, Arokkyam would be in a terrible state. At least ten pigs' heads, between fifteen to twenty sheep's heads, four or five cows' heads and intestines besides, would arrive; one basketful following the next. Savuri's father and his youngest brother, Diraviyaraj, were the ones who broke up the heads and splintered them. They would wash out the intestines. The different meats had to be cooked separately in three or four huge vessels; it was like cooking a wedding feast. Arokkyam scarcely had the strength to grasp the big wooden ladle. All the same, she thrust it into the different meat-pots and kept stirring and turning the meats. She would not even know where Savuri was. She took no notice of him, in any case. She was continuously busy. There were always jobs for her to do. In fact if the jobs weren't there, she'd create them herself.

Delighted with her, Savuri's father would frequently pat her head with affection. Mother-in-law, Mutthammal, would come to the fireside only to distribute the food that had already been prepared. Arokkyam would carry out the dishes into which the food had been shared out, and place them one by one before each person sitting outside in the front street.

Savuri's father died in the very month that Mary was born. Two months later, Savuri's younger brother died of jaundice. After that, there were the weddings of Savuri's two other brothers and his four sisters. Both the brothers went northwards in search of means of survival. Because of this, it was Arokkyam who continued to see to all the rites that were necessary at good and bad times, for all four sisters' families. She never became weary of it. 'It is our people who are our wealth,' was her maxim.

***

Some time before Josep and Sahayam went away, there was a bitter quarrel between Sahayam and Arokkyam. Somehow it was the worst quarrel they had ever had. Josep had gone by himself to collect the evening's cooked meal from the street. And Arokkyam had only asked why Sahayam had not gone with him.

Sahayam and Arokkyam usually started their disputes over very ordinary everyday problems. It might be that Sahayam had not placed things in their customary position. Or that some objects had been put down with a clatter. Perhaps some earthenware pots might have broken. Or she did not know where different items were kept; in which of the mud pots stacked one on top of the other and standing tall as a palmyra tree things were. Each pot would contain several different kinds of grain, tied into little bundles, like knobs of roots. It was only in the months of Thai and Maasi that a single pot would contain only one kind of grain. Arokkyam would name a particular grain and ask Sahayam to go and fetch it. Sahayam would take down the pots one by one and undo each separate bundle to examine its contents. The contents might get mixed up while undoing and redoing the bundles. Sometimes she would not bother to tighten the knots properly. Or the pots might not have been put back in the right order. Because she had put things back in haste, one of the pots might have cracked. The water pot, perhaps, had not been closed properly. The clothes brought in for mending might be scattered about. Her face-powder might have spilt on the floor like kolam flour. Her mai might have been daubed on the wall's surface in stripes. She might well have spilt her pottu colouring powder.

Sahayam had a habit of combing her hair frequently. Of gazing at her reflection in the mirror for a long time, as if it was only possible to tidy herself up in front of it. She ate very little, now and then, like a bird. She slept during the day. She told Mary the stories of films she had seen, and taught her the songs. Arokkyam would pick on any one of these things. A quarrel would then ensue as if between lifelong enemies.

'Do you think it's enough for you to look after yourself, and make sure you are all smart and shimmering? There's a life to be lived, you know. Is the mirror going to teach you to survive? Is it going to show you anything that isn't there, after all?'

Of course there were times when Arokkyam wanted to show off to the townsfolk. 'We might be humble people, but have you seen my daughter-in-law?' Immediately, though, like the nagging pain of a forgotten wound, her anxieties would return. What's the good of cutting such a fine figure? Don't our stomachs need to be filled? This one is not going to be of any help. What was going to happen after she, Arokkyam, died? How would she sustain the family? She would wonder anxiously, whether Sahayam would abandon them all in the middle of the street. The very next instant she would decide that Sahayam should go with Josep to collect the evening meal, and insist upon it stubbornly. Of course Arokkyam was fond of Sahayam. But there were times when she picked a quarrel out of the fear that Sahayam would actually become aware of this fact. Sometimes, as she walked along the street, the people would speak admiringly of Sahayam's colour, her hair, her figure. Sometimes Arokkyam would pick a quarrel precisely because of her own pleasure in hearing this.

Sahayam too really liked Arokkyam. But although she was truly happy in her heart, face to face with Arokkyam, she was all spit and fire. She was always ready to fight, for fear that Arokkyam would ask her to go and fetch the dirty washing from the street, or to collect the evening meal.

'Who cares whether you are the daughter of some wealthy man?'

'Did I ever claim that I was a rich man's daughter?'

'I'll sew up your mouth for you.'

'Go on, do it then, let's see. Ah...'

Sahayam came screaming at Arokkyam. Arokkyam had not expected this. Shaken, she stared back at Sahayam, wide-eyed with shock. She hesitated for a moment. She thought to herself that this was all her own doing.

'So why is it shameful to go for the food?'

'Are you asking me to go and stand in front of each house, with the rice-pot on my hip and the vessel for the curry on my head, calling out, "Ammov, it's the vannaati, give me food"?' She mimicked this, as if she were carrying the pot on her hip.

'Then who is to go?'

'Not me. I won't.'

'It's the girl who has married into the family who should go. What will you do if I'm not around?'

'I can look after myself.'

'When this block of wood finally reaches the ground, then the rest of you will have to take up your begging bowls, that's all.'

Arokkyam lamented softly:

When everyone else held out their pots at wedding-time, they grew as large as elephants; when I held mine out, the elephant diminished to the pot's size.

She gained everything; I gained nothing.

What do I care if she is the District Collector's daughter?

If you give away a large gift, then you can't manage the small charities.

Now everything I had has wasted away.

She's wiped the floor with us.

She's kicked us away.

She came like a monster and destroyed us all.

What is to become of me now?

I am nothing but clay and earth.

Did I ever go to anyone claiming kin?

Did I presume upon a relationship?

If the horse-gram disappears in the fart, you have to let it go.

The tears came welling up. What was going to happen to this family, after she herself died? What was going to be the fate of her innocent son Josep? She thought to herself, it looks certain that this arrogant girl will never see the family safe ashore. Nobody in the family had so far spoken in opposition to Arokkyam. Josep would never so much as say a single word against her. Nor had Arokkyam behaved towards any of them in a needlessly argumentative or deliberately fault-finding manner. She could not speak to Savuri about these constant tensions, either. He would only blame Arokkyam. 'It's all because of you, di,' he'd say. Now she muttered to herself in a low voice, 'I hadn't the wit to see that the whole family would go to ruin.' She did not wish to shed tears in front of Sahayam, but she wept all the same, scolding Sahayam and blaming her for everything. And in the same way, Sahayam wept, scolding and blaming her brother Albert.

'I insist that you go, at least to collect the washing.'

'Never, impossible. Every man from every house stares at me, wanting to know what's under my sari. Do you think I will go and take the clothes from these fellows' houses?'

'What can they do by staring at you?'

'If you haven't any shame or self-respect, must you think that another woman doesn't?'

'Don't shoot your mouth off so rudely. That's enough. I've told you now.'

'Did I come running to you?'

At last Mary shouted at both of them, 'Are you going to shut your mouths this instant, or aren't you?'

Instantly, Sahayam and Arokkyam fell silent. Mary had kept quiet until that moment. But there didn't seem to be any hope-that the argument could possibly have an end. It had begun in the late afternoon, when they returned from the thorapaadu. Sahayam spoke disrespectfully, and without showing any likelihood of giving in. Mary grieved for her mother. She was moved to the point of tears. Arokkyam had been the one who had insisted obstinately that she would only have Sahayam as Josep's bride. Now she was suffering the consequences. What was to be done? You couldn't take her back and exchange her as if she were a cooking vessel! Well, maybe the Melnariappanur Saint Anthony would look after everything, Mary thought to herself. She felt angry and fed up with all of it.

'You wouldn't talk in that way if you realized how I spend each breath of my body, every day, just to keep the kitchen stove alight,' Arokkyam began once more.

Mary managed to calm down Sahayam, spoke comfortingly to her, and took her inside. But Sahayam was still not prepared to give up her attitude.

'I'll go. You don't have to,' said Mary to Sahayam.

Arokkyam sank down in the pathway in front of the house, weeping and lamenting out loud: 'I thought I had found a good thing, but I stuck my hand into stinking shit.'

Inside the house, Sahayam sat in corner near the bundle of clothes that had come in to be mended, weeping. After a while she stopped sobbing, spread out the torn clothes, and lay down upon them. Mary came and sat by her side.

Although Mary, for the most part, felt a resentment against Sahayam, yet she also knew what was necessary. She determined that she would never again ask Sahayam to go to the street with her to collect the evening meal, nor the dirty washing; nor even to go to the thorapaadu. With the same impulse, she said to Sahayam, 'Place your hand on my head and promise me that for the rest of your life you will never again go to the street and collect food or clothes.'

Sahayam did not understand any of this. The two girls looked deeply into each others' eyes. Then Sahayam saw that Mary's eyes were troubled, and she gathered her into her arms, weeping softly. She said, 'Don't cry. I will never go into the street to collect cooked food or dirty washing. It's that mother of yours who torments me because she wants to bring me to heel.'

'You stay as you are. I like you to be what you are. I promise you that in the name of our Lord Jesus.'

Sahayam and Mary talked to each other throughout that night. They talked some more the following morning. After that, they found things to talk about every day. Mary described each person in the town and what they were like. And even though Arokkyam and Sahayam continued to be at loggerheads, Mary and Sahayam spoke to each other. Mary told of all the songs and plays that were performed at festivals and funerals. She taught Sahayam the traditional laments. She taught her the appropriate songs for a dead mother, father, elder brother, and younger brother. In her turn, Sahayam taught Mary the plots of cinema plays, and many cinema songs. Whenever Sahayam described in detail what was shown in the cinema, Mary would stare intently at her. Mary had not so far been to the cinema. She began to feel a greater affection for Sahayam. Sahayam taught Mary to write her name. They chatted together. They laughed. They helped each other at their tasks. Sahayam helped with the mending. She even accompanied Mary to the thorapaadu.

When she went away with Josep, Sahayam said she would write a letter. Mary was taken aback. 'A letter for me? But you'll come back immediately, won't you? Then why bother to write?'

'True enough,' Sahayam had said, as she left. But to this day, she had not returned. As she sat alone, Mary wrote her name in English and in Tamil, in rows upon the earth, as she had been taught.

***

Many hours passed since Susai Manikkam left. Arokkyam had not risen from where she sat, her doorstep. She looked as if she were in a trance. Mary too was silent. Suddenly Arokkyam spoke, as if coming to her senses, 'What a performance it's been!'

'The performance is yet to come, really.'

'O Anthonyaare!'

'How is Saint Anthony going to help when these are all your own son's antics?' Mary asked, with inward laughter.

'I know that times change, but should it come to this?' Arokkyam struck her mouth in wonder, thinking of all that had happened. 'O Jesus, Lord. O Saint Anthony, our boy is smoking bidis now. Has he got used to dealing in cash and coins? They say he never removes his shirt. It seems his shirt is as white as a jasmine flower. Can that really be true, Thambi? O God! O Saint Anthony!'

After Susai Manikkam told his story and left, Arokkyam had to tell it over and over again to the women of the leather-worker family. It was enough for anyone in the street to forget themselves so much as to ask, 'What's happened to your eldest son, we haven't seen him for some time.' She settled down to tell the whole story again and in full detail, before she moved on. She wept. At times she laughed. If people mentioned Josep, she forgot about embarrassment, an aching jaw, the business of the moment, and chattered away. Tears came to her, and laughter. There was some happiness, too.

'Yet how am I to survive by trusting these people any more? It looks as if they won't so much as care to give me a little gruel in my last days, when this piece of wood is ready for the cremation ground. O Anthonyaare.'

Mary said, with troubled eyes, "The strength in our bodies is our only wealth. The only thing that we brought with us. In your last days, when you are completely broken, is the child you bore going to offer to sustain you? Is your community prepared to do that? The moment you fell upon this earth with a cry, you knew that you were alone for ever.'

Arokkyam raised her voice and wept. 'It's all just emptiness, that's the end of the story,' she said, picking up the bundle of washing that Savuri had left, and walking towards the thorapaadu. In a little while, Savuri brought two more bundles, carrying them on his head, and over his shoulder. When Mary and he set off again, with a bundle each, Peter went along with them, driving his goats.

As they sorted the clothes, put them to soak with the cleansing clay, and then started beating them, Arokkyam kept up her complaint. She wondered why on earth Susai Manikkam had come that day. Had he not come, she would have continued with her uncomprehending song of woe. When Josep first left, she had said, 'He has lost his only livelihood and ruined his life.' As days went by, she said:

My child is lost.
My innocent child, heaven knows how he is getting on.
He ran away like the running stream, murderous
chandaalan.
How can the snot become the nose?

Now when she came back from the thorapaadu, she dropped the bundles of clothing, and sat down immediately at the threshold, weeping and lamenting:

> What use are a thousand men, an army, a crowd, a gathering?
> O my first-born son!
> I tended a tender green parrot
> I lost it in flight
> I bred a baby parrot
> I lost it in its bird-call.

Mary knew that once Arokkyam started her laments, she would not stop easily. She felt really sorry for her. But she was angry, too. She was impatient at the thought that Arokkyam forgot her, Mary, who was always ready to reply to her voice throughout the day; to do any of the chores laid to her; but instead, yearned after her son Josep who had forsaken her and followed his wife so meekly. And now Arokkyam lamented like this, night and day, refusing food and water.

'Why do you have to poke yourself in the guts and cry like this because your son has left you, the likes of whom you can't find anywhere in this world? Are you so heartbroken because there is no one to inherit and rule over all this wealth that you've gathered, or what?'

'Witch of a medicine-woman! She made off with my son. Heaven knows what potion or spell she used. He won't even show his face here anymore.'

'If he had truly been an affectionate and loving son, how would she have caught him in her net? What does she know? You are the one who drank healing medicines and pushed him out from your body, so you are the one who must keep howling like a donkey now. Why should they come to see you? Is it their bad fate or destiny?'

'My son doesn't know anything. That mischief-maker worked on him. Foreign whore.'

'Why do you have to complain about other peoples' children? Which of your own children has actually listened to you? However many times you shut your eyes and open them again, you can only see what's there.'

'Shut your mouth, di.'

'Stop living like this with your soul over there and your body over here; mind your business now. The child in the womb had to climb down and out one day.'

'Wretch! Murdering whore!'

'If you chase a dog, it's not only the dog whose legs will hurt. Even if the rains come from the heavens, the water has to flow along the earth. How long can one man wash another's bottom?'

'Did I bear children in order to have them question me?'

At last, Arokkyam undid the four big bundles of clean washing, and sorted out each family's clothes, tying them up into separate little bundles. It had darkened completely. She realized that neither Savuri nor Peter were in the house.

Mary could not endure the sight of Arokkyam sitting there in the darkness, chanting Josep's name. Mary too would have liked to cry. Josep's and Sahayam's absence made her sad, too. But she did not feel any anger towards Sahayam. Truly, this was what she had expected. Only she had not thought that Sahayam would make it happen so soon. Sahayam was all right in her own way. She had managed to escape from the people of this town.

The very week after Josep left, Arokkyam had declared she would go and fetch him back. Mary had offered to go with her. But to this day, she had not been able to make the time. Their work was unceasing. Each week she would make up her mind, fixing on a particular day of the following week when she could set off for Josep. As if it were predetermined, something requiring urgent attention would crop up, just the day before the journey. Again Arokkyam would pick a day of the next week. And yet again something new would turn up. Every day there was something: a death, a coming of age ceremony, a birth, a wedding. What would happen if Arokkyam wasn't there? In any case, Savuri would never let her go out of town. He'd mutter, 'So she's left everything as it is, and pushed off, has she? Let her come, I'll show her. She thinks she's the tax collector's daughter, does she? Let her come.'

Savuri came back from his wanderings finally, and set off for the colony street with the bundles that Arokkyam had rearranged. He accepted that Arokkyam had not been quite well since that morning, and went off now to deliver the clothes and to collect the food without actually saying anything. Savuri, too, was not his usual self. Ever since Josep went away to Chinnasalem, Savuri too had gradually worsened. He acted as if there was no connection at all between him and the rest of the family, and hardly any contact. Arokkyam noticed with anxiety that his hunched back looked even more bent. She thought to herself that it was true, his body was not what it used to be. Mary lit the hearth. When Savuri returned home after delivering the clothes from house to house, and collecting the evening meal, he expected his kundaan full of rice and a chembu of water, placed ready for him at the entrance of the house. Otherwise, he'd immediately start shouting in anger. He could never endure an empty stomach, even for a moment.

Arokkyam sat in the darkness, alone, thinking many different thoughts. She did not wish to weep any more, yet the tears came. She longed to see Josep. Yet she had no desire to come face to face with Sahayam. How to face a woman who enticed her husband away to her own parental home, even were she a millionaire's child? Yet she had to see Josep. Was it going to be a case where the child makes the mother eat dirt? Her mind refused to give an inch. After all, her daughter-in-law had spoken against her.

Josep was her eldest child. She had brought him up with loving care. When he was a baby, how many people had vied with one another for the opportunity to carry him about! Savuri had four younger sisters; three younger brothers. None of them was married at that time. Mary and Peter had grown up by themselves, in an ordinary way. Josep remained the same as he had been as a little boy, even after he was married. Wherever Arokkyam went, he would go along with her, hanging on to the pleats of her sari. And he who had once been like that, never even came to see her anymore. She wondered if something that the girls of their town had once said to her could possibly be true.

It seems that Sahayam had said to Josep, 'I'll only come to you as a wife if we leave this town and go away.' Could this be true? How was it that Josep had not told her of it?

At last Arokkyam asked herself why she had quarrelled so bitterly of late with Mary and Savuri; why she had beaten Peter so harshly. It had come to the point that no single day passed by without a conflict between her and Mary. And because of these daily battles, Mary wept bitterly when she was alone, or when she was doing the cooking. How will I bring this girl safe ashore, Arokkyam wondered, sorrowfully. She thought of Savuri who refused to notice anything, and of Peter who wandered about all day long with the street boys, cutting down palmyra fruit, and she wept.

'As for me, I can look after my stomach even if 1 just wash the odd vessel in one or two houses. But what is to be this Josep's fate? O Saint Anthony, the son I bore!' Arokkyam had kept repeating this all these days. But now she began to think differently. Now it was Mary who began to be of concern to her. 'I trusted these children. They've let me down. If Mary were another boy, I wouldn't worry. A son could even mind cows for a couple of households and take care of himself. But she's a female chick. If those who speak well of her today call her names tomorrow, she is lost. O Saint Anthony!'

And it was Mary who disturbed her reverie at last, calling her to come and eat. 'If there is a nose, there will be snot. It's not going to go away. No point for women such as us to weep, what do we gain? Come and eat.'

My beautiful son
My golden child
My beloved son, how shall I know about you
O Saint Anthony.

Peter ran away to play without even washing his hands. Arokkyam refused to eat. When they had finished all the work of the day, and sat down to eat, Arokkyam said, 'Joseppu.' Mary immediately covered all the dishes and went in to lie down. She wanted to cry. For the first time the darkness frightened her. She shut her eyes.

For a long time the subdued sound of Arokkyam's weeping continued to be heard. Savuri fell asleep in the place where he had eaten. Then Arokkyam too spread out her sari pallav and stretched herself out.

In the middle of the night, Arokkyam came in to lie down next to Mary, saying, 'Chi, get away. At this age, and with grown up children about, you have to come to me with lifted tongue.'

When Mary woke up in the night, wanting a pee, she was startled to find Arokkyam there, hand at her breast. After that, sleep eluded her.

Although Mary had tried to stop her, Arokkyam would not give way. Taking only Peter with her, she entered the colony. After three days of continuous fever, she had somewhat wasted away. Three more days had passed. By this time, the entire street had begun to protest. They began to carp and complain. Some were ready to pick a fight. They abused her roundly.

For two days the washing hasn't even been collected. The clothes which were taken away the day before that have not yet been returned. We have to hang about without even a change of clothes.'

The way this vannaan carries on is just not right. A dead loss.'

'We'd do better to replace him.'

'There are lots of men out there, competing with each other to come and serve us.'

'Very true. This one is absolutely useless.'

'How can one expect a vannaan to be a true vannaan these days?'

So Arokkyam went from house to house, collecting the washing. Peter went behind her, tying up the clothes into bundles and carrying them. Because it was the sowing season, there weren't too many clothes. Only the very young and the very old were left to establish any signs of life and movement in the colony. But they brought out enough clothes, by the armful. Arokkyam reached the last street where the kothukkaaran, Chadayan, lived. Suddenly she began to shiver and to feel faint. She sank down to the ground where she stood. She told Peter to go by himself to the houses that were left. Her tongue felt dry. There was a strange itching at the pit of her throat. Her legs trembled and she broke into a sweat.

***

Arokkyam felt like crying. She could only blame her own self. She thought to herself that everything that had happened was her own fault. It was she who had sent Savuri to look up Josep, and then, on his return, to go to the saamiyaar and ask when he would visit them. Savuri, having refused at first, left at last, thinking his own thoughts. The very afternoon that Savuri went, Arokkyam was struck down with a fever at the thorapaadu. She weakened rapidly.

Still, Mary had refused to go on her own to the main street. But Arokkyam would not let her off. Now it was all over. I alone set about to ruin myself, mourned Arokkyam. Everything that had happened ran through Arokkyam's mind: the state in which, day before yesterday, at this very time, Mary came home, terrible as a ghost; all that she had said to her, sentence by sentence.

Something similar had happened once before. Natesan's son, Sivaraman, had sent Rani to speak to Mary on his behalf. Mary had got into a terrible fight with Rani.

'Don't come to me with talk like that.'

'Why, di?'

'It's got to be possible. You should only talk of such things.'

'Are you saying it's not on?'

'Of course.'

'Why, di?'

'I'm a woman who makes a living by washing the polluted clothes from that family. Why do you talk as if you don't know anything?'

'He's a good man.'

'If he is a good man, will that stop him from putting a child into me?'

'Chi. Haven't you ever dreamt dreams?'

'I don't know how to weep inside the water. You come with the story of an elephant marrying a mouse. You can drink the water from a running stream, or bathe in it, that's all; what else can you do with running water? Is it enough for a beggar boy to have big eyes? Even dreams have to be appropriate to the eyes.'

Natesan had offered a meal of rice to Josep, after his wedding. He had given Josep the obligatory present of ten rupees, as well as a vetti and a sari. Nobody else in the town had given them anything more than the obligatory presentation money. Mary had driven away the son of such a man. Arokkyam had thought that she need never again fear for her daughter. But what had happened day before yesterday had been in stark contradiction to that hope.

***

'Who's at home? I'm here; it's the vannaati; please give me your washing.'

'Where's your mother, di? Why are you here?'

'She's ill.'

'O God!'

Bhakkiyam brought out the family washing, rolled into a ball, and flung it at Mary's feet. Thinking that Mary might protest because it was such a big bundle, she hurriedly exchanged another couple of words, 'That's why I asked. I was thinking to myself, where's she gone, she's usually up and down this street a hundred times an hour.'

'She's not even got the strength to walk. She's lying at home, helpless.'

Tell your mother to come this way if she's in town.'

'Very well.'

'O Anthonyaare.'

Mary stood outside each house in turn, collected the clothes, and then turned into the next street. She found she had already gathered two bundles. She tied them up, left them at the street coiner and went on.

'Ammov, I've come; it's the vannaati.'

'Ammov, vannaati,' she called out, once more.

'Wait, I'm coming,' called back Susila, as she went in and returned with the washing. Handing it to Mary, she sat down at the doorstep, motioning to Mary to do likewise.

'It seems that you won't even peep into my house these days to see whether I am dead or alive.'

'Akka, I'm never rid of it, from the moment I open my eyes, to the moment that I shut them; there's always something or the other to be done.'

'Have you had any news from your brother?'

'No, akka. My father went to ask what and wherefore; and now we haven't had sight of him either, for two days.'

'Maybe there's a feast at the son's house?'

'Leave it, akka. But what about you? There isn't the sparkle in your face that there used to be. You look as if you've been struck by a ghost.'

'What should happen to me, di? I'm the same as usual.'

The sun's rays suddenly fell sharply upon Mary's face, and she remembered that there were two more streets left. It struck her that Arokkyam would be waiting for her, and immediately she rose to her feet, lifting her bundle.

'It's getting late. I've still got work to do.'

'Come again, later.'

'Very well.'

Mary called out in front of the next house. She took the clothes and walked on to the house after that, calling loudly.

'Ammov, give me your washing, it's the vannaati's daughter.'

'Ammov.'

'It's me, the vannaati's daughter.'

For three days Arokkyam's health had completely broken down. She had been confined to her bed, as if she were paralysed on one side. She had become incapable of doing anything. This was the first time, since Peter's birth, that she had taken to her bed, admitting that there was something wrong with her health, and that she could not carry on. And it had happened at a time when Savuri, too, was not at home. Thinking of all this, Mary grieved. Please, Saint Anthony, nothing should happen to her.

Mary didn't even have time to draw breath. Within two days of Arokkyam's illness, she was exhausted. Every chore in the house fell to her. She had to collect the clothes in the morning, take them down to the thorapaadu and wash the entire lot. She had to deliver the clean clothes, collect the evening meal, as well as see to all the other chores. If Arokkyam had not lain down, Mary would not have had all these worries. She was usually happy to do all the jobs that were allocated to her every day. And Arokkyam never gave her anything that was really difficult to do. This new trouble must be to do with some disturbance in the stars. The saamiyaar had promised to come. If he came, everything would still be all right. Arokkyam had sent Savuri to visit Josep, but also, most importantly, to see the priest on his way home. Mary walked on from one house to the next, thinking that once Savuri returned, everything would be all right.

'Who's at home, the vannaati's daughter has come, bring out your washing.'

'Ammov, it's me, the vannaati.'

'Vannaati daughter, the sun is at its height, is this a time to come for the clothes, when everyone has gone to the fields or the river bank? I can't get up now, come back tomorrow,' the old woman Mutthamma said, laying her head down again.

'Ammov, put out your washing.'

'Here, little one, come and collect this.'

Mary usually collected all along one side of a street. She had not quite finished that side. But Chadayan called out from the opposite side, from the thinnai where he was seated. The minute she heard his voice, Mary felt as if her breath was draining away.

'I'll just take these clothes to the end of the street and then come back, saami.'

'Come and take this as well.'

'It's heavy, saami; let me take these away and then come back.'

'Vannaati girl, are you so impertinent?'

'No saami, please...it's very heavy.'

Chadayan's bullying tone frightened Mary. She was always terrified by the very presence of Chadayan. Startled, trembling within, she dropped the bundles of clothes from her head and waist on to the middle of the street where she stood. She came over to the entrance of his house, shivering with fear. She remembered that very often when she came round to collect clothes or food, he would speak provocatively to her.

Chadayan was a kothukkaaran, a long-established resident of the colony. He could do what he pleased to Mary. Nobody would be able to question him. When the panchayat met, he always handed out severe penalties and beatings, so people did not have the courage to cross him. He was always on the lookout, with his snake's eyes, to pick on people who were doing wrong. So all the kothukkaarar and karaikkaarar were in his hands.

Chadayan could easily find an opportunity to call her family to stand trial in front of the panchayat, on the pretext that they had not done the washing properly. Arokkyam's family was the lowest servicing clan for the whole town.

'Tell them to bring out the clothes, saami.'

'She's out of doors. Go and take them yourself, from the corner where they are lying.'

'Saami!'

Chadayan sat in the front verandah, fidgeting with his leg continuously. Mary never came here by herself. Arokkyam would always send Peter along with her. Now Mary wished desperately that she had brought him. She made a prayer, in her mind, to Saint Anthony of Melnariappanur.

'Saami, push the clothes out with a stick.'

'Chi, who can touch all that pollution? How can a man do it?'

'Where are the clothes, saami?'

'Inside.'

'Ammov, I've come; it's the vannaati's daughter. Who's at home?'

Mary went inside to look. Chadayan's wife, Amaravari, was nowhere to be seen. Chadayan's was a big house with an upper storey. In the whole colony, his was the only house with rooms upstairs. Everyone in town called Chadayan, 'the owner of the house with the upper storey.'

Don't, please, saami.

It's wrong, saami.

It's not right, saami.

I'll lose my reputation, saami.

I won't be able to show my face in the street, saami.

The family will be finished for ever, saami.

Mary did not have much physical strength, in the first place. More than that, she was simply paralysed with fear. Her body quaked all over, as if she were caught in some terrible cold. She held on tightly to his foot as she pleaded with him. She was trapped against the last corner of the house. She was in a room full of old bundles and pieces of luggage. She prayed desperately to Saint Anthony.

When she thought to herself that the townsfolk would accuse her of having set out deliberately to seduce the kothukkaaran, her eyes began to dim in sheer terror. Her tongue could not move. She could no longer utter a sound. She thought his entire body gave off a stink of toddy. For an instant she wondered what would happen even if she were to shout out aloud. What if the whole colony were to know? But what could they do to Chadayan? And what would happen to Arokkyam? O God! Anthonyaare! O Arokkya Mary! Mother of Good Health!

Chadayan could do whatever he wished. He could put it about that this vannaan was no good. He could say they definitely needed a different vannaan in this town, and drive them away. He could install a new vannaan in their place. He could do anything. And he would. Savuri's family was a very lowly one.

It seems that even Savuri's father did not know how they had first come to this place as vannaans. It was possible that his father's father knew who it was who had been established as sole vannaan to this town; how the townsfolk had brought him here; the terms of that contract. Arokkyam did not know the details either, when the people of this town had realised their need for a vannaan, what the elders of the town had said amongst themselves; neither did she know who had been installed, nor how all that had happened. To this day, Mary had never asked about it. She didn't even think about it. No such thought had ever crossed her mind. Nor had Arokkyam ever talked about these things. So where was it that Mary actually belonged? This town was where she was born. But was it the home of her ancestors, through seven or eight generations? Mary began to weep. If the townsfolk chased them away now, where were they to go?

When everyone in the colony worshipped the gods Maariaayi, Murugan, Venkatachalapati, Kaliyamman and the others, why should they alone worship the Lord Jesus? Why did they belong to the Christian faith? And as vannaans? If they were Hindus like the others, they would not need to wash clothes. They would have many more relations. The men would not dare to pester the womenfolk like this; they would be afraid of causing real fights. For the first time she thought, why do they say we are Christians, and Roman Catholics, at that.

The grip on Mary pressed down and tightened.

It's the vannaati, saami
I'm a woman who will soon be married, saami
My whole family will be ruined, saami
I could become pregnant, saami
I'll kill myself, saami
I touch your feet, ayya
Think of me as the daughter of your own body, ayya
If you want, you can kill me, burn me to ashes
O Saint Anthony
O God O Saint Anthony O Mother Mary.

Mary crouched in the corner of the house and wept as if she were dying. She looked again and again at each part of her body and wept aloud. She rained blows upon her own head and chest. She did not notice that her sari had slipped away from her breasts and her waist. She beat the ground again and again with her fists. She wept continuously. There seemed to be no end to her weeping. The sweat rolled off her body, making the earth wet.

Mary walked slowly back along the streets of the colony as if only the wind could shift her. Her eyes were like that of a corpse. Deep within, they were full of death. That stark look seemed to pierce its way beyond the skies in an attempt to find something, somewhere there, that she was seeking.

At first, Arokkyam was startled. Then she thought that surely someone in the street had scolded Mary. But, besides the loud weeping, there was no answer to Arokkyam's question. After a while, Arokkyam grew very frightened. She could not bring herself to say anything more. Her fear only brought tears and rage. Her eyes filled with darkness.

When Mary continued to weep as if her whole life were leaving her, Arokkyam could no longer stay lying down. She climbed down from the front bench and came to sit by Mary. Still no reply. Ceaseless weeping. A terrible weeping which grew out of helplessness, humiliation and extreme loss shook the hut.

Arokkyam understood everything. She too was a woman. She who lived in this town, what did she not know? The meaning of Mary's tears could not be hidden from her. There wasn't a single secret which women of that town kept hidden in their hearts that Arokkyam did not know. Now she became as still as a stone. Then she moved a little, took Mary in her arms, consoling her. She too wept. But Mary began to weep even more fiercely than before. Arokkyam led her away, and made her lie down.

Mary sobbed, lying curled up like a child. How was she to be comforted, with what words? Every time Arokkyam opened her mouth in an attempt to say a word, tears overcame her, in spite of herself. Yet she kept muttering the same thing over and over again:

Saint Anthony
Saint Anthony

Saint Anthony
O God O God
God should have led her, but even he has no eyes. Now he has destroyed and betrayed us.
Is he likely to rub off and re-write the fate he wrote for us at the moment of our making?
Is this like a head-load that we can remove or change?
Our lives have changed forever
Saint Anthony
O God O God
Blind God, without eyes to see.

Arokkyam slowly shuffled to the front pathway and looked out. There wasn't a single bundle of clothes lying there. Her heart beat fast. What would happen to them if someone stole all the good clothes? Arokkyam forgot that she was ill and walked towards the main street of the colony. She wept as she went, all along the way. She was careful, though, that nobody should notice it, outwardly. If anyone were to ask, what could she say? She thought to herself that she alone was to blame for what had happened. Mary should have taken Peter along with her. She felt irritation and anger towards Peter. Hereafter, she must never send Mary to collect food or the washing. She decided she must not even take her to the thorapaadu. Nobody should know what had happened; they must not even tell Savuri. I'm a sinner, she thought, my very birth was a sin. Everything I do is a sin, everything I desire is a sin. O god, it's like crushing a flower...

Thinking many thoughts, resolving upon many things, Arokkyam picked up each bundle lying there in the main street, and carried it home. She could not be at peace any more. Her treasure had been looted from her. The one thing that she wanted to protect and cherish had been destroyed. Now there was nothing left. Except darkness within.

'Ammov.'

'What's the matter with you, sleeping on your haunches!'

Arokkyam came to herself only after Peter shouted loudly at her for a second time. Her eyes filled when she realized she had been sitting in the middle of the street like this, lost in thought. Peter had collected all the clothes together, from the different street comers. She stood up, pushing away her memories and her fatigue.

Arokkyam and Peter brought all the clothes to their front door, in two trips. As soon as it was all done, Arokkyam lay down just there, exhausted, in the pathway.

As the sun was setting, Savuri came home, carrying his bag. Nobody asked him anything. Neither Mary nor Arokkyam asked him a single word about Josep or Sahayam, nor whether he had visited the saamiyaar or not. They never spoke a word to him. As for Savuri, he thought that they would not speak to him because he had been away for all of three days. Then, seeing all the clothes lying there, he was startled, then frightened; he demanded the reason. For three days the clothes had not been washed. They had accumulated into a very big heap. He was filled with anxiety. What would the townsfolk say?

Savuri ran into the street. Then he came back and questioned Arokkyam. He looked for Peter. He was infuriated that Mary was lying down inside the house, and Arokkyam on the outside ledge, and that neither would speak to him. He calculated that Mary and Arokkyam had quarrelled with each other and asked, 'What's the matter with mother and daughter,

I want to know? It's like a house of death around here. Ei, little one, I'm talking to you.'

Arokkyam asked Mary whether she would light the wood-stove and make a little gruel. Mary was extremely exhausted and weary. She washed her swollen face, she left the house and came outside only after it had darkened completely. She sat down in front of the stove, still in tears. In the light of the burning stove, her face looked anguished. She cooked a handful of rice, making gruel for Arokkyam alone. The evening's collection of food would be sufficient for Savuri and Peter. Savuri had called out to Mary three times already. It was only at the fourth call that Mary heard him. As if she had come to herself at last, she came to the threshold of the house.

'What is it?'

'How many times must I call you? Why are you putting on these airs?'

'Didn't hear.'

'All right, all right. Bring me some rice or whatever.'

'There's only some leftover rice.'

'Bring it. What do you get up to, magic or trickery, that you can't even cook some rice?'

Mary went about her business like a machine. Then she strained the old rice from the water that covered it, and brought it to Savuri who was sitting out in the street. She did it all as if from force of habit.

'Why is the rice slimy, child?'

'Don't know.'

'What do you mean, don't know. I'm asking you why the rice has gone slimy, and you can't tell me. Are you a woman?'

'If the rice has gone off, what can I do about it?'

'Is there a hair or anything that has fallen into it? Hm...' Savuri kept poking at the rice and turning it over. Mary stood in front of him, solid as a tree. She felt neither sorrow nor anger. She stood there in an utterly strange way.

'It must have gone off because it was handled. How would a hair have fallen into the rice, I ask you.'

'You are the one who combs her hair a hundred times in a single hour. There's another one out there who's the cause of all this. Combing her hair all the time, and making her pottu, and putting on her face powder by the handful, shoving a cartload of mai on her eyes. Is that what a family woman should be doing? If you behave like a street performer, then of course there will be hair in the rice. It doesn't look as if she is making a family.'

Mary thought of Sahayam. She realized that all this invective was actually aimed at Sahayam, and had just turned to go inside when Savuri addressed her again. 'If you have a couple of chillies, just pop them into the fire and bring them here. My tongue can't taste a thing, it's dead.'

Mary knew that when Savuri asked for a couple of chillies, he really meant about ten. She scooped up a handful of dry red chillies, put them against a corner of the still burning stove and roasted them. Before she could toast them to the perfect point without burning them, he shouted at her, 'Why does it have to take so long? Are you roasting a pig or are you roasting a handful of chillies? You'll never be able to make a household for a man. At your age shouldn't you be as quick as a spinning top? Is this the way she brought you up?'

Mary brought the bunch of roasted chillies and placed them in front of Savuri. Savuri bit into one before each mouthful of rice. When he looked up and found Mary standing there, he could only feel irritation. He thought to himself, why is this child standing there in that unkempt fashion, as if everything is lost and gone? It was because of this unease that he spoke sharply to Mary. He had never before this, picked a quarrel unnecessarily with Mary, nor been severe with her. Equally, it was the first time that Mary had talked back to Savuri.

Savuri finished eating, picked up the vessels for the evening food, and went through the darkness, towards the main street.

Mary served the food that Savuri brought to him and Peter. She poured water over what was left, and covered the vessels. Arokkyam refused even the freshly made gruel in a muttered voice, and laid herself down. Mary herself did not eat, although Arokkyam argued with her. Savuri lay down in the front path. Peter ran away to play in the street.

Four or five times in the night, Arokkyam got up from where she lay in the front verandah ledge, looked at Mary and returned. Finally she came inside and lay down by Mary's side. Mary lay staring at the inner ridge of the roof; confused, yet aware of all that was going on around her. Tears ran down her cheeks.

Her gaze seemed to pierce through the roof and seek something beyond.

Throughout that week, Savuri was required elsewhere, out of town. Twice he was asked to take out the vaaykkarisi, the rice for the dead. One day he had to carry the news of a death. Then he had to attend a wedding. So when Diraviyaraj came to visit, Savuri was not at home.

It was amaavasai when he returned. There had been rather a lot of washing. Arokkyam had laundered and delivered all of it by midday. Savuri and Arokkyam went together to collect the food in the evening. Both vessels, for rice and for kuzhambu were full. Every month, at amaavasai, Arokkyam received enough food to last them for three days. Otherwise, such plentiful helpings of rice and kuzhambu came to them only on festival days. Can every day be amaavasai? If it were, then nobody would be so stingy that they would not even offer them the food left sticking to an unwashed hand.

Savuri ate a handful of rice, then took himself off to sleep. He asked about Diraviyaraj's visit of the day before. Arokkyam lay with her head against the front steps, and told him in detail about the visit of Theresa's son, Diraviyaraj. She told it like a story from start to finish, and he listened, interrupting her every now and then, with a murmur of assent.

***

'Anyone at home?'

'Who is it?'

'It's me.'

'What do you mean, "it's me". Who is it? I can't make out your voice.'

Diraviyaraj entered the house, pushing aside the door of woven palmyra leaves which had been left slightly ajar. For a moment he stood silent, stock-still. He looked at Mary as if he would swallow her up. Then he sat down at a little distance from her.

Mary tucked her legs under her, making some space for him. They looked at each other intently. Neither spoke a word; they were confused about what to say. Diraviyaraj had come in the certainty of finding Arokkyam there. Now he told himself that she must be at the thorapaadu. Mary pulled down her petticoat which had ridden above her knee. She began to sew, still not knowing what to say to him. For some reason, her eyes filled with tears. At the same time, she was resolved to prevent them from falling. Suddenly her heart grew heavy.

She was mending a blanket. She held one end of the tear between her toes and was sewing it from the other end, with a big needle. The strain showed every time she pushed the needle in and pulled it through. The blanket was a rough one. Matted dirt added to its weight, and it resisted the entry of the needle. At times, the needle bent, almost as if it would break. Had it been the needle that she used for mending saris, it would have broken at the very start. But this was a long thick needle, such as cobblers use to sew water-skins. A heavy, tough one. Her thumb and forefinger began to ache.

Diraviyaraj watched Mary sewing without once blinking his eyes. Noticing this, Mary felt shy, and asked with a little smile, 'Is there something on my face? Why are you watching me like that? What's the matter?'

'Yes, there is something.'

'Chi.'

'Why do you say that?'

'Move off.'

Anybody who observed from a distance the way Mary sat, her legs outstretched, holding the blanket with her toes and sewing, might have made a bet that it was an old woman they saw there. The way she sat, leaning against a wall for greater convenience; the way she held her threaded needle; the beauty of those regular stitches...She sat there as if she had been born only in order to spin out a living by mending torn clothes in return for a couple of measures of grain.

It was now five or six years since Diraviyaraj had left Arokkyam's house. Before that, it was at this house that he had grown up. In those days, he would go to the thorapaadu with the rest of them, every day. They had two donkeys then. The bundles of washing used to be tied to the backs of both. Mary and he would ride a donkey each. Mary would chatter unceasingly, all the way to the thorapaadu. She would clap her hands and laugh spontaneously. She would start to shout for no reason. Diraviyaraj would deliberately urge his donkey on ahead. Sometimes he would lean forward and kick the young donkey that Mary rode. The donkey, having been kicked, would start to howl. Mary would start weeping loudly, along with it. Diraviyaraj would laugh at this. Mary, furious at his laughter, would weep all the more, and scold. She would run up and hit him.

Savuri would walk ahead of the donkeys, with a bundle of clothes on his head. Arokkyam came at a little distance behind them. Peter sat on her hip. Behind her Josep sauntered along, lost in his dreams. Arokkyam walked along with a smile, as if observing everything for the first time. Every day it was as if they were making a long journey elsewhere. The way they went seemed to suggest that they had nothing left to do in that place, and might as well move on.

Wherever Diraviyaraj went, Mary would run along with him. Arokkyam would catch hold of her as she ran, and wrap a little cloth about her waist. Even that was a token, just reaching her knees. 'How can a female chick go about naked? It doesn't matter for the boys, they can run about the streets as they please, ringing their bells,' Arokkyam would say.

Arokkyam, Mary and he would all three sleep on the same mat at nights. Mary used to wet the bed every night. As soon as dawn broke, he would tease her, 'Piss-pot, ei piss-pot.' Half laughing, half in tears, she would rush at him, wanting to hit him. Clutching at the cloth that was slipping down from her waist, she would complain loudly. Arokkyam would scold him, but laughing at the same time, 'Why do you get at her, da, even before the sun has risen? Once the little nuisance starts crying, she won't stop the whole day.' With that, she would take the piece of sacking, all wet with urine, and put it out in the sun. The earthen floor beneath would be swollen and cracked. Arokkyam would repair it with cowdung. 'Look how this child pours out the urine in such quantities,' she would say.

Now Diraviyaraj wanted to talk a lot to Mary and ask all sorts of questions. But Mary behaved as if he was someone whom she had not met before. She had not expected his arrival. The sight of him troubled her heart somehow. He comforted himself with the thought, She is grown up now. That's why she feels shy. As Diraviyaraj had grown older, many responsibilities fell to him. He had to do all the jobs of taking up the washing and delivering it, collecting the evening rice, as well as doing all the business of weddings, funerals and final obsequies. He could hardly ever leave home. Only his mother, Theresa, would attend at family occasions. He had not been able to visit, even when Mary came of age. But he thought of this family, whenever possible. Above all, it was Arokkyam he remembered and thought about. Theresa could no longer cope. He had come to inform them about the state of her health.

'Why are you sitting there like a lump of oilcake?'

'O, for no reason.'

'Will you eat or drink something?'

'No thanks, I ate my fill before I set out.'

'In that case, why don't you lie down and sleep?'

'When will Athai come home?'

'Only at sunset time.'

'And Maama?'

'He's gone to get some cleansing clay.'

'All right then. Hand me that, I'll sew it.'

'No thanks. Just move further away.'

'Why shouldn't I sew it?'

'Did you do my sewing for me all these days? Or have you given me a couple of measures of grain in return for my sewing?'

'You want me to give you something, do you?'

'Yes, yes, just move away.'

Diraviyaraj plucked away the needle from Mary, laughing, and began to sew the blanket. She held on to the other end. When he moved forward a little, in order to hold the blanket firmly without stretching it, she moved further back. Again he moved forward, and again she shrank back.

'I can do it on my own.'

'If you hold it so taut, how can I sew?'

'You don't have to do anything for me.'

'Leave it. Let go, I tell you.'

'I know how to sew. You just move off.'

As Mary pulled at one end and Diraviyaraj at the other, the thread snapped. He raised his arm as if to slap her, and she dropped the blanket and turned away to the other end of the hut where the cooking fires were. Diraviyaraj threaded the needle once again and began to sew, holding the blanket taut with his toes, just as she had done. His stitches were neither tight, nor close together, but stood out separately. After a while, Mary returned and held the other end of the blanket for him. He went on sewing.

'Is everyone keeping well?'

'They are.'

'And your mother?'

'She's all right.'

'And how is the work doing?'

'We pull along, somehow.'

'And why is your mouth going like that, as if you had eaten something bitter?'

'There isn't even a bitter neem fruit to eat in these parts.'

Suddenly Mary broke out into loud tears. He could not console her. Weeping more and more, she said to him, 'Nothing is like it used to be. Amma takes the clothes away and washes them every day. But she doesn't have the strength any more. As for Annan, he's gone off to live in Chinnasalem. It must be more than six months now, since he went. I've been doing some mending, collecting a little—a quarter or half anna here and there. Amma bought a little goat out of the money. It's just had two kids. Now even this mending has gone. There's a tailor who has come and set up shop. And it's over two months now that another vannaan has come here and started up a laundry business.'

As she wept, Mary leaned down and drew lines on the earthen floor with her fingers. Her fingers would freeze momentarily, then begin those lines again.

'What happened to the donkey? Why is Athai carrying the clothes herself?'

'The old one died the year after you went away. We've sold the little one because of our money worries.'

'So it's all gone. That donkey was like a baby elephant.'

And it was a handsome beast. However many bundles were slung on to its back, it carried them without grumbling. It always moved on, moved forward. The little one was as good as its mother. It did not lag behind while carrying its burden. Diraviyaraj thought to himself that they should not have sold off such a well-bred donkey. Without those donkeys how were they managing to carry six and seven bundles—at the very least—every day to the thorapaadu?

'Once the donkeys went, we lost all our good fortune. We'll never be able to get such fine animals again, even if we begged for them. It was only after we got those donkeys that this family progressed. Since they left their tethering place, we've lost everything.'

'And how are all of you, since the donkeys left?'

'O, we just keep alive.'

They were excellent donkeys. Arokkyam had bought the older one when it was still a young animal, in return for eight marakkaal of cholam, from a kuravan who made grindstones and mortars and pestles out of stone. There was a fierce famine at that time. There wasn't such an animal to be obtained elsewhere. Because of the famine, the kuravan had sold the donkey. Savuri had been hesitant to buy it. But Arokkyam had fought to have her way. It was a good-looking donkey, with a patch of white on its head. When Arokkyam first claimed it, it was only a baby, and quite thin. Within months of coming into Arokkyam's possession, it had grown sleek. Peter, Mary and he would ride it every day. They would take it to graze. They would fight with each other, each claiming sole ownership of it. Each had a different name for the donkey. They bathed it. They twisted its tail and made it run, and then chased after it, laughing. They wandered all day, taking it to graze along the side of the stream.

He stopped sewing and asked, 'What was the hurry? Were things really so bad that you had to sell the donkey?'

'We sold it because of the wedding.'

'And how are you carrying the clothes?'

'Who gives us their washing as they did in the old days? They are all running to the laundry-shop now.' She began crying once again. Then, wiping her eyes and nose, she asked resentfully, 'You didn't even bother to come to the wedding. You're busy being an advocate, I suppose?'

'But my mother came, didn't she?'

'Who asked about her?'

'The work has been endless. I seem to have to give up my entire being in exchange for just three quarters of a paisa. There seems to be no way one can even stand quietly in a corner to gulp down a small amount of gruel.'

'Saint Anthony doesn't have eyes, you see.'

'He doesn't have the eyes or the heart even to take a quick glance to notice whether people are alive or dead. What good can your family or community do for you? Even if you can command an army of a thousand men, in the end it's your own arm and leg that will do your bidding.'

'One's body is one's only wealth. What use is anything else?'

When Diraviyaraj's father died, Arokkyam had brought him away. Within a year of her husband's death, Theresa had begun a relationship with his youngest brother. That clandestine affair had gone on for ten years. After that, Theresa had left this brother-in-law. For some years she had lived alone. But six years ago when her illness became so much worse that she needed someone to care for her, she had come to fetch Diraviyaraj. After he went with his mother, he found he had so much to do that he had not been able to come back and visit Arokkyam.

'Hereafter I intend to stay here always.'

'Whatever for?'

'For your sake, that's why.'

'Chi, you don't have any shame or respect. Move off. My mother will be angry.'

Diraviyaraj laughed. This made Mary even more annoyed. Suppressing her anger, she said, 'You don't have to hang around for my sake.'

'Who are you to say that to me? Let my athai tell me.'

'This is like the tale which goes "I'll give you a pearl necklace; don't hesitate to come to me." If you want your aunt, then run to the thorapaadu. Go on, get a move on, run.'

'I'll go in a little while. What happened to the house? Where are all your bundles and belongings? It looks as bare as a cremation ground.'

'Who is there now to take pity on a starving family and give us a couple of handfuls of grain so that we can just survive? There isn't even a handful left in the storage barrel as a token of next year's harvest.'

'How can you say these things?'

'Do you think I say all this as some kind of joke? I tell you these days it is difficult even to get enough to eat. It is by Saint Anthony's grace that we still stay alive on this earth...It would be best to close one's eyes and end it all. After all, there is no wealth that is coming to us in this life...And what use is this life when everything else is lost.'

'Whatever are you saying to me?'

'Nothing. You just move off.'

'You are behaving like a cow that will only take a step forward after its tail has been twisted, and tortured.'

'It's got to be like that everywhere; we have all become like those obstinate animals.'

Diraviyaraj couldn't believe anything. He had come with other expectations. This town wasn't as miserable as his own. It wasn't so small either. It served as a feeder for seven or eight villages. You didn't have to go elsewhere to buy goods because you couldn't get them here. There were five, six provision stores, and all sorts of other shops. There never was a bad famine. You always saw a greenness surrounding the town. And there was a bigger paraya settlement here than in other towns. So it should not have been difficult for one servicing vannaan family to survive. The townsfolk weren't such rowdy people either.

However severe a famine in those parts, Arokkyam's granary always used to be full. It contained varagu most of all. She would pour in the varagu first, then place in the cholam, kambu and ragi, each tied into a separate bundle. Finally she would replace the lid of the granary and smooth it over tightly with cowdung. The granary was there long before she came to live in this house. During the rainy months of Kaartikai and Aippasi, people who had no grain left would come and buy supplies from her. During times of famine, it used to be Arokkyam alone who was in a position to sell her grain.

Even the people known to the panchayat as prosperous householders did not possess the bottles, baskets and what not that she did. In Arokkyam's house there used to be different sets of baskets and bottles and winnowing trays. They would all contain one sort of grain or the other, at least in a small quantity. Or there would be tiny bundles of different kinds of pulses. Her pots and her baskets held as wide a variety of grains as a field mouse's hole at harvest time.

There was a big hole at the base of the granary as if made by a rat. Mary sat beside it now. Nothing seemed right anywhere. Diraviyaraj thought that it was the same everywhere these days; one had to leave the country entirely in order to find some means of survival.

'Why don't you mend this hut? With the rain and the damp, this wall looks as if it is going to fall down.'

'And even if it is built up again, whom will it support?'

'Why do you talk like this?'

'Don't say anything; just go.'

The wall next to the granary was leaning to one side, weakened by the rain. It would surely fall in the next rainy season. If the roof were thatched, they could continue to live here. Otherwise, they might as well drain the water out with a bucket and a pulley. And in the midst of all this they had set aside a corner to tether the baby goat. Thinking wearily that everything had indeed changed, he rose to his feet.

'Well then, I'll go to the thorapaadu.'

'Very well.'

Mary came out into the street and stood awhile, staring after Diraviyaraj as he walked away. Tears began to stream down her cheeks. She was startled by this. Then she laughed. Again, she wept because of her own laughter. Her face was swollen. She picked up her mending and began to sew again. The needle sank into her finger as she was mending a flimsy sari. She put her finger into her mouth and sucked it; then continued to sew. Her fingertip began to throb with pain. She pressed on with her sewing, knowing that her mending would bring her a quarter or half measure of grain, or perhaps something to add to the curry—chillies or dal or tamarind. Her waist ached as if she were being pulled apart. Her legs had lost all feeling.

After Diraviyaraj left, thoughts and memories kept playing in her mind.

How grown-up he seemed now, with his moustache and beard! He had been as thin as a stick, always clinging to Arokkyam's sari-pleats. However firmly a cloth was tied around his waist, it never lasted there for long. He would sit astride the donkey and get up to all sorts of tricks. Mary and Diraviyaraj had quarrelled over every single thing, from the right to cling to Arokkyam's sari-pleats to the right to sleep next to her at night. It was always competition, quarrelling, fist-fights and tears.

Mary had been shocked when she saw him now. At first it was just surprise. But as he kept on talking to her, as he kept coming close to her, she had wanted to keep adjusting her sari across her breasts and at her waist. She couldn't believe that this was the same snotty-nosed lad she had known. Only Theresa had been to visit them, both on the occasion of her coming of age, and when Josep got married. Both times she had teased Mary with her questions. 'Well, di, my beloved daughter-in-law, when are you going to give me a grandchild, then?'

'Chi.'

'Look at her, how shy she is. Get on with it, di. Don't blame me later on. The girls are already queuing up for him.'

'Who'll marry your son? He's as black as charcoal.'

'You say that now!'

'Ayya, no never. Look for someone else.'

'Look at the way she jiggles about and runs off.'

'Black as charcoal! Black as charcoal!'

Theresa had talked like this always on her recent visits. Mary would get angry; the tears would come. She'd start wailing even more loudly when Arokkyam joined in the laughter. But when Diraviyaraj had lived with them as a small boy, Theresa had taken a different tone then.

'Have you got round my son already, taken him over?'

'Amma, listen to her.'

'Say yes,' Arokkyam would goad her on.

'You have neither conscience nor feeling.'

Mary stopped sewing suddenly and began to weep again.

***

It was high noon. Diraviyaraj walked on, silently, his eyes roving about the scene surrounding the footpath. This path wasn't strange to him by any means. He took the cloth that was slung over his shoulder and twisted it into a turban about his head. He had walked along this very path many years ago. Every day; and several times in a single day. Often he had run along it at a single stretch.

Every day he had walked beside this orderly row of karuvelam trees. He had gone in procession, riding his donkey. The people who lived here, the stream, the vannaan's pond, the temple, the houses, the fields and their boundaries—he had known them all. What did he not know about this place? Well, possibly, some people who were already very old when he was living here, were no longer about. He knew how to assess—from the washing they put out—everything about each family, its members, its state of affairs. But of course, it was Arokkyam who understood this best. Somehow she knew everything.

He left the town behind him and descended into the path that led to the thorapaadu. He picked up a stone and threw it along the path that stretched out in front of him. He smiled to himself. He walked on, throwing stones ahead of him, again and again.

The path was just wide enough for the passage of bullock carts. It went up and down, bending and twisting like the track of a snake. If you kept along it, you came to the stream, then the fields, then a waste space staring at the skies. After that, there was the Aadanur stream. A few houses belonging to the people there. Beyond that, Pulivalam, Kizhceruvaay, Thittikudi and so on.

On the other side of the path, palmyra and date palms in dense rows. Between them icchapputtru, cactus, karuvelam trees and flowering bushes such as oleander and wild jasmine were tightly plaited and bound together, as if they were strung on to a single rope. Amongst them small insects and dark coloured bees roamed, humming, echoing and reverberating.

With Mary and Josep he had plucked wild fruit that grew in this dense, jungle-like hedge. Josep was a skilled climber of trees. He would pluck and throw down naaval, jujube and even palm fruit. Arokkyam would shout and scold after him, 'Josep, don't climb those trees, da.'

'There might be a cobra in the anthills, da.'

'The wasps would have built their nests in the trees there.'

'There could be an adder, green as the leaves, coiled within the oleander bush. It could make straight for your eyes. What will I do then?'

'Josep!'

'How did this boy come to be born from this womb which only pleads for a plate of gruel?'

'What kind of life is this? God gives me nothing but sorrow.'

As soon as the bundles were lowered from the donkey, the children would claim that they would graze it, and drive it along the river bank. They would leave it in a safe place. It would stand there just where they left it, grazing as quietly as if it had been tethered.

Having left the donkey, they would not so much as show their faces at the thorapaadu until the evening, when the clean clothes were ready to be tied to the donkey's back again. They would rove like bees, from tree to tree and all along the woods. The nuna fruit made them produce utterly black faeces. If they ate too many palmyra fruit, they would suffer from violent pains in the stomach and diarrhoea. Mary usually folded her skirt into an apron to pick up the fruit. She never seemed to be bothered by thorns. Tucking a small sickle into his waist string, Josep leapt from tree to tree, never ever hurting himself. But Arokkyam would keep on calling after them:

'Ade, Josep
Ei, Diraviyam
Ei, little one, Mary.'

Where have the little devils gone and hidden themselves? 'They never ever listen to me, look,' she'd scold. Then she'd say, 'O Jesus, O Lord.'

What had been common grazing land for sheep and cows was now cultivated fields. Everywhere there were pump sets worked by electricity. When he had lived here, the irrigation was still done by old-fashioned lift-wells. How delightful they used to sound, the pull of the kamalai, the steady beat of footsteps treading the etram, the seven or eight voices joining in a chorus as the water splashed out at the end. Now there were engines and motors; electric wires surrounded the small town, twisting and looping over the land as if there were streets there. They had made a casuarina grove in the saline ground. In fact, it was casuarina that could be seen in great abundance. That, and eucalyptus. Several kinds of trees stood about as if they had been planted in burial holes.

Diraviyaraj folded up and tied his vetti, left the cart-track and stepped down onto a footpath that branched off from it.

Little children who were out grazing cows and goats as well as old people, were sheltering in the shade of trees, fearful of the heat of the day. And like a snake's track, the well-worn path went, bending and curving through the densely packed plants and trees, stretching forward endlessly.

It was the same path they had to take, even during the rainy season. At those times, the mud and mire would come up to their knees. Once it grew dark, the people who lived in those parts never used the path, fearing snakes and insects. But Arokkyam never cared about the time or the season. She would walk along the path whenever she needed to. Nothing had ever happened to her. Just as most people spend the largest part of their lives asleep, so Arokkyam had spent the largest part of her life walking that path. The heat of the day suggested that it might possibly rain later. Such humidity! Such sultry heat. For some time the skies had remained just like this, gleaming like a freshly washed bronze pot, white as stretching salt-pans.

As the vannaan's pool came within sight, he hastened, eager, taking longer strides. Along the river-bank, brown sheep grazed and cleared their throats, their mouths dripping with spittle. In the shade of a neem tree, a small boy was plucking the ticks off a cow. Diraviyaraj too had plucked ticks off the donkey, with Josep and Mary. He himself would always pick them off from behind the ears. They would squash the ticks against stones, smell them, and try to smear the black blood upon each other, fighting and squabbling. He smiled as he remembered this. He laughed to himself with the embarrassment of one who remembers a night-time dream, and tries to explain it to others during the day.

Even from a distance, he could hear Arokkyam pounding the clothes. The sound alternated with its echo in a rhythmic series. Always when Arokkyam beat the clothes, you could hear a particular kind of echoing wave of music. The dense jungle standing on either side of the river-bank would keep echoing the sound of the beaten clothes. Before the sound of each slap of cloth against stone could die away, the echo of the previous slap would begin.

He stepped on the burning sand of the river beach and walked on. It felt hot enough to scorch his soles. Not a single cloud in the sky. The river bed lay dry and exposed. He was astonished at this. There must be just a little water left in the vannaan's pool at least, he thought.

Each year, during the summer season, Savuri would dig a large pool in the riverbed. Once the rains came, he would have to remake it again and again. During the high summer, there would be water only in the thorapaadu, known as the vannaan's pool. This water never dried up, even in the months of Chittirai and Vaikasi. The cattle and goats would need to come here to slake their thirst. And those people who grazed their cattle and goats too would drink the same disturbed water, kneeling and stooping down, as if their lives depended on it. They would drink again and again, breathing deeply. On the opposite side, the animals too would drink.

Dropping the sari which she was just about to beat against the stone, Arokkyam gathered up Diraviyaraj in her arms and kissed him. She began to pour out all her troubles, weeping and sobbing.

'Could you find your way here only now?'

'It's not that.'

'Can't you even bother to cast a glance at us, at least because we belong to the same folk.'

'...'

'How is your amma?'

'She's still there.'

'What do you mean?'

'We'll know in another ten days. I came because I know you will want to see her while she is still alive.'

'O Saint Anthony! Is this true?'

'Mm. Yes.'

'What a terrible thing, O Jesus!'

Arokkyam began to cry again. They sat under the shade of a pale green nochi tree. Peter, who had been wringing out and twisting the clothes, came and joined them.

'How is life in your parts?'

Times are changing.'

'What do you mean?'

'Families there too are just like the families here. Wherever we are, we have to manage by our own hard work.'

'And that's true too. Our fate is like that.'

Arokkyam asked again about Theresa. She listened, and wept from time to time. She talked at length of the times when she and Theresa were young. She could not believe that Theresa might be dead in another ten days. They talked for a long time and then went back to the water. Diraviyaraj picked up the clothes which Arokkyam had yet to wash and began to beat them against the flat stone.

'No, don't. You go home now. I'll be back very soon.'

'Leave this to me now.'

'Go and sit there, then, in the shade.'

'Let go, leave it.'

'O God, O Saint Anthony.'

Diraviyaraj and Peter beat the clothes for Arokkyam who rinsed them and put them out to dry. There were four large containers with wide mouths. Three of the containers were used for the cleansing clay; the other was full of water coloured with laundering blue. Arokkyam dissolved the cleansing clay with water in the three vessels, soaked each piece of clothing in it, wrung it out, and left it twisted, on the sand. The clothes fell, wrung out and twisted, one on top of the other, making a small mountain. The white clothes had already been washed, blued and laid out to dry.

Savuri would go once every week to Cherunesalur and bring back a used cement sack full of the cleansing clay. He had to go past that town, to a wood where the cleansing clay could be found. In former days, Savuri would bring sacks of it home on the donkey's back. That amount would do for a month's washing.It tasted as sharp as salt. And when the clothes were put to soak in water in which it was dissolved, the dirt simply disappeared from them, like salt in water. After that, they would beat out the clothes and rinse them.

'Why did you have to start on the clothes the moment you arrived?'

'What are you saying? Am I an outsider? Do you think I am working for the government in my village?'

'Did you go home?'

'I did.'

'Did you see that girl there?'

But when Diraviyaraj told her in detail about his visit, and his conversation with Mary, and how he had left the house, telling it like a play, Arokkyam fell silent. Suddenly she wanted to weep aloud.

There wasn't a lot of water. It was only a little pool, stagnant water collecting there briefly during the rainy season. It must be a while since Savuri worked at it. The rocks lay piled about, as if by design, some as flat as planks of wood, some sharply pointed. Nobody knew who had first discovered this place, whether it had been Savuri's father or grandfather. They had always laundered the clothes here, at this place, against this very stone-slab. Possibly this stone had been used for four or five generations. But people had changed, as the sound of a bell does, as it rings in sequence, changing its pitch each time.

On both banks of the river, the arali grew in abundance. It had a bright yellow flower. The vegetation was abundant: palm trees, naaval fruit trees, screwpine bushes, other plants and creepers. When the floods came, half the trees would disappear into the water. Arokkyam could calculate the depth of the water according to the different trees that had disappeared.

'What does Arokkyam lack, lucky thing! She's like a pious vellachi, neat and tidy after her puja. If you keep working in the fields and boundaries as we have to do, what's left of your body? Look at her, though, firm and round as a stone! What good does it do us to own five kaani of wet or dry land? Look at me, I look like a leather-worker.'

'Does she have to worry if the fields don't yield or the rain doesn't fall, tell me? What does she care? The entire paraya street's rice is hers to claim. Why won't she have a fine figure, then?'

In the old days, women would look at Arokkyam and say things like this. But now, Diraviyaraj thought, she had changed so much, and lost so much weight that you could scarcely recognize her.

Savuri, though, looked only half the size of Arokkyam. He was thin and wiry, as if he would fly away in the wind and bent over, with a hunch. Arokkyam strode proudly like a man. It was she who would demand the vannaan's yearly dues, or the odd gift, from the families of the town. It was she whom the townsfolk feared. Savuri went with her only for the sake of form. Now, Arokkyam's cheeks had sunk into hollows and her ribs stuck out. She used to have a novel way of beating out the clothes. With each stroke, she would call out, aa su aa su aa su. These sounds would rise, spreading over the stream, and echoing around the surrounding jungle.

Arokkyam never differentiated between people. She never made a fuss about who was her own, who was not. It was her practice always to be generous in giving. But she would not accept less than her due, either. Always there would be some event going on in one house or the other in the town. Food would be distributed. She would keep what she was given, however late it was, and distribute it to all the family. She liked to eat well. She wasn't one for keeping things until tomorrow. She wanted a full belly. She wanted plenty of laughter and song. If anyone was in tears, she joined in, weeping as if her very life was at stake. She would respond as if part of her own body was hurt. But like a child, she would forget it all the next instant.

As soon as the clothes were washed, Arokkyam rested for a while in the shade, and then separated the dry clothes, first according to each house, and then tied them in bundles according to the street. Then she hid away the four large containers within an enclosure, out of the sight of the small boys who herded the cattle and sheep.

Peter untied the sheep and goats which had been allowed to graze in circles and let them go home. Then, carrying one of the smaller bundles on his head, he too started homewards. Arokkyam piled three bundles on Diraviyam's back, one on top of the other, and then picked one up herself. And so they began their walk home, one following the other, each the other's shadow.

However much Arokkyam pleaded, Diraviyaraj would not listen, but set off home the same night.

When Theresa had delivered Diraviyaraj, the afterbirth did not descend, but stayed inside her. Eventually it grew into a tumour and gave her incessant pain. It was said that the tumour had even sprouted hair. Now her condition had worsened, bringing her to the point of death.

***

Arokkyam recounted all this. Savuri who had been listening to all of it, barked out, 'Did I ask you to tell me the whole story, di?'

'Never mind all that. You'd better go and see her tomorrow. Poor thing.'

'We'll see. And what's the matter with that child?'

'Which child?'

'Your daughter.'

Arokkyam and Savuri kept talking about Theresa and Diraviyaraj until it was time to collect the evening meal. But Arokkyam made no reply to Savuri's question about Mary.

The sun was setting when Arokkyam reached the chettiyaar's grocery store in the main street. She had just come from the thorapaadu. Her head was absolutely bursting. She thought that if she made a piquant rasam to drink, it would set it right, and so she had set off with a small twig-basket full of varagu, intending to exchange it for garlic and chillies.

Since the day before, Arokkyam had been feeling unwell. Perhaps it was because she had rolled about on the streets, beating her breast and wailing, after Theresa's death. She had left Savuri behind, and had returned home the previous evening. And Savuri himself had returned at dawn that day. Arokkyam was full of thoughts of Diraviyaraj. She talked incessantly about him that day.

On her way back with the garlic and chillies, it suddenly struck her that she would take a look at the new laundry man Periasaami, who seemed to have cast a spell over the whole town, like a magician, and also at the new tailor. Instead of turning her steps towards the colony, she kept walking along the town's other caste streets.

She asked everyone she met for the way to these newcomers. And suddenly she found herself getting angry. She was distressed that these people had so easily ruined her own means of livelihood. When this thought struck her, it was immediately followed by an impulse to turn around and go back after all; yet her feet impelled her forwards.

She could not follow the ways in which the townsfolk were thinking. One family had served this town; a vannaan family. Couldn't they understand that it was only by depending on the townsfolk that the vannaan and his family lit their kitchen fires? That it was through their generosity that they filled their bellies? How could they have the heart to betray the low-caste vannaan who lived by trusting them, who served them to the very end? Truly, people had changed. Not just Arokkyam, but those whom she knew, and her forefathers and mothers, had all worked here and served these people in an unbroken tradition. Arokkyam had never, to this day, caused any trouble. There had never been a serious delay or a hindrance in her work, serving the people here. And her very pulse-beat lay in the food and drink that they gave her. How unjust of them to change in this way. Arokkyam thought of all this. The thought that her entire means of livelihood had changed, and all the consequences of this, kept appearing and disappearing in her mind, like a vision that would not fade, however tightly she shut her eyes. Her feet did not seem to press down on the earth, they felt like a puppet's limbs.

Under what tree could she find shade and shelter? Where were the roots for her to cling to? What was there left for her to cling to?

The entire street had belonged to her.

Arokkyam went up to everyone—people walking towards her, the Gaunders and the Udaiyaars sitting in their front verandahs, and their women—and asked them about their families, their relatives, the crops growing in their fields, everything she wanted to know.

'Has it gone out of your mind, saami, that there is a vannaati woman here?'

'O Saint Anthony, how is it you have grown so thin? What has happened? Are you not keeping well?'

'Tell me all that has been happening to you, saami, good or evil.'

'There's not a thing to mix with the rice; throw me a couple of chillies, amma.'

'Don't forget the vannaati woman, saami.'

'It's your paraya-vannaati, saami.'

'Yes, yes, saami.'

'It's your paraya-vannaati, Arokkyam.'

'Don't forget the vannaati from the paraya household.'

'Yes, saami.'

'Keep me in mind, aandavare.'

'Yes, sir.'

'It's the paraya vannaati herself.'

'Arokkyam.'

'Where else can I go and stand, except at your feet?'

She measured the length of the street, looking at each house anew, as if she belonged to a different species of life. Her feet would not tread the earth firmly. She went along two streets, but could not find what she was looking for. Nor could she bring herself to ask anyone, any longer. The heat of the sun, fierce as flames, became unendurable; she loosened the sari across her breasts, and spread the end over her head as she walked along. Even the wind blew hot.

Sayibu had set up his tailor shop in front of the Picchaandavar temple. Fearful of the heat, he had hung up a curtain right across the shop front. She could only see his feet, yellowish, moving up and down on the pedals. There seemed to be a few clients inside the shop. Arokkyam walked away from the place swiftly, as if preparing for battle. She hastened, as if she were walking against the wind.

Suppressing the tears which accompanied a fury that seemed to rise from the very pit of her stomach, she walked on, speaking only a few words now to those whom she encountered. She no longer knew why she was walking on like this. Stumbling, she walked on, as if she had lost her common sense and consciousness.

It was scarcely two months since the tailor, Sayibu, had arrived here. Although his house and shop were in the main street of the town, he mended and sewed clothes for the people in the colony too. Mary had told her that people from many of the small towns roundabout also came to him as clients. Before this, it used to be Arokkyam who did the mending for the entire colony. Always there would be bundles of mending, waiting in heaps in Arokkyam's house. She could scarcely finish it all on her own. Savuri would never give her a hand with this. It was Arokkyam who got on with it endlessly. Except for the time that she spent at the thorapaadu, all the rest of her time was taken up with the mending. If she finished the mending and delivered it in time, she'd get perhaps half a measure of grain, or the ingredients for a curry. After Mary came of age, her job was to stay at home and do the mending all day long. By selling the goods that Mary received in exchange for her mending, Arokkyam had bought her a baby goat. It had grown up now, and had borne two little kids this past month. But nowadays, not a single soul brought them torn clothes to mend. Mary bewailed this. Because, before you could blink, in a trice, Sayibu sewed together clothes which were torn right across, or split along the seams. In former days, if they had wanted their clothes to be sewn by machine, they would have had to go to Thittikudi, Chinnasalem and such faraway places.

Arokkyam went past the streets with their alleyways and hideaways, and came at last to the house of the laundry man Periasaami. Her head began to swim; she felt bilious. At last she set off for home. Her heart was filled with darkness.

Periasaami's house was newly built on what was once a waste area between the colony and town streets. There wasn't a soul to be seen there. Extending outward from the front verandah of the house, an enclosure had been set up, made up of palmyra thatch. A long bench stood within. Some two or three sheets had been spread over it. On top stood a box-iron with a handle.

'The reason for all this is that the school, which only used to have five classes, has been made into a really big one, it seems. And all the teachers come wearing trousers, you see. It seems that there are even women in the school now. It's not like in the old days.' Mary had passed on all the gossip of the town to Arokkyam.

She could just about endure the thought of the tailor. It was the laundry man Periasaami who really agitated Arokkyam. The very thought of him being there shook her, as if something like a heavy stone rolled within her.

It must be barely two months since Periasaami opened his shop. Already, in that time, her situation had deteriorated. The clothes from the colony as well as the town now came to him. In the town, only a few of the old people continued to send their clothes to their own caste-vannaan nowadays.

As for the colony, the young women were giving Periasaami even their everyday cotton saris to be laundered. Only the sheets came to her to be washed. People were reluctant to give her their clothes any more, complaining, 'You beat them against your stone and tear them to shreds, vannaati woman.' Arokkyam called at the houses every day, and brought away only a few items. But they delivered their clothes to Periasaami, taking them there themselves. 'And it seems he returns the clothes folded and pressed, blued and crisply starched. It seems the clothes are brilliantly white; fresh as flowers. O God!'

When Arokkyam returned home, she was exhausted. She woke Mary up and asked her to make a rasam with the chillies and garlic. Then she sat down at the threshold, removed the sari end which she had used to cover her head, and wiped the sweat streaming down her neck, her chest and arms.

'Where have you been, in this baking heat?'

'Where would I go? Who is there on this earth that I can call mine? I can only look for a pond or a pool, fall into it and give up my life.'

'Did you go to the main street?'

'It's like the story of the farmer with one plough who lost out though he worked, and the farmer with two ploughs who lost out because he stopped.'

Mary's eyes filled. She went inside, peeling the garlic as she went. Sadly, she wished that Arokkyam had not gone to the main street. Mary had only told her mother that Periasaami did his ironing in the early morning and the late evening. She had not said specifically that Periasaami was never at home at midday.

In a little while, Mary brought the hot rasam in a brass-carrier. Rotating the carrier to stir the rasam, and blowing on its surface, Arokkyam drank it down. Although she pleaded that she had drunk enough, Mary would not let her off. Sweat streamed off Arokkyam.

'All these family cares have turned into lice on my head. Just scratch my scalp a little.'

Arokkyam loosened her hair from its knot, spread it out over her shoulder, and came and sat in front of Mary. Mary parted Arokkyam's hair, which was reddened through malnourishment, untangling it carefully and lifting it lock by lock as she looked for lice. As she picked off the lice, she would place them on the ground and squash them with both thumbnails.

Since Arokkyam had been to town and seen it all for herself, Mary felt able to ask, 'What if we too should take to the box-iron, Amma?'

'O for God's sake!'

'Why not, Amma?'

'Is that a suitable thing for our community?'

'But my brother does it, in Chinnasalem!'

'It's like the tale of the Lord God asking to share the beggar man's rice.'

Arokkyam jerked her head away sharply, gathered her hair up and tied it, then moved some distance away. Mary was frightened. She reprimanded herself for asking that question. Arokkyam was silent for a while, then began to sob quietly. It seemed she had forgotten about laundry man Periasaami and the tailor; her attention focused solely on Josep.

'I bore a child with love and reared him with care. But what happened? He just ran away and disappeared. Why did you have to mention him now? The rascal chose to come and be born in my womb. Now he's lost his head. That arrogant woman has turned my son's head. He'll lie there, soft as clay. What did he know, do you think? I tell you, he knew nothing. He'd be there as still as a stone in a well. I don't know what spell she cast on him, what potion she gave him. Child of a useless father! My eye always searches for him. I look for him all the time. But he won't even show his face here, the murderer. Heaven knows what potion she gave him. O Saint Anthony.'

Arokkyam kept on wailing and lamenting. But although she castigated Josep roundly, he was not the real target of her anger; actually her anger was directed against the laundry man, the tailor and the families in the town. It was they whom she meant to scold. She even reprimanded Jesus Christ. For the very first time she began to doubt the priest.

The sun was sinking. Darkness fell. Arokkyam wiped her face and moved off towards the colony. She moved like the dust borne along by the wind. She had no particular work to see to, but she walked into the colony all the same.

Mary watched her mother disappearing towards the colony. At that moment Periyaan came to sit by her side at the threshold, wrapped entirely in a sheet that left only his face free. Darkness descended, heavy as a curtain, between earth and sky. Mary went indoors.

***

Every day, whenever they could find the time, Savuri and Periyaan would sit together at the threshold of Savuri's house, and talk. Their conversation was ceaseless; no hour or season put an end to it. It would begin by their reminiscing about their first loincloths, the sprouting of their moustaches, and so they would go on to talk about marriage, the coming of children, their masters, the families they served, and so on. Nobody had lived to such an age as Periyaan, in this entire district. As the Elder of the leather-working chakkiliyaar community, he was famous.

'It's a good thing that there is an old tree like that in the town.'

'He's got a body like a teak tree.'

'It's the energy from the beef he eats that makes him so strong.'

If Savuri was quiet today, it was because he was thinking of Theresa, the first of his three younger sisters, who had died yesterday, and of her son Diraviyaraj, now orphaned. Periyaan knew that Savuri had returned only this morning, after completing all his duties at the funeral. He kept sucking at his leathery, toothless gums. Except for his eyes, his skin was as fine and as wrinkled as the peel that is stripped off a boiled tapioca.

Periyaan of the chakkili family never removed his wrap, come rain or sun. He never got around much these days. The most he journeyed was to Arokkyam's house. For the past ten years, he had not travelled very much further.

Savuri felt his head spinning in the most extraordinary way. He thought it must be because he was hungry. Having returned from the house of mourning, he had headed straight for the thorapaadu. He hadn't eaten properly as yet. Besides, there had been an unusual amount of washing. Before the entire lot could be washed, the joints of both his arms and wrists were aching. They felt as if they would come apart and drop off. In former times, Savuri had washed many times this amount of clothes. Nothing had happened to him then. He thought to himself, A taste of gruel will drive away this tiredness. He called out to Mary, 'Is the rice ready?'

'Not yet.'

'If there is some rice-water left, throw a couple of lumps of salt in it and bring it here. My stomach is rumbling away like thamru drum.'

'O, I poured out the rice-water for the baby goat; it was turning sour.'

'Your attitude gets worse and worse.'

Mary stood still at the threshold, muttering in open defiance of what Savuri had said. Crazy with hunger, Savuri began to talk wildly. 'So you have started to talk back to me, have you?'

'I'm not saying a thing. I'll lock up my mouth.'

'And do all females in the world talk like this, challenging every word that is said to them?'

'Now why do you drag in everyone else in the town? And why do you have to jump at me like this? What is this terrible sin that I have done?'

'Who? I? Should I not ask for so much as a little rice-water? Is that wrong, I ask you?'

'So what am I to do if there is none?'

'And what use is a woman who can't even cook some rice?'

Mary raised her voice and began to weep aloud. Savuri fell silent, neither his hunger, nor his fury appeased. Had it been Arokkyam who was talking back to him, she would have received four good blows by now. But Mary was only a girl. One should not hit girls. Arokkyam would scold him roundly. Savuri was quiet. Then he opened the three bundles lying in front of him, and began to tie up the clothes separately. Periyaan laughed gently and teased him, 'The araa fish and the korava fish were fighting in the middle of the lake. But the viraa fish which went to separate them was the one that got its head smashed...Savuri...My dear son-in-law...'

Periyaan's fable was in response to the angry looks he got from both Savuri and Mary when he begged them not to quarrel. He was always full of such fables, appropriate to any situation.

Periyaan lived a little distance to the east of Arokkyam's place. This family was the single leather-working family serving the town as well as the colony. Just as Arokkyam served the colony families, so Mutthusaami served as vannaan to the caste streets of the town. Mutthusaami's house was at the end of the gaunder street. There were three or four families working along with him. They divided up the town between them, each vannaan having his own particular streets. A thicket of karuvelam trees surrounded Periyaan's house, similar to Arokkyam's place. The trees stood densely together. Because they were so closely packed, the cheri or colony girls would relieve themselves there. Sometimes they could be seen even from Savuri's house. It became a place where pigs roamed about. In the summer season, both men and women would cut down the thicket, felling the karuvelam, tree by tree. But in a short while, the bare ground would be covered in green once more. There would hardly be enough space for a single person to squeeze through. Always there was the loud buzzing of insects there.

Between the town and the vannaan's and chakkili's houses, a path ran, splitting the thicket. It curved and twisted through, like a creeper. It allowed only enough space for a single passer-by. In the rainy season, this path was knee-high in mud and mire. One had to wade and splash one's way through it. Whether it was the summer season or the time of rains, always one heard the grunting of pigs, the barking of dogs. On certain nights one could also hear the howling of wolves. But none of this affected the members of Periyaan's and Arokkyam's families.

Neither of the two families received the free brick housing that the government had offered to build early that year. They had stipulated that you had to own your land. People who had made their dwellings by encroaching on wasteland were not eligible for the scheme, they said. Arokkyam got nowhere by falling at the feet of all sorts of people. You had to own the land; you had to have some record of settlement; you had to have some proof of inheritance.

All of Arokkyam's informal giving and taking, as between neighbours, happened with Periyaan's family alone. And Periyaan's sons too, limited all such exchanges to Arokkyam's family. All the same, Arokkyam negotiated all her needs within the colony streets for the reason that Periyaan's family did not collect their evening meal there every evening. Neither were they called upon to winnow the grain. They only went there to receive food on special occasions such as Pongal, Deepavali, the auspicious Eighteenth day of Aadi, and at other festivals and weddings.

In former days, Periyaan could at least see a little, in the daylight. Now, though, he had lost his sight completely. At one rime, he had been an expert maker of all manner of water-skins, ropes and sandals. There had not been anyone in all the villages in these parts who could sew a leather basket with the same skill. He would make fine leather sandals, using tassels and nails. Now it was as if he had completely forgotten the use of needle and thread. He never so much as touched these things. Since motors and engines had come to be used for irrigation, nobody wanted leather buckets and bellows for their etrams. And who was there, who came asking for a new pair of leather sandals these days? Only a few old people came, bringing sandals which had been cast off a long time ago, and which the younger people did not wear any longer. Periyaan's eldest son Ambaayiram alone still wielded needle and thread, in spite of all these difficulties. And because of this, he and his wife quarrelled every day. Periyaan's other two sons made a living as bonded labourers for gaunders. Before this, no one from the chakkili community had worked as coolies. Periyaan would remark, in regard to this:

He who forgets the skill he was taught will end up destitute.

He hoped to belch from feasting, but his stomach will only rumble from fasting.

Must you listen to everyone's word? Would you drink anyone's piss?

During the day, Periyaan lay about, silent and bored. He would send his grandchildren to find out whether Arokkyam's family had returned home from the thorapaadu. And later, he would come to sit with Savuri to chat with him. Savuri agreed with everything Periyaan said, complementing him with his own stories. Arokkyam, meanwhile, would come and go, busy about her work.

Periyaan, realizing now that Savuri was silent because of his sister's death and his quarrel with Mary, tried both to pacify him and to draw him out.

'Ei, Savuri, why should a man bandy words with a female chick, da?'

'Don't ask me maama. It's gradually become the reign of females here.'

'Why should it matter who reigns, when there's nothing in the house? If you plant your fields with groundnut, it doesn't rain; if you go to your mother-in-law's house for a feast, there's no grain. The times are such. So who's reigning, and where's the kingdom? Look here, son-in-law...'

Periyaan was off. After this, he would not leave Savuri alone. Savuri sat there as still as a stone, as if admitting his need of Periyaan. Arokkyam appeared just then, and picking up two of the bundles which Savuri had rearranged, turned as if to go. Stopping her, Savuri asked angrily, 'And what were you doing all this time?'

'Mm. I've just been leaping about, that's all.'

'O, really?'

'Yes. Really.'

Mary picked up the rice containers and the remaining bundle and followed Arokkyam.

Periyaan felt a sudden leap of energy. It would be a long time now, before Arokkyam returned. Thinking to himself he could have a really long conversation, he cleared his throat and began. Savuri too gave the impression of having waited just for this moment. He started, 'Maamov, in those days...' But Periyaan cut in with his low bass voice, shaking his head and pulling his covering tightly about him, 'Those times or these times, then or now, what difference does it make to me, I ask you. What hour can I name? When can I say this is night, or this is day? When your belly is crying out for gruel, what does your common sense tell you to speak about? Tell me that. All time is the same to me. I can't see any more. I've gone completely blind. I don't know the difference between night and day. And what would I do if I knew? What place have lice and nits on a bald head, I ask you.'

Although Periyaan's head shook all the time, like a spinning top before it leaps off from its string, his words were always clear. An audience was meat and drink to Periyaan. And Savuri never contradicted anything he said. It was the same now; Savuri watched Periyaan intently, without verbal response. Periyaan could persuade anyone who was willing to converse with him. Very often he would turn quarrelsome, too.

'Why have you turned into such a silent creature, son-in-law? It seems that you are not going to look after my girl.'

Even before Savuri was married, Periyaan would call him 'son-in-law', teasing him affectionately. And Savuri, too, always called him 'maamov' in return.

'What you say is true enough, maamov.'

'One has to do something to earn the food one eats.'

'Even if you beg for it, bowl in hand, who puts rice into it any more? Times have changed and gone beyond the hills, maamov.'

Periyaan laughed aloud like a rattle when he heard Savuri's words. All of a sudden he stopped and began to sing:

I combed and bound my hair and came out
my mirror is broken.
If I see small boys out and about
I take small coins from them
If I meet some innocent lads
I relieve them of five or ten

and if it's an old greyhead
I'll take perhaps two or four
They call me the most virtuous wife!
Just one short of ninety.

'No, it's not the times that have changed, it's people who have changed. When I was a small boy, during the months of Thai and Maasi, when they were winnowing grain, I would go and stand there, pointedly. They would give me a handful of varagu or cholam or kambu. 'Look, it's the chakkili lad, let him take this,' they'd say. Every day I would go round the threshing floors, one after the next. Without fail, by the end of Thai, I'd have gathered a whole bundle. Who has such a generous hand nowadays? They never give the chakkili his traditional dues any more. But that was the way I grew up. Son-in-law, do you hear me?'

'Yes, what changes there are, maamov.'

Savuri listened as Periyaan carried on, sunk into a silence. How many families had Periyaan known before Savuri's time. He had a way of making even his lies sound credible. Enthused by all he said, at last, Savuri began to speak.

'Maamov, have you heard this tale? When my father helped with the winnowing, he was allowed to take five murams, brimming over. But see here. Within ten, fifteen years, it has lessened to four, then three. This Thai, it's come down to two. What will happen next? When I see all this, I think it's best for me to shut my eyes and die. When I was a small boy, I used to hang on to my mother's sari and run after her. In those days, where were all these houses? There used to be only four houses to a street. And yet they called it a street. You just had to go and stand in front of any house and ask for food. All sorts of good things would appear immediately. Ah, I never had to open my mouth and ask for this or that. In those days, they gave generously. But also one had the stomach to eat what was given. Now, there is neither one nor the other. All those people without malice or deceit have gone now. There's just us left, burdening this earth.'

'True, true, son-in-law.'

Normally, Savuri was not one who talked much. But on that day, somehow, the words came pouring out. One reason for this was Arokkyam's absence. And Periyaan didn't interrupt or muddle him. Savuri had inordinate respect and regard for him. Periyaan would tell him a number of things which he had never known about. His conversations were mostly about himself and matters that concerned him most. But he always included Savuri among those concerns so he was never boring. He was such a clever talker.

There were different vannaans who served the upper-caste people and the colony people. Besides, the vannaan who lived in town was a Hindu. The colony vannaan was a Christian. How did this happen? Yet in all towns, only one chakkili served both groups. Periyaan would talk of matters like this. It was only after he had listened to Periyaan that Savuri could begin to understand these things. He had never had time to reflect seriously upon his own position.

Periyaan rolled his empty eyes and stared; then pulled his covering tightly about himself. The light drizzle didn't quite agree with him. He held on firmly to the stick lying at his side, lifted his face in the direction of Savuri's voice, and spoke into the wind.

'One cock joined another, and so it seems they all climbed up to the roof! All these youngsters, how they smoke their fancy cigarettes, how they sprawl in front of their houses with their legs crossed, as if they are saying, "What impertinence of these people to ask me to marry their daughter". Men are trying to ape the gods, son-in-law.'

'Maamov, how well you speak, even at your age; your voice is as clear as a bell. Look at the youngsters of this age, like undernourished infants, deprived of mothers' milk!'

'But who eats more than a couple of mouthfuls of rice these days? And they just sniff at even that much, like mice nibbling at grain. They throw all sorts of things on the fields these days, claiming it's medicines and magic. But what flavour does the rice have now? You know, when some women are pregnant, they actually like eating clay. And even clay has a taste and a smell. Who gets any nourishment from today's rice?'

'These fellows enter a woman, and then get up and run away before she can pull down her sari.'

'Don't speak of it, son-in-law. Women of those days used to have breasts as firm as palmyra fruit made of stone, even after they had borne ten children. Nowadays, look, as soon as she has dropped a child, her breasts have started hanging down a whole arm's length.'

'And that's true, too, maamov.'

Periyaan's breath came fast. Then he coughed loud and long. A dog came and sheltered by his side. From the karuvelam thicket the loud sound of pigs fighting could be heard continuously. In the skies, the moon was as bright as it is in the months of Chittirai and Vaikasi. There was one more day left of the month of Kaartikai. The heavy monsoon had not come. There was only mist and dew. Only a cold wind kept blowing. Taking no notice of it, Periyaan continued to speak. 'In my prime, I used to mix a vessel full of cholam rice, so thick that you could mark your forehead with the gruel. For that much choilam, one good dried chilli would be enough. I would place it my mouth and chew on it while tipping the whole vessel full of cholam down my throat. It was like a cow lapping water. The cholam would disappear like magic. And my stomach was as taut and firm as stone.'

'Very true, maamov.'

'Beef was my very favourite. If I didn't eat any for a month, my face would swell up. I would eat a whole leg on my own. Even before it was completely cooked, I'd pop it into my mouth boiling hot, and wolf it down in great mouthfuls. Cattle in those days were well fleshed. Look at them now, are they cattle or are they lizards, tough as anything and tasteless to boot. Who butchers a cow these days? Nowadays, if a cow dies, they bury it. In those days they would give it away to the chakkili. It's the strength I got from the beef I ate in those days that keeps this body on earth even today.'

'Too true, maama.'

'In the old days, you could see dry beef strips strung together on ten and twenty foot long straw ropes, hanging in festoons. If you placed a piece of it in a tempering spoon, with a couple of grains of salt and some oil, and just roasted it in the fire, then it would just slip down your throat by itself if you tossed it into your mouth. Can you find enough meat on a cow these days to make such a festoon?'

Periyaan and Savuri spoke together, and in turn. Each looked back on the past as they exchanged stories.

'However much you sweep and gather it all up, rubbish is still rubbish.'

'What's to be done, son-in-law, Bhagwan won't open his eyes.'

Arokkyam and Mary arrived with the evening's collection of food. Periyaan's eldest son Ambaayiram's daughter Kosalai came to fetch her grandfather for his meal. She stood her ground saying, 'Appa is calling you to come and eat.' Then she took him home, holding on to his stick. Periyaan left with assurances that he would return. He was disappointed he had to end his conversation so abruptly.

Arokkyam was in a grand confusion about the jobs that needed to be done. The month of Thai was always like this for her in any case. There were the Pongal chores; more clothes to be washed than usual; weddings as well. By chance, it happened that this was the time when there also were an unusual number of births. Next, there was the local festival. In the same month, there was also the festival of Saint Anthony's Church of Melnariappanur. Above all, Mary's wedding had been fixed for the day following the festival of Saint Anthony. There was the winnowing. Clothes needed washing. Money and goods had to be collected for the wedding. All this had to be done. In the end, everything fell to Arokkyam alone.

Theresa had died in Kaartikai. Since then, Diraviyaraj had cooked for himself and lived alone. Suddenly one Friday he had turned up, his chithappa and chinnamma with him.

At first Arokkyam could not understand what was going on. Then she wept a little. After that she remained silent. Then Diraviyaraj's uncle said, 'He has no other stay or support. If you forsake him too, who can he turn to?' At this Arokkyam began to weep out loud. Savuri too spoke on Diraviyaraj's behalf.

Diraviyaraj came up to Arokkyam all of a sudden, threw his arms about her and wept with her. He did so, half afraid that she might refuse him. There was reason enough for his fears. He and his uncle had divided their colony into half, each working separately, and only for the families allocated to him. They also went halves on business that fell to them commonly, as on festival days. Considered plainly, he had barely a hundred households. Besides, he had nothing whatsoever by way of goods and chattels. He lived alone. In the same month that he himself was born, his father had died. As Theresa stood in front of her, blowing her nose and wiping her eyes, Arokkyam had made up four bundles of varagu and some rice to take away to her in-laws. And it was when she was living in her brother-in-law's house that Arokkyam had brought away Diraviyaraj. He thought she would go over all this in her mind now. But she said straightaway, 'He who has a tuft on his head can decide whether to grow it or shave it. But what is there for a family which possesses nothing to discuss?'

'Arokkyam, it's not like that. Let us talk together. Tell us your wish.'

'What decision can there be? This is the story of the blind leading the blind.'

Hearing the sound of conversation in Arokkyam's house, Periyaan came by. When he understood what was going on, he brought the matter to a successful end by overpowering Arokkyam with his counter arguments. He declared that the wedding should be held at the end of Thai. Arokkyam could not oppose it any longer. She wept. After a single midday meal, Diraviyaraj left for home that same evening, with his uncle and aunt.

For the entire month following this visit, Arokkyam went rushing about without ceasing. She sent Mary to do the winnowing with Savuri, and went to the thorapaadu herself with only Peter to help her. Pongal arrived in the middle of all this. There were endless chores. She stored up all their regular payments of grain, as well as the extras they received from the winnowing, for Mary's wedding. At each threshing floor she pleaded, 'Your little vannaati is getting married this Thai; give us another couple of measures of grain, saami.'

'Your little vannaati is getting married, saami.'

'It's my daughter's wedding.'

'My one and only girl child.'

'If even you refuse me, then who is there who will be generous to me?'

'When you came into this world, it was my lap that caught you, sir.'

'Think of this child as your own sister, and be generous, saami.'

'Where will she go, when she leaves you?'

'It is at your feet that she must spend her lifetime.'

She went to one household for firewood. She asked for tamarind at another. A hundred times she walked back and forth, asking for chillies, dal, paddy; asking for money: to cook, to buy goods, for each thing she needed. Gradually she collected it all. She sold the goats. As the grain accumulated, she began to sell it and turn it into money. Because it was the month of Thai, the grain went at a low price. But she made good money by selling the goats off on a meat-eating day.

She had sent Savuri to fetch Josep and Sahayam. Both of them had just arrived. She had deputed them to buy a box, woven mats, pillows, and vessels made of bell-metal. By the time they had chosen a sari and jacket for Mary, and a veshti and upper cloth for Diraviyaraj, Arokkyam's entire yearly income was used up. They had to buy a tali worth quarter of a sovereign, out of the money they made from Mary's goats. Arokkyam complained that Sahayam had thrown away most of the money on the wedding clothes. Sahayam had ordered all these things through her brother, and brought them with her from Chinnasalem.

Arokkyam had been careful right from the beginning, to keep the elders of the town informed about the wedding to come; she had talked to the karaikkaarar and kothukkaarar as well as the members of the panchayat. But in the end, yesterday, they had all turned on her instead and betrayed her. Now she prayed to Saint Anthony, and kept on repeating the words, 'O Jesus, O Lord.'

When Josep got married, the town had presented the couple with a tali worth a quarter-sovereign, as well as a couple of veshtis and saris. Arokkyam had hoped that this time too, Mary would be given something out of the money commonly held by the town panchayat, and gained by various levies and fines. It was against that hope that she had worked day and night and ordered these goods. But in the end, when she asked for help towards Mary's wedding, they rounded on her.

'Our town's money has gone to a man who went off elsewhere to make his living. You had better return all that we gave you in the first place.'

If all of her family went elsewhere, they said, there would be no vannaans left in the town. This could not be allowed. Either the ornaments should be returned, or Josep must return to serve this colony. Seeing that they were adamant, Arokkyam found no means of escape.

I survive only by trusting you, saami.
I spend my life in your service, saami.
It is you who must see to everything.
You are everything to me saami; kin, kith and God.

Nobody yielded to Arokkyam's prayers. They heaped blame upon Josep. They claimed that Arokkyam too was most likely to go off and join her son in a little while, and on that score, refused to allow her any money from the commonly held town coffers. They excused themselves, saying that if Mary were a bride coming to their town, it would be appropriate for them to make a presentation to her, but in this case, the girl was actually leaving them and going elsewhere. And so they drove Arokkyam away. Besides, they made it an absolute order that Peter should stay in the town. Arokkyam raised her voice and wailed as she had never done before. But her anger was all directed towards Sahayam and Josep.

Savuri was not much concerned by all this. He kept on muttering, as he always did. He firmly believed that there was no need for all this expense. And he said so to Arokkyam, at every opportunity. He believed that it was quite enough to provide a tali and sari for the bride, and a veshti for the groom; there was no need for all the other goods. From the moment that Arokkyam sold their entire store of grain, keeping nothing back, not even for their own food, Savuri would not speak to her. He behaved to her as if towards a sworn enemy. 'Would anybody sell the very food they should eat in order to buy clothes,' was his contention.

Arokkyam had not expected this at all. Of course she was anxious too. What would they do for food during the coming year? She had placed absolute faith in Josep and in the townsfolk. Both had now shown their empty hands to her. So long as they had kept their fists closed, she could hope.

It seemed that Josep had left his brother-in-law last month and set up shop on his own. Because of that, Sahayam declared, they could not spare a single penny. It was at that point that Arokkyam made up her mind and sold off the grain, even at a low price.

Sahayam had selected a sari and jacket such as women of well-off communities might wear. Arokkyam had never expected Mary to look as pretty as she did. Yes, the clothes had been expensive. Savuri grumbled and complained. But Arokkyam did not worry on that score. Mary was her only daughter, the child she loved. Her heart should not be troubled. Arokkyam knew that Diraviyaraj was in no position to buy a tali, and so she had agreed to have it done herself.

The relations began to arrive at dawn. It was Sahayam who did the cooking herself. Arokkyam had sent invitations to all of them, with betel leaves and areca nuts. She had gone to every house in the colony in the same way. The plan was that they would set out on the evening of the next day to Melnariappanur, and spend the night there. The tali-tying would take place on the following day. But before the bride set off, she must go to each house without fail, and receive their blessing, on bended knee. Arokkyam had calculated that she would receive a few coins along with the blessing; some two or four annas, perhaps. She would send that with Mary as her own housekeeping money, she thought.

So the wedding was to be held not on the morrow, but on the day after that. Not sure how busy she would be on the day following the wedding, Arokkyam had asked permission from the kothukkaarar, karaikkaarar and the panchayat, that she might leave the washing for three days. At first they refused entirely. On their insistence, at last, that she must do the washing on the first of those days at least, she set off with Savuri as her sole help.

***

The sun was climbing high in the sky. As Arokkyam and Savuri walked along the cart-track towards the thorapaadu with their bundles, the upper-caste vannaan, Mutthusaami and his wife joined them. They walked on, chatting together. Arokkyam told them about Mary's wedding and how the townsfolk would not donate anything from their coffers, recounting it as part story, part lament. But Kunjamma told a more tragic tale than that, evoking Arokkyam's surprised interjections, 'Saint Anthony! Can such things happen! O my God! Jesus, Lord!'

That morning, the wedding of Thangaraj, an important landlord's son, had taken place. Everybody was delighted, sweepers, basket-makers, street-performers, barber, vannaan, chakkili and paraya. Mutthusaami, the town vannaan, and his wife Kunjamma, expected at least a coarse cotton sari and veshti. Because the family belonged to a more prestigious community than others in the town, they hoped for more generous gifts. But what actually happened was something else.

During Savuri's childhood, if ever weddings happened in the colony, the couple's families would distribute veshtis and saris. This custom had stopped a long time ago. In these days, you were given rice and curry, enough for two days, and nothing else except a handful of betel leaves and areca nuts.

Perhaps soon they would refuse even this much. Who could say? Anything could happen. The times were such.

If a wedding or a special event happened in a particular caste in the town, the vannaan serving that particular community used to be in a fine spin. There would be a number of jobs to be done: streamers to be tied to the pandal, mango-leaf festoons to be prepared, the bridal chamber to be decorated; coverlets to be laid for the guests to sit upon; cloths spread out to catch the presentation money. According to their capability, the families would give veshtis, saris and uncooked rice in return for this service. But when weddings happened in the colony, there was no differentiation between who belonged and who did not, the rice and curry was dispensed to everyone alike. Even if Savuri and Arokkyam refused, people would not listen; the food came in abundance.

On this occasion, for Thangaraj's wedding, people from elsewhere had been hired to do all that was required: to set up the pandal, to decorate it and to fix the loudspeakers. Even the palm leaves for thatching the pandal were brought in by lorry. Mutthusaami and Kunjamma went up and stood beside one of the pillars of the pandal. Someone called out, 'Serve out a meal for the vannaan;' and they were sent away, just like that, with a meal for one. Even the presentation of money had finished early in the morning. Kunjamma repeated this tale again and again, dying of shame.

It was the same with all the rest: koothu performers, basket makers, barber, vannaan and chakkili, each was given a serving of food on a leaf, and they all left through the backyard, bundling what was given into their veshtis.

'O Saint Anthony.'

'Why stab about at a festering pain,' said Kunjamma resentfully, lifting up her bundle with both hands to cool off the top of her head as she walked along.

'Get a move on,' Savuri chided Arokkyam. At this point, Mutthusaami said in a tone of weariness and boredom, 'At least the have-nots are better than this. If there is just one vannaan family serving the community, they'll give him several vessels of rice.'

'My children, who had stayed at home, were downright disappointed when they saw that single serving of rice; their very faces changed,' said Kunjamma.

Savuri remarked, as he walked on, 'Nothing is in our hands, saami. We can only go along the path that God has put us on. He is our only help.'

'And how are things in your parts?' Kunjamma asked. As if she had been waiting for that moment, Arokkyam poured out her story in a single breath.

'O Saint Anthony, do you have to ask? Do you think we lead a right royal life? It's like patching up a broken sandal and carrying on walking. Is this a life? And look here, saami, if it's like that with even those people who possess a couple of kaani of land, some property or whatever, what can you expect in the paraya community? It's all a matter of grab and snatch. The month of drought goes on for ever. Last Friday, it was our talayaari's son's wedding. In a completely new ritual, they just sat on a bench and did the tali-tying, and then got up; there was no bridal room or anything. To whom can we go and complain? We weren't asked to decorate the pandal, or to spread the cloth for the presentation money. There was just a spoken word of invitation, "There's to be a wedding, come there, di, vannaati woman." And I must say, though they didn't have this and that, they did give us food enough to last a couple of days. Why would I deny what the maharaja gave us, saami? I speak as one upon whom the earth is about to fall. Then they scooped up a handful of betel leaves and nuts for us. There was nothing else.'

'Times have changed,' Mutthusaami said to Savuri.

'Yes, saamiyov.'

'But it's not so bad for you, vannaati,' Kunjamma said.

'How can that be saami,' Arokkyam wailed. 'Will the Nariappanur Saint Anthony ever open his eyes?'

They had arrived at the water-hole. By this time, Arokkyam's spine was throbbing with pain. Because she carried a bundle under her arm, it had not been possible to cool off her head, or even to ease the bundle upon it, a little. The upper-caste vannaan and vannaati departed to their own washing place, having said their goodbyes. Arokkyam went to her own thorapaadu. The sun had not even crossed half the sky. It shone down fiercely. The earth felt baking hot.

Before sunset Rani came to Mary's house and looked around in all directions to make sure she was not being observed. Then she slipped inside swiftly.

Mary sat by the hearth, cooking rice. As soon as she saw Rani, she handed things over to Sahayam, and the two girls went to sit by the grain-store.

'So why are you sitting here doing nothing?'

'Well, what do you want me to do?'

'O. Very well then.'

Mary was silent for a while. Then she went and fetched needle and thread from the crossbeam and took the underskirt that Rani had brought to be mended. Always, when Rani wanted to come and chat with Mary, she would roll up some clothes and bring them along as her excuse. Often they did not need any sewing at all. It was the same today. There were no tears in the underskirt. Mary gave Rani a playful slap.

Rani teased, 'It's true what they say. The vannaati knows all the weaknesses of the town.'

'What do you mean?'

'What a proud creature! You don't even bother to look at me. The shy bride indeed!'

'Fine wedding it's going to be.'

'Why do you say that, di?'

'After all, am I going to a rich man's house as you are? It feels as if all of this is in celebration of a corpse.

I ploughed the dry land
I sowed firm seed-paddy
When the paddy began to sprout
Dark clouds began to gather
And the whole field was ruined.'

The tears streamed from Mary's eyes. Rani too was distressed by this. She wept, but at the same time she slapped Mary gently, saying, 'Don't cry.' After a little while she was able to laugh. 'You donkey, as if you could hide it all from me. I can even make out tracks in water, really. Did you know that?'

'Never mind now. But what happened about your business?'

'They decided the date today.'

'And have you seen the bridegroom yet?'

'All sorts of girls get all sorts of bridegrooms. I have to go and get a lump of charcoal. Look at my luck!'

'O my Lord, really?'

The wedding guests who had arrived at the house asked Sahayam who Rani was. One woman, who was combing her hair with a fine-toothed comb in order to catch the nits, seemed especially eager to know. 'Do these people actually come inside our houses? Can there be such friendship? Not bad; our bridegroom is a lucky fellow then!'

But in this entire town, it was only Rani's house that Mary would enter of her own accord. Those two had been friends since their childhood. But Mary, too, would look carefully to see if anyone was approaching along the street, before she went inside. And that was only when she knew that Rani was alone in the house. Although Rani's mother was a good sort, she would never allow Mary inside. She was fearful of the townsfolk. If anybody were to see Mary going in, a big fight might follow. Mary's family could be in grave danger.

Rani took out a small packet which she had kept hidden in her lap. Oil had soaked through the wrapping paper. Fritters made of cholam and bananas. Then she handed Mary a jacket. She rolled up the underskirt that she had brought with her, and stood up.

'My mother will be looking for me.'

'Have the bridegroom's party left?'

'Mm. Yes.'

'Why are you giving me this?'

'I don't have any money or coins of my own. But as to this, I can always tell them it was lost. You must wear it when you get to your husband's place.'

'I don't want it.'

'Shut up, girl.'

Mary's eyes showed a trace of tears. Rani wept openly now. Still weeping, she said, 'I thought I'd be the first to get married.

I hoped when I moved to a different town, you could marry the vannaan there. We could have been in the same town together.'

'We weren't lucky enough for that.'

'I wanted to tell you all sorts of things. Now I've gone and forgotten most of it, on the way here. It seems there's to be a cinema show in the main street. Come there. We'll talk some more.'

'Very well.'

'Don't forget.'

'Chi, as if I would.'

'Will you come, really and truly?'

'I promise.'

Mary went to the doorway to check whether anyone was coming, and then gave the signal. Rani hastened to the street, entered the karuvelam jungle, and then ran home. Mary looked at her and at the blouse she had brought, in turn. As Rani's form dissolved into the woods and disappeared, the tears flowed from Mary's eyes.

In a little while, Periyaan came by with his granddaughter Kosalai, sat down at the doorstep and called out, 'Savuri!'

'I'm the only one home, thaatha.'

'Where's everybody?'

'Appa and Amma have gone to the thorapaadu.'

'Even today?'

'What else can we do, thaathov.'

'Have you finished cooking the wedding food?'

'It's done.'

'You're a lucky girl. You've truly been fortunate.'

***

Arokkyam and Savuri returned with their bundles of clothes. While Arokkyam greeted the wedding guests who had just arrived, she invited them to eat; she did so herself. Then she sat down amidst them, and talked to everyone. She asked each one there about the rainfall in their part of the country, how their crops grew, how their business went. At last she shed a few tears and told her own tale. With some she quarrelled. She asked if they had only just discovered the way to her house. One by one, and in private, she talked to each visitor who arrived later.

Josep suddenly made an appearance and came into the house. Arokkyam gave a start when she saw him. Every time she glanced at him, it was as if she saw him afresh. She had been watching him since the previous day. Yet she could not feel that she had looked her fill of him. They had said in the street, when she went to collect the washing, 'Do you think he looks like a vannaan's son any more? He looks a deal better than a child from a well-off family.' And it would be true, Arokkyam thought, stunned, as she sank down in the very place where she stood.

Savuri was talking, as usual, to chakkili Periyaan. Some of the relations were scattered about; some stood listening to Periyaan's conversation. Mary was plaiting Kosalai's hair. Earlier, Sahayam had plaited Mary's hair, powdered her face, and touched her eyes with mai. Arokkyam did not care in the least for all this. Knowing it to be largely Sahayam's work, she asked Kosalai, 'Why all this combing and dressing of hair today?'

'They are showing a cinema picture, it seems. We want to go.'

'So why look like a gypsy, smearing your face with all that flour and streaking a cartload of mai along your eyes?'

As Arokkyam was probing Kosalai for all these details, Mary came up and asked in a soft and pleading voice, 'Ammov, me too.'

'No, I shan't let you.'

'Well, I shall go anyway.'

'So, have your husbands invited you girls? Run, then. Chi, how can all of you call yourselves women?'

Mary rose with a start and went inside immediately. Arokkyam was left with a feeling of awkwardness and disharmony. Tomorrow evening, Mary was going to be a bride, and here she was, wanting to go to a cinema show in the main street today! More annoyingly, since Sahayam's arrival, Mary would only speak to her indirectly, through hints. It was Arokkyam's anger against Sahayam that had prompted her to speak so sharply to Mary. She had not intended to hurt her.

The picture to be shown on video was part of that morning's celebration of the big landlord's son, Thangaraj's wedding. They were actually in the process of building a touring cinema theatre. It had been their intention that the first showing should happen on the wedding day, and be a free one. But for some reason, the building wasn't quite complete. So they were showing a film on video instead.

Since Arokkyam had scolded her, Mary was sulking. She sat in a corner, in tears, sobbing. Arokkyam began to feel extremely distressed. The relatives had all finished their meal and set off, providing themselves with mats and sacking for seats. Periyaan's son Ambaayiram went as well, with his wife Rajathi and daughter Kosalai. Arokkyam saw Sahayam inciting and prompting Mary. She thought to herself, Very well, let them go and be done with it. But she still would not say anything. She waited for either Sahayam or Mary to ask her, once again. Had it been a street theatre performance, she would have taken Mary herself. She had done so several times during the festival season, when Mary was a little girl.

Mary's sobs increased; Sahayam invited her repeatedly to go with her. Let them go and get lost, Arokkyam thought once again, and so she said, turning her face away, 'Everyone's gone. If you want to go, then you'd better go in good time.'

'I don't want to go now.'

'All right. All right. Go on. I spoke only for your good. I don't know how you are going to survive in this world. If it were a koothu at least, you could see people performing in reality. How can you watch these dolls in a picture? How can people sing and dance and perform in pictures? Are times so bad you can't tell the difference between real people and their pictures?'

'You come too!'

'All my time has gone into worrying about providing food and clothes. What am I going to achieve by watching cinema pictures in a box? What practical use would that be?'

Mary walked out, dragging her feet. Sahayam went with her, carrying an old mat. Arokkyam watched her go, staring intently, the tears gathering in her eyes.

How is she going to survive, once my time is finished? How am I going to live without her? Will this life even stay in this body? Arokkyam asked herself.

The path that Mary took through the jungle was melting into the darkness. Arokkyam continued to gaze in that direction. All that she saw, and all her thoughts, were touched by the newly descending harsh darkness.

She grew afraid suddenly. How could she have let Mary go? To reach the place where the cinema show was being held, Mary had to go past the Dwarf Karuppusaami temple. This saami was known as the evil deity in these parts. Menstruating girls would never go past that temple. If they suddenly got their periods while walking there, they were finished. They would get the most fearful aches and pains. They would suffer a terrible flow of blood. Unceasing, it would be. Only after their fourth day, after their bath, might they walk along that path safely. There wasn't another path either. To reach the main street, you'd have to go right round the town.

A girl from the colony had walked there last Kaartikai, forgetting she had not had her ritual bath. She started foaming at the mouth even before she could reach home, and she died within two days of falling upon her bed.

People carrying uncooked meat, women who had just borne children, young unmarried girls walking past at midday or at night were all vulnerable to evil spirits. So they always had a bunch of neem leaves tucked into their waist or into their hair. She should have sent Mary with a couple of sprigs. Arokkyam thought to herself, If only Mary were a girl with some commonsense, she would have kept a couple of twigs handy. The next instant, Arokkyam began to run towards the place where the cinema show was happening, neem leaves in hand.

Five or six months had passed since Mary's wedding. It was only now, after all this time, that Arokkyam was able to speak with some animation once again.

After the tali-tying and the priest's blessing, when Diraviyaraj was preparing to take Mary home, Arokkyam had burst into laments. Even the priest had not been able to restrain her. Immediately after the tali-tying, Josep and Sahayam had brought Arokkyam away to Chinnasalem, insisting that she stay with them for a couple of days. Even now, Savuri complained that Arokkyam was no longer her usual self. And she did seem strangely detached from the days that passed. Mary had not yet been to visit them.

Arokkyam spoke about her at every opportunity. Whatever job she set off to do, she would think of her daughter. Every time they cooked rice, or a curry, or anything good to eat, Mary would come to mind. She had not returned home even once. Nowadays it was Peter alone who was a companion to her. As for him, at evening time, he sold off the different grains in the storage jars and went off to the cinema with the other boys. Arokkyam. would weep, telling herself again and again that Mary had never talked back to her. Nowadays there wasn't a great deal of work. The sowing season was over. One night, as Arokkyam lay awake, anxious that although it was weeding time, there had been no rains as yet, she heard the Malayalam-speaking astrologer. He had come in the morning, rattling his hand-drum, the gudugudupai, received his share of grain, and gone away.

When he returned, it was nearly midnight. Sleep fled as soon as he came to stand in front of Arokkyam's house, rattling his drum and calling out. But Arokkyam did not rise up and come to the door. Ghosts and evil spirits often followed the gudugudupai man. People would never come out at that time of night, fearing they might be caught. He only told his predictions in one street, and always, only at midnight. At daybreak he would come for a few coins or for some grain. Even if asked, he would never make his predictions during the day. At midnight, he made puja at the cremation ground. Then he would come to a particular street and tell the future, house by house. The older people would never allow their children anywhere near him. When he stayed with his family under the tree in front of the temple, or next to the school, nobody would go near him during the day. They said that he might cast a spell or work black magic, or use charms and potions against them. He certainly looked fearful enough.

Afraid that an evil spirit might catch her, Arokkyam lay on her mat without making a noise, listening carefully to what he said, accompanying himself on his drum. Savuri slept through it all.

Kali...Kali...Kali...
gudu gudu gudu gudu
A family that once flourished has now fallen on evil days
gudu gudu gudu gudu

Nothing to be gained by hard work, no profit in return for your pain
with all your drudgery you cannot fill your belly
gudu gudu gudu gudu

You dissolve away like salt, you wear yourself out like a tile,
you run like the wind, you circle like a paper-kite
gudu gudu gudu gudu

With both hands you gave generously, but now you hold your hands out
asking whether they will be filled and your cares diminished
gudu gudu gudu gudu

For one who has a generous heart, even a stone will dissolve
the dry earth will yield; by her hand even diseases are cured
gudu gudu gudu gudu

Your husband is no consolation to you; your children bring no happiness
gudu gudu gudu gudu

Once you had goats, cattle, a home, relations
A family and a house which people looked up to is now a common thoroughfare
like river-water all things have flowed away
gudu gudu gudu gudu

A young woman has left this house and gone away
gudu gudu gudu gudu

> You stand alone as a stone. But it does not matter. You have strength in your heart
> gudu gudu gudu gudu
>
> You have your own commonsense. There is no strength in family, nor in relations nor in husband
> gudu gudu gudu gudu
>
> You have not believed in vain. Many people give you their goodwill
> gudu gudu gudu gudu
>
> Above all else, Kali...Kali...Kali...has already looked upon this family, eight days ago
> gudu gudu gudu gudu
>
> Your illness will pass; that which you have lost will return and come to fruition; your family will improve its fortunes and prosper once more
> gudu gudu gudu gudu
> Kali...Kali...Kali...Kali
> gudu gudu gudu gudu

Some time later the guduguduppai sounded outside the chakkili elder's house. Then it returned past Arokkyam's doorstep once again, and went into the colony street.

Arokkyam could not sleep any more after the Malayali astrologer had gone. Last year too, this same man had spoken one night in the month of Panguni. He had said that a young woman of this family would be persecuted. That was what had happened to Mary, Arokkyam thought. This man came every year, and year after year. He spoke; he chanted. And it happened as he foretold. Arokkyam determined to do something in response. What would it cost to do a kazhividai to revoke the spell.

At earliest dawn she spoke to Savuri. She went and consulted the chakkili elder. She talked about it to Ambaayiram, his wife, and even to Kosalai. She found out what the Malayali astrologer had said at their house. Her heart was full of anxieties about her family. What more could happen to all of them? But at the end he had said that they need not worry, the gods would watch over them. Yes, that was good.

All along the way to the thorapaadu, as she carried the clothes there and washed them, she spoke continually of the astrologer. Then, because there was going to be a procession in the town, she returned home early.

The entire town had turned out. For the very first time, and as never before, they had decided to carry the deity in procession in the month of Aadi, praying for rains. A huge crowd had gathered in front of the Mariamman temple. The whole town was bustling. The women were in a state of high excitement. From midday, the youngsters had begun to drive home the cattle and goats from their grazing. The cattle raced forward, their tails lifted up, raising the dust with their hooves.

Women began lighting their fires to cook the pongal. Some made an impromptu cooking hearth with three stones. The women of some families walked along the street, trying to borrow a little raw rice. Many were pounding unhusked paddy in stone pestles. Small children flew between home and temple in order to find and bring ingredients that had been forgotten or left behind. Some boys pushed along long stalks of dry cholam, the ends bent back, between lines drawn upon the earth, pretending they were driving cars.

There's rain in all the surrounding villages. But not a single drop of water here. Not a spot of rain to refresh the eye. It looks as bare as a cremation ground everywhere. How are families to survive, they and their small children? It's all down to the gods. What does it matter which month it is? There has to be a procession.'

'What else can we do?'

'Exactly.'

On the previous evening, the town crier had gone from street to street summoning the elders to a meeting. Later the panchayat met. After a whole night of argument and wrangling, it was finally decided that the procession must be held.

'It's all up to the gods.'

'Of course.'

'Let's see what happens after the procession. Why should we leave anything undone?'

'What can a man do on his own?'

'We can only talk.'

'And talk won't gain us anything.'

They had summoned the pujaris serving Katavaraayan, Kali, Mariamman, Tundi Karuppan and Chelliamman, and asked them all for their predictions. They had invited Datchinamurti Aiyar to make his forecast. After all, it had been he who had said at sowing time, 'This year the god is riding on a pig; the darker grains should yield plentifully.' They had tried to tell the gods' wishes by the way the flowers fell. They had looked for omens and portents. At evening time they had gone some way beyond the boundaries of the town and gazed at the sky, noting the direction in which the birds flew, calculating whether it indicated the coming of rain. None of this had yielded a result, so at last they had come to this conclusion.

'Yes, it is the gods complaining. Once we have made a blood sacrifice, cooked the offering, and taken out the god in procession, we'll see. The next day the rains will pour down in all their strength. There is no other way.'

'True enough. Five, six years ago, it happened exactly like this in our town. We had such a fierce famine. A famine so complete there are no words to describe it. They looked for all sorts of omens, they made all kinds of offerings. Nothing. At last we sacrificed a pig, cooked the pongal, and then took out a procession. That was it. No sooner was the procession over, and the god returned to the front of the temple, than it began to rain. That very instant it rained down hailstones. We have never had such rains again.'

Several people chimed in, 'What you say is true.' Many others nodded in agreement.

People said repeatedly, 'The grain that has sprouted stands at the same level. There's not a single drop of rain. It looks as if it's all going to wither and fly away in the wind.' They watched the skies constantly. They looked at the earth and shed tears.

There were by now crowds of women on all four sides of the Mariamman temple, laying more firewood on their hearths and stirring the pongal rice. Children were raising a hubbub and playing all kinds of games. When they heard that there would be a cinema show that night, they began to leap about with excitement.

The Mariamman temple was roofed with country tiles. In front of it stood a large and shady neem tree. Upon its spreading roots, there stood two tridents. Ripe limes had been stuck into them newly, and they had been decorated with kumkumam. They had been hung about with scraps of red cloth which looked like tassels. The idol had fine sickle shaped moustaches, sticking out on either side of the face. There was his horse, with a head which had partly fallen off. A big crowd surrounded all this. A joyous crowd.

Arokkyam and Savuri set off for the temple immediately after returning from the thorapaadu. Peter ran towards the temple, jumping and leaping as he went.

Arokkyam gazed at everything and everyone as if she were seeing it all for the first time. Savuri asked her, 'Why don't you go home and cook some gruel?'

'In a little while, we're going to get cooked rice here by the bowlful. Why should I rush to cook food which will be wasted?'

'Yes, that's true.'

'Is it ever possible to be hungry in spite of ourselves?'

Arokkyam asked a woman who was busy with her cooking, 'Is there going to be a koothu performance today?'

'No, no koothu. They say there's to be a cinema show.'

'O, I see.'

'O God, everywhere you look, they are talking about cinema shows these days. They've completely forgotten the old ways.'

'People don't care any more for what happened yesterday.'

Arokkyam walked on towards the next group. Savuri followed her. Suddenly she asked him, 'Shall I walk to the child's house and visit her? It's as if she is always in my vision. And it's not a busy time here is it? Nothing much is happening.'

'Is it a child you gave birth to, di?'

Arokkyam was shocked. She never expected Savuri to shout at her like that. These days Savuri had begun to scold Arokkyam and to find fault with her all the time. Mostly they tended to quarrel over Peter. He roamed about the streets every day. He would come and eat his meal after Savuri had left for the thorapaadu, and promptly go back to the street.

Every woman in the town gave birth to a child, but I went
and gave birth to a stone.
One person after another dies a good death. Why can't
I die even a horrible death?
The Lord who puts an end to all lives seems blind to
my life.
I wish I could put down all my troubles and find a place
to rest
O Anthonyaare.

The pig had barely half a life left. They had tied its legs together and passed a pole through; two men, one in front and the other at the rear, carried it with some difficulty, but came running up, all the same. The pig was screaming with the blow it had received on its face.

Viramuthu was the one who had caught the pig. Now, he was second to none when it came to catching pigs. However large the pig, however fast it ran, it would never escape him. How expertly he would grab it by its hind-legs, lay it on its back and give it a single blow to its face. And that would be it! If Viramuthu was coining to catch a pig, you wouldn't even need to fill its water trough.

They brought the pig now and placed it in front of the tridents. They garlanded it and decorated it with kumkumam and sandalwood paste. As soon as they sprinkled water on its face, it shook itself vigorously as if with renewed life, and began to squeal again. Yet the tight knot on the rope about it didn't give way in the slightest. The pujari of the temple, Kannan, circled it with camphor, scattered sacred ash upon it, and then went in with his camphor tray. Arokkyam and Savuri accepted the sacred ash, smeared their foreheads and the base of their throats, and then went and stood at the place where the pig would be slaughtered.

Ramasaami was hurrying the proceedings. 'Come on you rascals. Get on with it. Hurry up and finish it.'

Viramuthu, bathed, wearing a wet veshti and garland, felled the pig with a single stroke. Only he was allowed to do this whenever a sacrifice was made to the gods. Before his time, his father Kumarasaami did it. Nobody else in the town was allowed to hold the god's sickle, nor wield it, nor make the offering.

Viramuthu's father it was who had the idol installed where only the tridents and stone had once stood. He also had the temple built. Although they had been married for eight years, he and his wife were childless. There were no temples they had not visited; no fasts they had not observed. At last, after they had made an oath to Mariamman to rebuild the ruined temple, their son Viramuthu was born. From that date, only people of their family were allowed to make the sacrificial offering.

Ramasaami rose to his feet saying, 'Divide up the carcass between all the clan groups, and make sure that each family gets a piece of meat.' Then he instructed them to auction the head and entrails.

Arokkyam and Savuri prostrated themselves in front of Ramasaami. After a while, Peter did so as well. He watched intently as the meat was being divided up. Arokkyam spoke to Ramasaami, 'Saami, please don't misunderstand me. But hasn't it always been the custom, whenever a goat or a pig is slaughtered, to give the head and the entrails to the vannaan?'

'This is not Deepavali, Pongal or the Eighteenth day,' Chadayan stared hard and spoke sharply.

'What does it matter when an animal is slaughtered? It isn't the custom in any town to auction the head and entrails.'

'You need to be whipped with my slippers. Bitch of a vannaati, how much insolence must you carry in your heart that you dare to oppose me in public! Have you gone that far? You monster! You whore!'

An unknown voice was heard to say, 'Talking back! How dare she, I ask you.'

Then Mottayyan flew into a great rage against Arokkyam. She was shaken, and inwardly terrified. Savuri stood silently, his arms folded. Peter had taken hold of her sari gathers and was twisting them.

'It's not like that, yejamaan.'

'What do you mean, illinge, nollinge, not like this, not like that?'

'Yes, ask her; give it to her properly!'

Arokkyam too was in a state of fury against Mottayyan. The crowd that had been making the food-offering to the gods returned and foregathered here. Arokkyam stood at their midst. Peter and Savuri were looking about them awkwardly, like thieves who have been caught red-handed. They were trembling slightly. A warm wind was blowing.

'You are our masters. There is nothing that you don't know. Throughout the generations, the head and entrails were always given to the vannaan. This is the business of the entire town, sirs. If you fail in this, who will give us our due when they slaughter animals at the ear-piercing rite, or at a funeral?'

'And that's fair enough. Hand it over to her. Poor thing, vannaati woman. There's only the one family for the whole colony.'

Savuri had untied his veshti from his waist, and re-tied it around his stomach, over his loincloth. Now he stood quietly, feet together, arms folded, stooping a little.

'What is it, woman? You have come to dispute with us, have you? You can ask, if you like, at Pongal, or Deepavali, or the Padinettu. If we don't give you your due then, you may whip us with your shoes and speak as you like. There might be justice in that.'

Ramasaami lit himself a roll-up and barked to everyone to shut up. Arokkyam asked, 'Would it be enough, saami, if I only did your washing on Pongal and Deepavali days?'

'Flog her! Scavenging bitch, I'll pull your teeth out!'

'Has it come to this?'

Several others in the crowd began to shout along with Ramasaami. They leapt about. Mottayyan shouted continually, without even seeming to draw breath. His two plough bullocks had not had any fodder or drink for a whole week. He wanted the entrails for the animals. If they were given pig's entrails, they would start eating their fodder with a good appetite the very next day. It was clear, from Mottayyan's words, that he would not let go.

Mukkayi, as the owner of the pig, now asked Ramasaami, 'Maamov, why don't you give it to me? My children will be disappointed otherwise!'

'You don't need it child, go away now.'

'O God, you'll go to ruin. It was I who reared it with love, after all.'

Mukkayi was overcome with anger and tears. Yes, she had reared the pig with affection and care, and had been loath to give it away at a low price. Had it been a festival day, she would not have been willing to sell for even a paisa short of three hundred rupees. But she had been embarrassed by the entire contingent of town elders who had turned up at her door with their request. Besides, she was frightened when they went on to say, 'How can you refuse to give to the gods? Be careful, you'll end up with nothing.' So she had given away her pig for the sum they named.

She had bought the pig out of the housekeeping money that she had scraped together. She had hoped to sell the animal when she had reared it, and buy her daughter some ear-studs and eardrops with the money. Then when her daughter came of age a week ago, she had wanted to sell it in order to do the dritti ceremonies to ward off the evil eye. None of this had worked out as she had calculated. So now, because she had given the pig at a low price, she felt that at least she had the right to ask for the head and entrails. When they refused her, she spoke abusively to the elders, and walked off in a rage.

Arokkyam was adamant. 'You have to give me the entrails, saamiyov. I come from the poorest people. Look at my misery and tell me how I am to survive.'

At Deepavali and the Eighteenth, they would get five and ten heads. On meat-eating days, there would be no less than twenty. There would be goat, cow and pig, mixed together. Savuri would chop up all the intestines into workable lengths and take them down to the river in a basket. He would dump out the faeces and urine and undigested material, and then rinse the pieces thoroughly. Filling them with water-like rubes, and holding either end, he'd tilt the lengths either way, cleaning and washing them out. Then he'd cut them into small pieces with a sharp double-edged knife, fill up his basket until it was dripping, place a large puvarasu leaf on top, and carry the basket home. Peter, carrying a large stick to drive the crows away, would accompany him throughout.

Mary would separate the different pieces and cook them in various containers. When Sahayam was there, it was she who would grind the chillies to a paste. She would grind them very fine, to the consistency of sandal-paste. If she sat down to it in the morning, she would need to be at it the whole day. The chillies had to be ground in time for each batch of cooking. Her hand would burn as if it were on fire. Three or four months' worth of chillies would be used up in a single day. Besides chillies, it was Arokkyam's household that bought the largest amount of meat masala spices from the Chettiyar's shop. She always added some extra tamarind to preserve the meat and keep it from going off. Not even the colony women were as expert at preparing the meat as she was.

Meanwhile, Josep would sharpen his sickle with powdered brick. Then he would lay each head on a wooden plank and break it into pieces. Arokkyam would stand there, driving away the dogs and crows, instructing him, 'Do it this way; break it just there.' Mary would bring two large earthenware pots to do the cooking. She would cook each of the different kinds of meat separately. She would stir the pots with long-handled ladles which she held with both hands. Once Mary grew up, Arokkyam stopped going anywhere near the cooking fire.

There would be enough meat for a whole week. Mary would only touch goat's meat, though. She would eat nothing else, although she would cook it. In fact, she did all the jobs up to covering and sealing the pots and putting them away.

When pig's meat was being cooked, Mary would collect three or four measures of the fat. The more the meat was allowed to brown, the more the glistening oil would float to the top. People would come to buy this oil in exchange for grain; it was said to be good for brain-fever, or for cattle which would not feed properly.

***

'Who do think you are, that you can talk about rules and regulations? Do you imagine that this is your father's wealth?'

'Why do you talk like that, saami?'

Mottayyan, standing behind Ramasaami, leapt out at this point. 'What sort of man are you anyway?' he asked Ramasaami. 'Do you have to act the naataamai and judge every soul in the town? Just arrange for the auction; I'll see to anyone who doesn't like it.'

Arokkyam pulled back Peter who had gone off to take a peek at the basket of entrails, gave him a couple of hard slaps and held him between her legs, saying, 'Son of a shameless one!' Then she continued to mutter to herself, 'All the good taste ends at the throat; after that it's shit. I had better just go away now, like the dog that has seen too much and has been whipped across the mouth.'

'Vannaati woman, are you still talking back to me? Have the rimes got so bad that people like you talk back to me?'

But Mutthusaami opposed Chadayan and said, 'Look, she's worked for our sake all the hours there are, never even distinguishing between night and day. She's taken a fancy to this thing; she's got her mind fixed on it. It would be right and proper to give it to her.'

'So you are the only one here who knows about proprieties?'

Mutthusaami got up and went away. But Ramasaami immediately started to gossip about Mutthusaami's wife who ran away with a Gaunder. Suddenly, everybody became deeply interested in this matter.

When at last the pongal offering was made to the god, the coconut broken, the camphor taken around, and just as the women were lifting the pots of pongal rice on to their heads, the old woman Mutthamma became possessed. Now the women with their pots and all the people surrounding Arokkyam thronged towards Mutthamma.

There were no set times when old woman Mutthamma became possessed by the goddess. It could happen during the day, or even at midnight. Inspired, she would chase ghosts and evil spirits right away to the end of the street. The goddess would leave her and return home only after having been worshipped with sacred ash and camphor. The old woman would be left exhausted. She never seemed to realize that only a few moments ago the goddess had entered her; that she had danced in a frenzy, like a street performer. That was not me, her actions would seem to declare.

'De! De! De!'

'Mother, thaaye, tell us why you have come.'

The Katavaraayan pujari beat his udukkai drum and began to question the goddess, where the goddess came from, and the reason for this manifestation.

'O ho ho...Dai!'

'Thaaye, mother!'

They all stood about in a circle, their hands together in worship, waiting expectantly with fear and devotion, for the words that the goddess would say.

'Ah ha.. .ha.. .haha...'

'Speak to us, mother, Mahamaayi.'

'What is your complaint?'

'Rain...Rain...we need rain...'

'In eight days, counting from today, the river will overflow its bank.'

'That is what we pray for, mother.'

'Kali.. .Kali.. .Mahamaayi.'

She continued to dance for some time longer, and then suddenly quietened down when she felt the warmth of the lighted camphor which the pujari took towards her, touching her face. A little later, she lifted up the vessel full of pongal on to her head, and went home with her daughter-in-law. Her whole body was spent and weary after the ecstatic dancing.

Once more Arokkyam dared to ask, 'What is your final decision, yejamaan?'

'Mottayya, you can pay twenty rupees. Take it away now, it stinks. As soon as you go home, get the money and bring it to me. I have to pay the video-man.'

Having chased away the surrounding dogs, Mottayyan's son chopped up the dripping head and entrails to the accompaniment of the buzzing of flies, and set off at last, carrying the basket.

'Give us permission, saami. May we go now?'

Arokkyam and Savuri prostrated themselves and then rose to their feet. Savuri ordered Peter to do the same, and he did so in a resentful and bored manner. And so they walked home.

'Ammov.'

'What is it, da?'

'Are we not going to have any meat at our house tonight?'

***

'Will you fry a piece of the entrails for me in the large tempering spoon?'

'Of course.'

'Crush the salt well in the grindstone, otherwise you crunch into the lumps. And add a lot of oil so that it isn't slippery...'

'Ammov, it's the vannaati; give us some food.'

'I've just washed the rice and set it to boil. Why don't you stop by on your way home, Arokkyam?'

Arokkyam and Peter moved on to the next house. 'Is that Arokkyam? What is the matter, we haven't clapped eyes on you for ages... Look at your timing! Just this once, I haven't lit the fire all day. The only thing on the hearth is the cat. There were a few leftovers. I let it go at that. Come tomorrow and take two days' worth.'

Peter walked ahead with the container for curry. Arokkyam followed, rice container tucked under her arm.

'Ammov.'

'I've just come in from the field; I've only just had time to wash my hands and face, and to light the fire.'

'It's the vannaati woman.'

'I haven't made a curry or rice or anything. At the rate at which tamarind and chillies sell, who can afford it, Arokkyam? So I've left the rice in its water. Here, take this.'

'Ammov, it's the vannaati woman.'

It was too dark to make out each other's faces. Cold, too. A light rain fell. It was always like this in the month of Kaartikai. It could darken even during the day. One's feet would shrink from treading the streets. Mud and mire everywhere. Because of the damp, the smoke from the cooking fires never rose from the thatched roofs, but swirled in murky clouds just overhead.

In former days, people would gather up and store away everything that they required for the rainy season, starting with firewood. Once the rains started, throughout the month when people had to stay indoors, they would cook rice and delicious curries in every house. Enough for one to crush some vadagam in the tempering spoon, add some oil, and thrust it towards the cooking fire. It would crackle and pop as loud as fire crackers. At once the aroma would spread and snake about the whole street, assaulting one's sense of smell. There is an aroma about roasting vadagam that is unique. Everyone in the town loved to eat a tempered curry.

At midday they would roast different kinds of gram. Or they would eat them boiled in their pods. Everyone would carry around, at the very least, a half-measure of gram, tied to their waists. Arokkyam would receive a little from each person she met. When all this was gathered together, it would make up two measures in all. Nowadays, even at festivals and holidays, people did not cook and serve such meals as they used to. Nor did they make such a variety of snacks. Food no longer had the flavour or taste that it once had. People ate their food as if they were eating hay.

'Ammov, the vannaati.'

'She only dips the clothes in water, and then brings them back. Yet before the sun has set she comes running here at top speed with her rice vessel.'

'Eldest daughter, it's me. Arokkyam.'

'Wait a minute, I'm coming.'

'Give us something to season our food, saami. Our tongues have become numb without salt or spice.'

'Who's at home?'

'No one. My mother has gone to fetch water.'

'The vannaati has come.'

Peter entered the next street in a great hurry. Arokkyam covered her head with the top part of her sari against the falling rain and walked on. In the dark, the wet mud splashed on her. Walls were crumbling and dissolving in the rain. Pigs ran about in the darkness.

'Sushila, Arokkyam has come.'

'Tell her to wait a bit. The child is suckling.'

'Come soon, amma.'

'Watch how you go, da. Mind that you don't catch your foot and take a toss.'

'Please...'

'I've just taken the rice off the boil; it hasn't even drained properly.'

'Amma, it's the vannaati. It's your vannaati who has come.'

Arokkyam stumbled through the mud and the darkness. It continued to drizzle slightly. Her feet were chilled through with the damp. For an entire week she had been given hardly any cooked food. And what she was given had barely sufficed for a single person. Every evening, Arokkyam was forced to cook at home, herself. She began to wonder whether anyone at all was actually cooking a proper evening meal these days.

It wasn't so bad in former times. Peter would accompany Mary when she went to collect the evening meal. They managed to get something, even if it wasn't a lot. After everybody had eaten, Mary would pour some water over what was left, and place it on the hearth with a heavy weight on top so that dogs would not get at it. They would have that in the mornings. If there was plenty, it would even do for the midday meal.

But today there wasn't enough even for one person. Peter carried the empty curry container, swinging it fore and aft as he walked along. Arokkyam was concerned mostly for Savuri. He was one who needed a lot to eat. His face would fall immediately if he saw a smaller serving of rice upon his plate.

Neither Savuri nor Josep felt the satisfaction of having eaten a proper meal unless they had at least a mouthful of the composite food of several kitchens. However many dishes were cooked and served separately, it never tasted the same to them. Such stomachs and tongues they had. They had to have at least a little mingling of the town's food to feel they had eaten sufficiently. However late at night, they would fall asleep only after they had eaten some of the town's food. If delayed, they would wait up, awake, until it was collected and brought home.

Arokkyam seethed with resentment against laundry man Periasaami and tailor-shop Sayibu. Peter asked, swinging the vessel he was carrying, 'Why do I have to bring this curry container? Tomorrow I'm not going to carry it, if I come with you.'

'Very well.'

'Should I go and work for the man with the box-iron?'

'Why?'

'O, for no reason.'

'What do you mean, da, for no reason?'

'Till I learn to iron, just like he does.'

'Heaven knows what spell he has cast, or potion he has used. Where five or six bundles of washing fell to me, I don't even collect two. Not a single sinner or slut is willing to give us even the rice from a spittle-ridden hand.

'He has that box-iron.'

'No, he must have used witchcraft. People don't speak a word to us any more. And these are the same folk who were always wanting the vannaati woman.'

'Why don't you go and have a word with the Aiyar, anyway?'

'O my God, why didn't it ever strike me to do just that?'

Arokkyam was overjoyed. She should go to Datchinamurti Aiyar first thing in the morning and ask him for his predictions about the family. Had she thought to check with him, he might have told her of some way of countering Sayibu's spell. She had forgotten all about Aiyar. She started to think of all the things she should ask him.

As they came to the footpath through the neem woods which took them home, she became anxious about encountering lizards, snakes and insects. There might be snakes slithering about, slippery underfoot, amidst all the wetness. Even as they were about to enter their home, the rain came down hard, in sheets of water. They were soaked through in the sudden downpour. Somehow she wrapped the rice vessel in her sari, and protecting it with her own body, brought it safely inside.

She was startled to see Savuri seated at the threshold, talking to the priest's cook. Having put away her vessel, she came to sit beside the cook, and began to talk to him. Peter, meanwhile, took himself off to sleep.

Arokkyam felt herself shivering with the cold. What should she say? How was she to speak? If the priest took the trouble to send his cook, could this be an ordinary matter? Some disaster or other kept happening to this family, one after another. Had Josep done something wrong? Or was it Mary's husband who was in trouble? Might it be that someone from this very town had gone and complained about them, declaring that they did not want them any more as their vannaans? It could be anything. If the townsfolk and their vannaan could not get on together, and if the leaders of the community spoke to the priest about it, then the priest would come and deal with it at a panchayat meeting. They would agree to impose a penalty on the vannaan. But if this were the case, who was their enemy in the town? Did they have such enemies? How could it be? Arokkyam called to mind every single face in the colony. She had not behaved in any special way towards anybody. It could be the kothukkaaran, Chadayan, though. He might have done it to cover up that business with Mary. He was certainly capable of it. Arokkyam was appalled at the thought of what he might have said to the priest about Mary.

I've been double-crossed, she thought to herself, and was too confused and anxious to ask any questions. She felt as if her very life had left her. The lantern continued to burn inside the house. But here no one could be seen clearly. There was only thick darkness. The sound of falling rain. Distant thunder.

'I am also of your community.'

'What does it matter, sir, who one is? You have to have a heart. That's all that matters. What's the good of anything else?'

'Haha. True enough. Haha.'

'And the reason for saami's visit?' Both fear and eagerness were mixed in her voice.

'Savuri, you tell her, pa.'

Savuri took Arokkyam inside the house. He told her of his conversation with the priest's cook. Although Arokkyam was relieved in one way, by what he said, she was nevertheless plunged into a deep grief. How could she bring herself to send Peter away? The priest is a good and kind man, that is why he is offering Peter a life and a vocation, she thought. All her previous anger and resentment towards him vanished without a trace. He had said, 'I wish to educate Arokkyam's son and make him a priest of some importance like myself. He will study. He will go abroad and travel around the world. He will be as good as a white man. Our Lord has said that to serve God is better than to serve man.'

Arokkyam came back and sat behind Savuri, at the entrance of the house. The cook was silent. It was Arokkyam who initiated the conversation. She asked after the priest. She spoke of all her worries and concerns. She gave a detailed account of the townsfolk's changed behaviour. She did not forget to describe the laundry and the tailor-shop. She complained about Josep's brother-in-law. She said it was because of him that her family stood to be ruined. She poured it all out in a single breath, and ended by asking, Why hadn't the priest come himself, after his assurances that he would. Savuri had been frequently nudging her in the ribs with the back of his hand, as if to say, shut up. But Arokkyam would stop only after she had said everything she wished to say. Savuri and Arokkyam treated the cook with the same honour and respect, and almost the same reverence they would have shown the priest himself. Savuri, particularly, was full of fear and anxiety that the cook might take away the wrong impression about them.

He was a big man, bloated and round as a kozhukkattai, with a big moustache adorning a face pitted and scarred by smallpox. He smiled at everything. He said very little beyond

'Good' and 'True enough'. Arokkyam only felt at ease with people who were willing to talk a lot. For some reason, she could not take to the cook from the first moment. The rain, the cold, and the darkness, all taken together had tired her out. But the matter concerning Peter troubled her deeply.

She made some rice for the cook's meal. She prepared the accompaniments. Wanting to appease him somehow, she made him come and sit by the hearth, and made desultory conversation with him. She minded very much that she was putting on a performance. Arokkyam never liked to pretend.

'How is your family getting on, sir?'

'My family...?' He laughed out loud. Then he stared intently at the lantern and said, 'The days just pass; that is my life.'

'Let it be, saami. God will be your refuge.'

He was one who grew up knowing neither his father nor his mother. When his mother was eight months pregnant, his father ran away with a young woman who made a living from lining cooking vessels with lead. When he was only three years old, his mother swallowed a poisonous herb and died with a swollen stomach, after she was punished in public for a clandestine love affair. After this he stayed in the home of his maternal grandmother. The old lady too died when he was eight. He took himself to the priest on the advice of some of the townsfolk. He started to work for him that very day. Now he was fifty-four. He was still in the same job, as cook. As time went on, the people who ate the food he cooked had changed. The current priest had been there the longest. Who would be next? He would still cook for him.

He told his story with plenty of amusing detail, but with a curious detachment. Arokkyam felt a sudden affection for him, mixed with concern that he should be like this. In the light given off by the glowing coals in the cooking hearth, her face looked flushed. A trace of tears gleamed in her eyes. She kept putting more and more sticks into the fire. Her scalp was perspiring. She turned to look at the outstretched figure of Peter as he lay there, asleep. She stroked him with both hands. She was astonished at the sturdiness of his legs. He lay asleep in the posture of a baby. For some reason, she touched her own breasts. Then she turned to face the darkness.

Savuri went out into the street and bought a leaf-plate. Arokkyam insisted on loading it with rice and curry. When he had finished, she took the leaf-plate outside and threw it away. The cook rose and went to wash his hands, and then returned. For a moment, suddenly he wept, shaken. Then he looked intently at Arokkyam. She felt very sorry for him. A man of his age, to weep like that! She looked at his squat body. Nobody would believe he was capable of tears.

Once again the cook went to sit on the front ledge of the house. Savuri sat on the floor of the entrance, and Arokkyam a little behind him. Suddenly the rain poured down again, with thunder and lightning. In a little while, the roof began to leak, right in front of the hearth. With a cry of, 'Ayyo, I forgot completely,' she ran to place containers underneath all the leaks. From the leaking roof, the raindrops fell in loud drips into the tins. It was nearly seven years since the roof had been thatched. It had been done properly then, with varagu straw. Now it had worn away. There seemed hardly a place where it did not give way and leak. A creeper had spread over the roof, covering it with green. Now the whole thing might fall down.

She gave the cook Savuri's wrapper. Savuri covered himself with a piece of sacking over his vetti. Arokkyam wrapped herself tightly in her sari. She laid an old sari over the sleeping Peter, and then at last came and sat down, looking steadily into the cook's eyes.

'What am I to say to the priest? The saamiyaar will be really angry.'

'From what I know, from what I have seen, my father, my grandfather and all my ancestors made a living out of this same work. I know this well. Even if we weren't as rich as Kubera, we didn't live by begging. My time too is running out, saami. But even if there isn't much strength left in our arms and legs, yet we have the strength of heart to believe we can look after this lad. We've lost our eldest son. One way or another, our girl's story too has come to a conclusion. He is the only one left to us. Who else do we have, who will go where we bid him and come when we need him? If I sink down to the ground with a headache, who else will stay by me? Let him be, saami. We don't need all that wealth and comfort. What was our hope when we bore our children, saami?'

'Very well, then.'

'He doesn't need to go into the priesthood, saami.'

Noticing his silence and his expression of dissatisfaction, Arokkyam became anxious. What should she do if he insisted on taking Peter away? She would be in a terrible position if the saamiyaar arrived in person. She could not refuse him then. She was happy that the saamiyaar had not come after all, but had sent the cook in his place. For an instant she imagined how it would be if Peter were to stand in front of them, wearing a cassock. She felt a deep bitterness. However parched or famished he might be, how could he manage without a wife and children! She looked fiercely at the cook. Then she looked away into the darkness. She was filled with apprehension. The rain continued to come down heavily. Water flowed in spate along the front pathway to the house. She could hear the intermittent drip-drip of raindrops falling into the tins. Thunder blasted her ears. Her mind was engulfed in darkness.

The cook's cousin had once roamed the streets aimlessly, having attended school only as far as the eighth class. A priest had taken him away and made him study. He was now an important priest himself. How many comforts and conveniences were available to him now! A house as big as a mansion. Servants to wait upon him. A congregation to listen to his words. He travelled by aeroplane. He had lived abroad for six years. When he returned, he behaved exactly like a white man. He had even forgotten our language completely. Everything he said was in English. Now he just gave money away by the handful. He helped all sorts of people with money, clothes, everything. His family and all his relatives were able to live in comfort now. The cook said all this in one great rush, implying why not let Peter have the same chance?

Savuri looked at the cook and at Arokkyam in turn. He only wanted to go to sleep. Arokkyam said to the cook, who still looked only at the lantern and its light, 'Saamiyov, while they were asking whether the curry had cooked or the pot had burnt, it was the ladle that actually broke. It's like that. All my life the needs of the stomach have come first. But it's done now. Am I going to ask for a gold coffin now that I am nearing my grave? I don't even have the means to buy a set of black beads. It is enough for us to have a little gruel for the time remaining to us. But who knows how that Saint Anthony has planned it? He has inscribed it deeply into our foreheads, saami.

Throughout my life I believed my children were everything to me. I don't need wealth, or comforts, or a big mansion. To this day, there is breath in my body only because of the thought that my children are about me. If it were not for them, I'd give up my life in an instant, saami.'

'Very well.'

Arokkyam did not like it that the cook remained silent and depressed. She wondered what, if anything, he was planning to do. She thought to herself that whatever it might be, she would never agree. She rose to her feet, collected the tins which were now full of rain water, emptied them outside, and returned them to their places. The entire house felt cold and wet, as if it had been washed throughout. There wasn't a dry place to put a foot down. At last the rain abated. The wind began to blow in strong gusts. She shut the palm-leaf gate. Now the wind felt less forceful. Savuri was trembling with the cold. The water along the pathway had risen as high as the doorstep, so she opened the gate once more to look outside. It was like a lake out there. She tried to make a channel with her feet so that the water would drain away. It would not. So she went inside, brought out the weeding hook and dug out a canal in the darkness and the pouring rain.

Josep, Sahayam and Mary—what would all of them think? Would they say to her, you have knowingly kicked away the goddess of fortune, now what are we to do? Or would they say, no, never, we don't care even if we starve; whether we live or die, let us stay within our nest? And all this time, Savuri remained silent, never saying a word.

When Arokkyam first began her conversation with the cook, she had thought that she might ask him to speak to the elders and leaders of the community. For an instant she had forgotten all her resentment against the community, and her sorrow about her own destiny. But the very next moment a thunderbolt had descended upon her head. Now she thought hard, taking no notice of the cold. What should she do? Whom to go to for advice? So far the thought of the priest had been her only support and solace. And now, he was asking her to do this. For the first time, she thought, I am going to be abandoned...

'Savuri, tell me what you wish. I must report it to the priest tomorrow.'

'If the saami has considered everything and tells us what to do, how can we oppose it?'

'Good.'

Arokkyam stared fiercely at Savuri. He, for his part, hid his face in the sacking. She was afraid that the evil fellow would go and give his permission. How could they send away the child born to them as if he were an orphan? Peter would surely yearn for them and die of grief. What good did it do to worry about it on her own? With this event, the family would be ruined, finally. She would be a mere corpse hereafter, abandoned by everyone, no one at all at her side. Who was there left to be her comfort? First Josep went away. Then Mary was gone. If Peter too should go?...and why should he stay? Had they all actually planned to isolate her like this? And would the townsfolk stand for it?

'Must you always stay like this?'

'Saami.'

Arokkyam did not care for the cook's question. Why did he ask that? At first she did not know how to answer him. But then she decided that he asked such strange questions only to mock her. That he wanted to torment her needlessly. Perhaps he asked these questions because he was contemptuous of her lifestyle, her family and their work. She asked herself for the first time if her life indeed deserved such contempt, and suddenly she began to lament:

> I suffered a thousand sorrows
> I endured three thousand struggles
> In the end what was left?
> Just a piece of cloth for my shroud.

She could not finish the song. She felt choked. Her eyes filled with warm tears. She dug at the floor, in her shame. Her whole body felt hot, as if she were in the grip of a fever. At first she prayed to Saint Anthony of Melnariappanur. Then she also made a prayer to Mariamman. Had they all made up their minds to leave her? Her own mind was painted with darkness.

'You mustn't lose heart.'

'My sorrow won't end with my tears; even if I heap it all up it can't be expressed.' Her entire body shook with her sobs. She had bent her face towards the floor. Her tears splashed in great puddles upon the cowdung paving. She did not want to look anyone in the face. She glanced at the granary which stood empty, riddled with rat-holes. She was aware that the entire house was covered in darkness. She listened to the rain falling drop by drop, cutting through the silence of the night; and to the reverberation of that sound. For sometime she listened only to that sound, beyond feeling. Then she rose again and emptied each tin into the water flowing below the gate. Because the water had dripped through the roof, it looked yellow. It didn't run clear, like tears, she thought, as she came and sat down once more. She struggled with the complexity of her problems. For the first time she was in the terrible position of sitting up at midnight, frustrated with her life.

'Tell me your decision.'

'Decision, sir, what decision? We have always spent our days together as mother and child. However many countries we roam, whatever authority we acquire, one day we put a handful of earth in our mouths, and become one with the earth. Is it so impossible to care for this body which stinks if the wind drops?' She looked at Savuri and the cook as if they were some kind of strange beasts. They were both still shivering with the cold. She looked at the flame in the lantern which blew wildly in the wind. Still drawing lines upon the floor, she spoke with a little more courage, 'All the people in this land, crore upon crore of them, do all of them possess land or property; do they even have a house to their name? There are lots and lots of people just like us. What land does a kuravan possess? Does he have house, property, goods or chattels? All these people who go around coating cooking vessels with lead, those men with the nodding cattle, the Malayali astrologer, the fortune teller with his guduppai, the snake-charmer, the gypsy with her wares, dancers and performers, basket-weavers, the voddar people who dig wells and quarry stones—do any of them possess anything? But even if they don't possess a single thing, will any of them abandon the child they carried in their womb, saami, leave it abandoned in the middle of the street? Our hearts are made of flesh and blood, saami, not of stone. When I brought him to life in my own body, I didn't do it with the thought that he would look after me in my later life. I did not know this pain even when I carried him in my body, nor when I delivered him, saami.'

Arokkyam looked up. The cook was staring intently at her. Savuri had fallen asleep in a sitting position. The rain was beating down more fiercely than before. Thunder sounded. Lightning struck across the skies in flashes of white light. There was no wind. If the wind blew strongly there would be no rain, for it would carry the clouds away in the direction in which it was blowing. She was not unduly distressed because of the rain. Of course the house leaked. Of course the vannaan's pool would rise up with the heavy flooding. They would need to dredge it out again. Until the flood abated, they would not be able to do the washing. Besides, there would not be much food in the town. And the streets would scarcely be passable because of the mud and mire. Yet, in spite of it all, she loved the rain. Because of the rains there would not be a famine. Even if the crops were damaged today, there would not be a famine in the end. Because of this rain, there would be further growth. If the land yielded well for the townsfolk, their families would flourish. Let it rain, she thought.

She excused herself to the cook, took the lantern with her and looked about the house. She put out a few more tins to catch the leaks. She spread out more sacking. Covering her head with another piece of sacking, she came outside and walked around the house. She put out her hand and checked to see at which places the walls could become waterlogged and perhaps fall down. It was still raining heavily. She dug more channels to drain away the stagnant pools. She wrung out the wet clothes she was wearing four or five times and came back in.

'Saami, have you gone to sleep?'

'What am I to say to the priest?'

'It feels as if this family is hanging in the air. What can I say to the saamiyaar when we are in this state?'

'We must not stand in the way of our children's lives, wilfully.'

'Saami!'

'You won't get such an opportunity again, even if you beg for it. And there won't be any use weeping, later on. It's because this priest is such a good man that you are being offered even this. The world we live in is a different one.'

'Saami.'

'Tomorrow I have to set off at cockcrow. Shut your eyes now and go to sleep. Tell me your decision later.'

'When I am laid out as a corpse, who will sit by my side, saami? Am I to be left without any support? O Saint Anthony.'

At last, Arokkyam wept aloud, saying she and her family had come to this terrible pass. If the priest became angry, what could she do? If he wished to do so, he had the power to excommunicate her, make it impossible for her to attend the church. He had the power to do whatever else he chose. Even Josep perhaps would have agreed to his wish, had he been here. And Mary too was not at home any longer. She kept casting about in her mind what she should do. She wept unceasingly. She wept because she felt unable to let her son grasp such a rare opportunity when it came seeking after him, which might give him the chance to live well. Her mind was so confused and perplexed that she could see no light.

'Don't condemn him to wash clothes for the rest of his life.'

'The God who designed the human mouth made it so that only the lower jaw can move. He decided that the upper jaw should never move. What are we to do about this, saami? We have to go along with our fate. If everyone becomes a priest, who will be left to do the washing?'

'O well, go to sleep. I must make a start at break of day.'

'O Jesus, O God.'

Arokkyam took the lantern inside, searched for a reasonably dry spot in its dim light, spread the head-piece of her sari, and lay down. She moved Peter as if she were moving someone whose life had come to an end. He felt as light as a baby.

Arokkyam's thoughts swirled about like paper kites that have lost their string. She would not be able to answer the townsfolk if she sent away this boy as well. Even if the townsfolk never paid her properly for her services, they would never let her go, either. But what if the cook misrepresented her to the priest? She thought of that light-complexioned stern face, instilling fear. This man came with the hour of darkness, accompanied by thunder, lightning, rain, floods. The roof leaked. The roof flapped in the wind.

In former days little girls who sold milk and old women who could barely stand would pound their paddy and other grain along the street. She would pluck away the pounder from their hands every time she walked along the street, and do it for them. And they too, if they saw her coming, would not let her go. 'Here, hold this for a moment,' they would say, and young mothers would take the time off to suckle their babies. Old women would catch their breath once more. Whether they were grinding varagu, or breaking the heads off cholam, they would hand over to Arokkyam, and go off to deal with their other chores. When she had finished, she would come away with curry seasonings, rice, curry, and other eatables. But nowadays, even if Arokkyam herself offered help, no one called her to pound their grain, grind it, or to sift it in the winnowing tray. The year before this, they had set up a machine that would pound paddy. This year they installed a machine for grinding varagu. Everyone ran off to the machine these days, even if they had only four measures of paddy or varagu. When things had come to this pass, it might be better to send Peter away. But what would happen if they had nobody at their side? She lay there, weeping and thinking, listening to the falling rain and to the rustling noises in the jungle. There really was no decision to be made. It was not possible. In their time of need, what had the priest ever done for them? When she went to see him that day, why, even at Mary's wedding, he had shown no great concern. He had smoked his cigars. No, it was impossible to do as he asked.

At daybreak, she woke the cook. He kept repeating himself, again and again. He argued with her. He attempted to advise her. He spoke of the world and its ways. Once again he explained about the priesthood. Finally he tried to intimidate her by saying the priest would be angry with her. He himself feared the priest. He was anxious that he might lose his job. But the priest knew nothing about women, nor about mothers and children. So the cook's efforts were fruitless.

By the time Savuri and Arokkyam had walked up to the boundary of the town with the cook, it was morning. Although it had stopped raining, the skies were still clouded over, and it was thundering. All along the way, Arokkyam wept. She was trembling with the cold. It would be up to the cook to explain to the priest with sensitivity about herself and the state of her family. So she behaved as if she genuinely felt affection and respect towards the cook. As well as this, she gave him a twenty rupee note. He tied it carefully into his vetti.

'Do go back now. I should be on my way.'

'Give us leave then, saami.'

'I'll speak to the priest.'

'Very well, saami.'

He moved off along the muddy foot path, slowly and carefully, like a duck. Hands folded in obeisance, Arokkyam watched him go. Some distance off, Savuri stood to one side, urinating. Then Arokkyam began to walk home through the mud, drying off her wet sari in the wind. And Savuri followed.

❋

'Why should I care?'

'My raja!'

'Why do you always make me run errands for you?'

'Who else is there for me to ask, da?'

'What about all of you, sitting on your backsides? No, I won't.'

'Just do it for me. Aren't you my saami?'

'You go yourself.'

Peter stood with his legs apart, straining forward, like a colt ready to run off. Arokkyam knew she couldn't do anything more with him. She too was fed up, ready to give up on everything. She had been trying to persuade him since sunset. He would not move. She felt a kind of anger and disgust towards everyone. A sense of emptiness overcame her.

She had seen off the priest's cook at dawn on Friday, and put herself to bed later. Since then she had suffered a fever and cold for five days. She couldn't even get up and walk about. It still rained intermittently. No clothes had been washed except those which were most urgently needed. For two days they had not collected any washing. There wasn't a soul even to ask after Arokkyam. The fever might have arisen out of her anxiety that the priest could come in person to take Peter away after he had heard what the cook had to say. The fever had not left her for five days. There was no strength in her body. Her glance flickered from the pelting rain to the waterlogged walls without any sense of attachment.

Peter too, was not to be blamed. In the morning he had gone from house to house with Savuri to collect the clothes at last. Then he went to the thorapaadu. In the evening he delivered the clothes to each family. He then collected the evening meal. He had grown up to be as good a worker as Arokkyam. He was twelve years old. Only a little child, really. Even though he was so young, he had said straight out, in answer to Arokkyam's question, that he would never be a priest. But he jumped up and down and said, 'I shall go to Madras.' Arokkyam was shocked. Had she been well enough, she would never have asked him to do any work.

Peter sat in front of Arokkyam opposing everything she said. Savuri had gone off elsewhere. These days he spent his entire time in the street. He had no desire to stay at home. He had made no effort whatever to mend the roof which had come apart in the rain. It would be done only if Arokkyam took the initiative.

Today, the dritti ceremony to dispel the evil eye was to be held for Minakshi's daughter, Sakuntala. She had menstruated eight days ago. If they went to Minakshi's house today, they would receive enough rice and curry to last them for two days. It would be good rice and a well-made curry, appropriate to a special occasion. But Peter refused to go. In spite of the cold, Savuri had gone out. If it was too late, the rice would all be finished, and the vannaan's share would be reduced. It was very cold. A howling wind tore through the roof. The walls were swollen with the damp. The water stood stagnant about the house. Even a person in sound health took a risk going out in such weather. The skies were covered over with dark clouds. She could hear the pigs grunting as they bristled and gathered together at the stagnant pools inside the jungle, and the leaves of the karuvelam trees swishing in the gusts of wind.

For the first three days, she had washed Sakuntala's clothes in the thorapaadu. Since she had fallen ill, she had washed out Sakuntala's clothes alone, at home, and sent them to her, every day. Savuri would never touch clothes that were polluted in this way. If she did too much washing in her feverish condition, Arokkyam would begin to feel faint.

If Savuri or Peter went to Minakshi's house, they would only receive rice. In the old days, when a baby was born, or if a girl came of age, Arokkyam would be given a new sari. But nowadays, whether it was an auspicious event or a sad one, they only gave her used and old material for a sari. If she did not attend the event personally, she didn't even get that much. As soon as this thought struck her, she wrapped herself in a sheet and began to get ready. She took some large vessels and handed them to Peter. They set off through the karuvelam jungle, splashing through the mud. In the darkness, they could hardly make out the footpath. The wet mud was knee-deep. The rubbish from the street floated in the water.

Peter entered the street first, with his vessels. She thought to herself, How could I have sent him away to be a priest... She watched over him carefully as he squelched his way through the sludge. She worried about what she would do if the priest or the cook should come again. At once she thought of Mary. Tears came to her eyes as she thought, this is why one needs a girl-child. It was really difficult for Arokkyam even to walk. The streets were pitted with potholes. Because the houses were built closely together, like stacked boxes, there was no way for the water to run out. Everywhere, there was mud and mire. They walked as the thomban walks upon a rope slung in midair, placing their feet carefully, one alter the other.

***

When Mary came of age, there wasn't even the space for her to be seated in exclusion. They had to seat her in the front thinnai-ledge, screening it off with old pieces of material and saris joined together. Arokkyam had wanted to build up Mary's strength by cooking rice with pungent curries, and making all sorts of foods such as vadai, paniyaaram and kozhukattai. But her own body had let her down. Arokkyam could not even leave her bed. The third day after she had been secluded, Mary had a bath, and returned to the house of her own accord. She saw to her own affairs as if she were a grown-up woman. She bound herself with rough cloth which cut into her thighs, and set about the household chores. And over and above that, she cooked a hot rasam for her mother. She gave Arokkyam a fomentation. She heated water for her bath. She served her with hot, freshly cooked rice.

None of their relations—neither mother's brothers nor father's sisters—had arrived with gifts of goods and new clothes, prepared to stay for two, three days, cooking for the family in turn. Had they belonged to a different community, at least a few relations would have turned up and cooked, at least for appearance's sake. Even the poor would have made a few fried snacks such as vadai and paniyaaram; cooked a little rice and vegetables, dal or gram. But there was no one for Mary. When Arokkyam first menstruated, she had been given the food that the relations cooked for her for eighteen days.

> No matter how many you bear, no child is like a girl child
> She'll look after you while you live, she'll see to you when you die
> She'll rinse out the cloth you wrap about you She'll think of you because you carried her in your womb
> When you stand before her, broken down and worn out she'll give you a bowl of gruel
> A woman is always a woman There might be any number of fellows with moustaches, but what use are they?
> They'll run off and abandon you; they'll betray the very mother who gave them birth for the sake of a pair of thighs.

The thought struck her that she ought to send Savuri to fetch Mary home. How many days had passed since the wedding! She had got her married in haste, thinking, Poor child, she has been exploited and betrayed. But Bhagwan will pay him back. After all, the vessel that has been blackened by soot has to be scoured. Josep too had not been back to see them. She had sent Savuri to Josep. They had looked after him well during his visit, given him every comfort. When he came home, Sahayam had sent a message with him that the entire family should go and stay there. Both Savuri and Peter had agreed it would be best. It was Arokkyam who refused. For the first time in her life the thought struck her that there might be no one to help her in her last days. And she began to believe it to be the truth.

She had arranged Mary's wedding, steadfast in the belief that Peter would still be at her side. Although four years had passed since the girl had come of age, there were no lads around, fighting for her hand. She had thought then, What will she gain if I keep her at home? She'll only earn a bad reputation. Is it to a hen's cackle that the dawn breaks? But now her feeling had changed to one of profound loss. During the last four days, whenever Peter had behaved stubbornly, she had threatened to send him off to the priest. She mourned that it had come to this. There did not seem to be any other way of controlling him. Yet she could not say that even such a threat was successful as a means of discipline.

As she reached Minakshi's house, she forgot all these things that she had been thinking about. She was exhausted. She wanted desperately to sit down. But immediately she realized that in this weather, and in the pervasive damp, there would be no place where she could sit. She walked on, supporting herself at the waist with both fists.

Minakshi's house was filled with the noises of a bustling, celebratory festival crowd. Arokkyam sat down at the front steps, tired out, muddy feet to one side. Ambaayiram the chakkiliyan went past with his daughter, Kosalai, having received his portion of rice. Sakuntala was walking about, all excited, resplendent in her new paavaadai and jacket. She kept walking between the street and the house as if it were a festival day. Her skin had a freshness about it and she had put on weight. You could scarcely recognize her. Somehow, when girls come of age, they look fleshed out. Their skin lightens in colour.

The important elders of the town and the close relations had been seated in the main room and in the verandah, and were feasting. In the pandal out in the street, there were two petromax lamps burning. Elsewhere, lanterns had been hung about. Minakshi was giving presents of food to each family. Her husband, Ezhumalai, was inside, standing at the centre of the guests.

'Rasam,' said a voice.

'Curry,' said another.

'Bring me some rice.'

'Water, water.'

'He's not like us with our five, six daughters. They have just the one. But look at the curry he serves, it's like cow's urine.'

'Does this look like rice to you, or does it look like date-stones?'

'I did a dritti for my middle daughter. You should have seen the likes of it. We cooked four kalams of rice. People loosened their waist chains and gorged themselves until they could hardly breathe. Isn't this rice as slimy smooth as plantain stems?'

'This rice is definitely going to tear your guts out.'

'Call this a curry? Look how the curry and rice fight each other, refusing to mix!'

'Ei, rice!'

'Water; it's too hot. O, O!'

'Bring the rice here, Vilangathur boy!'

'Who's the lad serving vegetables? I asked him for a serving, and he just pretends to put it on my leaf.'

'And it's only plantain—just gas and air!'

'Do you think I have any savings? It was only by pawning the rice vessel for ten rupees that I could find the presentation money.'

'Bring the curry this way.'

'Don't narrow your hands into a leper's fist; spread them wide and scoop the rice generously with both hands.'

'Ei, curry.'

'Water, water.'

The place resounded with shrieks and cries, like the noises that children make at the Perumal temple in Margazhi, when the singing of bhajanai ends, and either pongal or boiled gram is handed around.

At a particular time, Ponnusaami came in and stood in the middle of the room where the people were feasting. As soon as he saw him, Ezhumalai hastened outside to summon all those who had not eaten as yet.

For long periods of time, Ponnusaami was not to be seen in the town. He was a man who had studied a little. Even as a student, he had been involved as a party member in the freedom struggle. Now he had joined another political party, and held quite an important position in it. He had managed to bring a minister to the opening of the new high school here. He had built houses in the colony. Now he was having the streets gravelled, one after the other.

For some reason, Ponnusaami had never married. To this day, there continued to be gossip about this.

'Minakshi showed her teeth, lifted her leg and seduced her brother-in-law.'

'Ponnusaami suffers from some mysterious disease. That's why he never married.'

'She used some potion to charm him.'

'Ezhumalai can't do it with her, it seems.'

Such whispers. Ezhumalai was Ponnusaami's elder brother and own sibling. But Ezhumalai's actions and

Ponnusaami's behaviour seemed to corroborate the town gossip. If Ponnusaami stayed at home, then Ezhumalai would be working in the fields. At nights, whether it rained or blew cold, he always slept at the entrance of the temple. According to the townsfolk, it was Ponnusaami who had fathered Sakuntala. The brothers had not yet divided their joint property. It was whispered abroad that Ponnusaami's share as well as his income would certainly go to Sakuntala and her brother. However that might be, Arokkyam was very fond of Minakshi. She always washed the clothes from Minakshi's household with particular care. It was only to Minakshi that she spoke of her own troubles. And Minakshi was actually well loved in the town for her fine character.

The rain started coming down again in steady drops. Arokkyam was chilled. She wrapped the sheet more tightly about herself. But the wrap felt really heavy. She found it difficult just to bear its weight.

Minakshi, having just given away a share of food, returned and caught sight of Arokkyam and Peter. The crowd had thinned slightly. Now it was mainly women and children who were there. Minakshi struck up a quarrel with Arokkyam immediately.

'What is it di, amma? Do I need to send you too a formal invitation, or what? So did you arrive in a grand palanquin from Mount Meru?'

'I wasn't well, saami.'

'Why, what's the matter with you?'

'Don't ask me, saami. Cold, fever. I just couldn't even open my eyes.'

'When you are like this, why did you walk through the sludge, di?'

'Who is there to come instead of me, saami?'

'Wait, I'll be back.'

Minakshi went inside, and returned in a little while to fill up Arokkyam's rice vessel. It was a big vessel, capable of holding three makaani of rice. She returned again, to pour the still simmering curry into Arokkyam's containers. It was a curry of brinjals. There were poriyals made of green banana, pumpkin and squash. She laid them in heaps on top of the rice. Minakshi looked up as if to ask, is that enough? Arokkyam tried hard to give her a wide smile in reply.

Arokkyam had deliberately brought her biggest vessels. And Minakshi too had filled them generously, thinking, She is the one who washes our polluted crotch-cloths. On special occasions like this, even those who had little for themselves would not stint when it came to serving Arokkyam.

'Ever since Mary left, your body has become half what it used to be.'

'What is one to do, saami? How long can one keep a girl child to oneself?'

'Does this lad at least give you a hand, keep you company?'

'He does what he can, saami.'

'Here, boy, at least you should stay with your father and mother and look after them.'

Peter nodded. Minakshi's voice broke. Arokkyam wept silently. Sakuntala called out for her mother, and Minakshi went in. Sometime later, when she happened to step out again, Arokkyam asked her, 'Shall I go then, saami?'

'Very well, di Arokkyam. Look after your health. It's a woman's only means of survival.'

'Then, shall I go?'

'What else is it, di, Arokkyam?'

'I haven't any decent clothes to wrap about me, saami.'

'O, goodness, I completely forgot. Wait a minute.'

Minakshi ran inside hurriedly. Children continued to bring the leaves upon which they had eaten their meals, and to throw them away at a distance a little beyond where Arokkyam sat. Peter stood, ready, the curry container on his head. Arokkyam lifted the rice vessel. She could scarcely stand. It was very cold now. Her jaw trembled. Her feet were numb. The skies were echoing like drumbeats. Minakshi brought out a set of Sakuntala's old paavaadai and davani.

'Saami, why can't you give this vannaati a new piece of cloth? You are a big family.'

'When the wedding is done, and she comes home for the delivery of her first child, I promise on your head you will be given whatever you want, Arokkyam. Don't hold anything against me. We've had such a lot of expenses.'

'I am one who washes out urine and shit and clots of blood, saami. It is only by your holding out your hand that my stomach is filled, saami.'

'You talk as if your family is tearing itself away. Come when all this is over. Must I give it to you this very moment?'

'Ammov!'

'Coming, di.'

'I'll go now, saami.'

Minakshi ran inside in answer to Sakuntala's call, without waiting a moment longer.

By the time Arokkyam and Peter reached home, she was exhausted. Savuri was not to be seen. Arokkyam lit the lamps. She swept the house. She told Peter to eat, and went and lay down. The ground was still soaked through and cold. In places, the cowdung paving had cracked and swollen.

Savuri finished his conversation with Periyaan and came home to eat. Then he poured some water into the leftover rice, covered it carefully against prowling dogs, and went off to sleep in the thinnai. He did not have anything to say to Arokkyam.

For the following two weeks and more, it rained without letting up. A whole month had gone by. Now and again, Arokkyam went and fetched rice and curry from one house or another. Peter did not stay at home, but wandered about in the colony. Savuri was engrossed in his conversations with Periyaan who was now bedridden. At last Arokkyam quarrelled with Savuri about all of this. After that, he went away and fetched a sackful of washing clay. That night, as they were going to bed, Arokkyam reminded Savuri that they had to go to the thorapaadu early the next day.

The sun was in the skies by the time she got there with Savuri, holding Peter by the hand; they had set off very early, because they needed to dig out the water-hole. They knew the path to the thorapaadu really well, and could walk there even in the dark.

She prayed to Saint Anthony. After that, Savuri began to dig out the earth with his curved spade. Arokkyam and Peter scooped it up with their bare hands, and threw it far away. The pool, which had been deep enough to submerge a man standing upright, had filled up now with silt, and was flooded over. Hunchbacked, Savuri dug it out in great haste. He did not work as fast as he used to in the old days. And he was silent, showing no enthusiasm. He was a shade thinner since Arokkyam's illness.

Arokkyam had borrowed the spade and shovelling basket just the day before. The basket was full of holes. She had tied a piece from an old sari across it. Even so, it leaked. Arokkyam's ill health would scarcely allow her to keep working, but her will spurred her on.

Now he could no longer scoop the earth up with his spade. Yet the soft earth kept falling off the sides of the pit. Savuri stood at the bottom of the pool, filled the basket and handed it up. Arokkyam and Peter carried it away, and tipped it out at some distance. Savuri kept widening and deepening the pit so that its sides would not fall in. But there was no way he could prevent them from sliding down from time to time. A strong wind was sufficient to bring down enough mud to make two cart-loads.

Arokkyam walked up and down, carrying the basket full of dripping mud. Seeing that Peter walked more and more slowly as time went on, she told him to sit down for a while. They would need to dig out about twenty cartloads of earth in order to make a pool that was deep enough and wide enough so that it would fill sufficiently. Because they would need to clear out the mud as the sides fell in from time to time, she asked Savuri to make sure the pool was wide enough. Savuri made no response, staying silent. Arokkyam was distressed at this. For some reason, he had taken to acting in this strange manner of late.

Soon, Savuri too grew tired. He had to lift up the basket and hand it to Arokkyam and Peter by turns. They had dug up perhaps seven, eight cartloads already. The water had begun to enter in a rush. They could not lift the wet earth easily. When the water running out of the basket soaked her right through, Arokkyam too sat down awhile, to rest and draw breath. They could have hired someone to dig the pool for them. But they could not afford to pay for such day-labour. They themselves had no other employment.

There was an all-pervasive scent by the river. Upon the trees and plants along either bank of the stream, muddy marks had been left by the rising waters. Arokkyam thought, from the evidence upon the trees, that the flood must have risen to one and a half times the height of a man. Savuri said it must have been more, perhaps twice the height of a man. Peter ran up to stand against a palm tree and checked. He called out that the water had risen only to his height. Then he asked Arokkyam, 'Where does all the water go, Amma?'

'Mm. It just keeps on flowing like this.'

'And after that?'

'People with pump-sets draw out the water and channel it to their fields.'

'And the rest of it?'

'It must keep on flowing through the woods and fields.'

'And then?'

'It keeps on flowing. That's all.'

'It seems it finally reaches the sea.'

'Who told you?'

'Arumugam.'

'Truly?'

'I swear on your head.'

'Maybe. Could be. Where else would all this water go?'

'Have you seen the sea?'

'Who has seen the ocean?'

'What would it be like?'

'Who has set eyes upon the ocean?'

'Are the sea and the ocean the same?'

'Ayyo, it's getting late! Come on, get up!'

Arokkyam hurried them on. She asked Savuri and Peter to carry out the mud, and began to work on the walls herself. There was a lot of water filling up the pool now. It was difficult to work the mud with the spade. She kept on straining the mud before packing the basket and lifting it up. In between all this, she tried to keep Peter's spirits up by telling him stories. She kept telling him he was a good lad, clever and sensible. Savuri remained silent.

As the sun rose up swiftly in the sky, the heat beat down fiercely. Everywhere she struck the spade, water sprang up, like the sap spurting from the banana stem wherever it is cut. Now the entire pool was ankle deep in water. Arokkyam stood in the water, building up the pool's walls. After this, the river would not be in spate for several months. It might not even rain. That was why the pool had to be dug wide enough and deep enough now. Four or five times during the year, they would need to dredge the pool and to deepen it. Besides, the walls might fall in when small boys brought their cattle and goats to drink there. That too had to be made good from time to time. Because of the recent floods and rain, the water lay close to the earth's surface now. In time its level would drop. They would have to deepen the pool then. As the sides of the pool slid inward, they would have to cut them back. It happened all the time.

Savuri spoke up finally. He said that the pool was now good enough for the amount of washing that came to them these days. Peter agreed with him. In the old days, they had to dig a pool deep enough to submerge a man. They used to wash no less than six bundles of clothes a day. Nowadays they received that much work only on Pongal and other festival days. In spite of what Savuri said, Arokkyam continued to dig for a little longer. She could not bring herself to stop, although she too thought the pool was probably deep enough. Her idea was that instead of struggling with it day after day, they should make a big effort now. Would the walls hold yet? A big gust of wind might make the sides fall in.

The sun's rays fell through and between the densely growing trees, and lay dappled along the sandy beaches of the river-bank, like the shifting shadows of clouds, broad and narrow, short and long, round, square, formless. The smell of the screwpine filled the air all along the stream. Yellow arali flowers shone and sparkled in the sunlight. The earth was not yet completely dry. The clean smell of wet earth rose up, after a long rime. As it grew warmer and warmer, birds, bees and insects flew out into the sunlight. They raised their voices joyfully, now that the rain had abated. The foam and tide marks on the trees began to disappear. Flotsam and dirt which lay in great waves on both banks of the stream also dried out. The entire stream gleamed and sparkled, freshly green. Except for the palm trees, everything looked bright and new. All because of the rain. Everything needed the rain. Yet, in a little while this freshness would vanish. This place would look like a barren wasteland. The parched earth would be riven; cracked open. It would yearn then, for a single drop of rain.

Peter began to whinge and clamour that he was hungry. Then Savuri started pestering her to stop. Before they could quite dig a pit that was waist deep and twenty feet wide, they had reached a point of extreme exhaustion. Water was seeping steadily from the bottom. Arokkyam's legs were numb from standing so long in the water. They had turned pale and bloodless. She threw her spade down and strengthened the walls of the pit all the way round, patting them firmly with the palms of her hand. She squeezed and pressed the palms of her hand again and again into the earthen walls, as if she were applying poultice. She smoothed and stroked the walls as if she were bathing a baby. She pressed it here and there, as she would an invalid's body, to relieve pain. At certain places the walls had slid down a little. She dissolved the mud into the water, and threw it away.

Arokkyam walked round and round, patting the walls. Where it was muddy, she scooped it out with her cupped hands. She heaped some of the earth together, and fashioned some steps so that they could climb in and out of the pool. Peter jumped into the neck-deep water, frolicking as he swam and bathed. Savuri, too, bathed, came ashore, and sat on the warm rocks, sunning himself. He was so hungry, he felt faint; his eyes dimmed. He was furious with Arokkyam for staying so long. But he didn't say anything.

The pond was perfectly square; it was beautiful. Arokkyam was filled with elation. As time passed, more and more water seeped into the pond. Arokkyam bathed and came ashore at last. She had wanted to revel in the water to her heart's content. All her tiredness and hunger had disappeared without a trace while she bathed.

She handed one end of her sari to Peter to hold, and stood with a single fold of it about her, letting it dry. She stood there, looking in wonder at the trees, plants and flowers on both sides of the stream, stretching as far away as the eye could see. She rejoiced to see the little pools of water that had gathered in small holes, and how their surfaces rippled in wavelets as the wind blew. Everywhere there was the pervading scent of the screwpine. She twisted her sari about her. Savuri walked on ahead of her. Peter set off for home at a run.

O Jesus, O Lord
Surya Bhagwan
Chandra Bhagwan
Vayu Bhagwan
Bhuma Devi
Saint Anthony!

Arokkyam fell to the earth in prostration. Then she brought her hands together in worship to the sun. Once again she looked at the newly made pond and the entire stretch of the river as if scrutinizing everything. She didn't have the heart to go home. She had ground some aavaaram leaves and massaged the paste into her scalp before bathing, so her head felt cool. There was its fine scent upon her body. She separated her hair into strands, and lifted the strands to the sun.

She crawled into the shelter where she had hidden away three earthenware containers before the rains came, to see whether they were still whole. She was shocked to see that two of them were broken and lay in scattered fragments. Either shepherd boys or gypsies hunting for fox and hare by night must have done it. O God, now what will I do for two more containers, Arokkyam thought, stunned for a moment. Then she hid the remaining container in a different place and obscured it with leaves. She picked up the clay shards and flung them away towards the river bank. They scattered and fell, shattering into still smaller fragments.

The worrying thought hit her that she needed kindling for her hearth and she began to pull at some of the rotting pieces of the fence. She broke them up and set them aside. Hoping to collect enough to last a couple of days, she looked for thorny twigs all along the stream. As she walked past a small pool, a crab peeped out from its hole. Immediately she threw down her kindling and began hunting for crabs. Even as a young girl, she had been particularly smart at catching crabs. However big the crab, its pincers would never bother her hands. Even if they pinched, she never gave in to them. Some days after the rains ended, she would set off to catch crabs as soon as she had washed the clothes and put them to dry. She would stroke their shells in wonder. She would put her fingers at the end of their pincers, between what looked like fine teeth, and she would laugh.

The crabs had increased in number, immediately after the rains began. Arokkyam lay along the river, thrust her hands into the hole and pulled. She did not mind the bite; in fact she was only too glad. As she discovered more and more crabs, she grew more delighted and excited; she laughed like a child, not giving up even when they bit, collecting them one by one into her lap. Seeking out one hole after another, she collected about twenty crabs. She left the little ones in their holes, or flung them back into the water. Her entire body, her face and her clothes were covered in pieces of caked mud. The crabs she had collected began to slither against her stomach. They irritated her skin. When she couldn't bear it any more, she tied them up into a bundle in a separate piece of cloth which she threw into the basket along with her pickaxe. She held the basket under her arm. Then she tied the kindling together, placed it on her head and set off home. The sun was sinking towards the west. She had forgotten her hunger and tiredness, but walked on at a good pace, looking forward to the crab-rasam she was going to prepare and eat.

***

'Have you seen that lad?'

Silence.

'Have you stuffed your ears with cotton-wool?'

'What do you want me to do, di? Daughter of a good-for-nothing!'

'He went ahead of us from the thorapaadu, and now I can't find the boy. Where can he have gone?'

'I haven't seen him, have I?'

'Do go and look for him. You'll be blessed for it.'

'You go yourself.'

'Where could he have gone? O Jesus, O God.'

This boy, who would snack on the sly ten times a day at least, hadn't eaten since morning. The rice she had left in its dish had not diminished. It was exactly as before. He was the one who had left the thorapaadu first, well ahead of them. What did he have to do so urgently that he could not even eat first? She began to worry lest he had wandered off somewhere in the woods with the shepherd boys. The crab-rasam was good and hot. She had looked forward to the rasam; she had caught the crabs and cooked them with love. Savuri ate the rasam. She could not, as none of them was there: not Josep, nor Mary, nor Peter.

Arokkyam went down to the street three times. Not there. He still had not come home, though it was time to collect the evening meal. She asked the boys he always played with, acquaintances, Minakshi, Susila, everyone. There wasn't a place left that she had not searched. There wasn't a single person whom she had not asked, adults, old people, boys and girls.

'Have you seen that boy?'

'Who do you mean?'

'Peteru.'

'O, no.'

'Saamiyov, have you seen him anywhere?'

'No.'

'Tejamaan?'

'No.'

'Thambi?'

'No.'

'Akka?'

'Haven't seen him, no.'

'Ayyavov?'

'Haven't clapped eyes on him.'

'Maama?'

'No, Arokkyam.'

'Baby?'

'I only saw him yesterday.'

O Saint Anthony
O Jesus, O Lord, he has filled my mouth with earth
Is this all that I have deserved?
What a wretch I am
People look at me as if I am denuded and isolated

Lord
Saint Anthony
I am left naked and exposed.

There was no news at all about him. Nobody claimed to have seen him here or there. She sent the boys to look for him in the Mariamman shrine. She went into the thorny jungle to search for him. Had he fallen into a pond and drowned? Perhaps a snake had bitten him? At every step she took, she called aloud to Saint Anthony of Melnariappanur. Until earliest dawn she waited up for him with lighted lantern, unable to sleep. He did not turn up. At break of day she went and searched once more at every well, thinking that in the darkness of the night she might have missed him. She had called out his name in the dark; now in the daylight she called out at each well and sugar-cane field, and all along the river.

Peteru
Ei, Peteru
Thambi Peteru
O Saint Anthony.

There was only the echo; no sign of Peter. She searched until noon, and then at last she came home and lay down. A stray dog had overturned the crab-rasam.

When Periyaan died, Savuri sat in the house of mourning the whole day, overcome by grief. For ten days after that he did not go out. His body shrank to half its former size. It was months since he had shaved. He looked as if he did not care about anything; as if he were only connected to a spirit world. There never was a response from him to anything.

Savuri had wanted to send word to Mary and Josep. But Arokkyam had stopped him. There was only Savuri left now, both to go to the thorapaadu, and to do all their other errands. So Arokkyam had rejected the idea. Just today they had received a letter from Peter at last. It was addressed to Arokkyam. This was the very first letter a member of their family had received. She had not even gone to the thorapaadu. She showed the letter to everyone in the colony who could read. She called out to people and told them about Peter's letter. Exasperated by Savuri's indifference, she picked a quarrel with him. She gave thanks to Saint Anthony that Peter was alive wherever he might have gone. She sat at the threshold of their house, the letter in her lap, silently weeping. Her eyes swept over and around the letter again and again. There was not a moment in the last four months when she had not wept for him. Every other minute she would say,

Peteru, Peteru
He's gone where the wind will take him
My life remained in this block of wood only for his sake
I took courage because I believed he was steadfast
O Saint Anthony.

Arokkyam had put together all the different sorts of grain and millet that she had received as payment at different times, and sold it all. She had saved this money in order to buy a silver waist chain for Josep and Sahayam's child, who was yet to be born then. It was this money that Peter had taken when he ran away to Madras with Arumugam. Arokkyam had not even mourned the loss of the money. She had just been anxious for any news of him. Now she could at least draw breath in peace, reassured that he was at least alive. Now at last she could walk about. She could go to the thorapaadu. For her, not going to the thorapaadu was like not eating. Arokkyam was like a withered leaf flying in the wind.

'It's like having ten kaani of wet and dry land together and yet going all the way to Panrutti for a piss,' she said, laughing. There was a renewed joy about her, as if her face and body had regained their lost youth.

She thought to herself that it was as the Malayali astrologer had said; everything had happened because of some planetary disturbance. She wanted so much to see Peter. She forgot entirely about choosing a waist chain for Josep's son, and sat there with Peter's letter upon her lap, touching it from time to time, and weeping. She needed to weep. She wept because of an excess of joy.

And as she sat there, unmindful of the intense heat and the height of the sun, Chinnasaami came along. He looked very tired and weary. He took off his upper cloth and wiped away the sweat that had gathered upon his face, his neck and his body. Watching him as he stood there awkwardly, hesitating to speak, Arokkyam herself was moved to ask him, 'What is the matter, saami?'

'O, nothing. Why don't you just come up to the house?'

'Why, saami?'

'A small matter...'

'Tell me, saami, don't feel shy.'

'Her breasts have knotted up.'

'You go on ahead. I'll be there in one leap, saami. O Saint Anthony, let it all be good news today.'

Chinnasaami hesitated a moment more, then he walked on. She stood up, reflecting for a moment on what she needed to do. She was just about to tuck away the letter under the eaves of the roof when she remembered that Susila could read, so she kept it in her lap thinking she would have it read out once again. She shut the hanging gate and went out. She was still full of happiness. Sprightly as a young child she sped along, and in no time at all she had entered Susila's house.

Susila sat leaning against the wooden pestle, her eyes shut, covered in sweat, tired out. Her face was twisted with pain; flushed and swollen. Arokkyam was shocked by the sight. She lifted her and with her own sari wiped away the sweat from her face. As soon as she saw Arokkyam, the tears that Susila had kept suppressed for so long came bursting out. She held on tightly to Arokkyam and wept. Her tears were like that of a child who howls as she flings her arms around the legs of a mother just about to leave on a journey. Arokkyam told Chinnasaami to go and see to whatever jobs he had in hand, and without a word he climbed down the front steps and went out, his cloth upon his head against the heat of the day. His gait reminded her of cattle with planks across their necks to prevent them from going through hedges, their gaze fixed earthwards, their legs knocking each other as they walked on.

Arokkyam struck a blow across Susila's shoulder blades. Then she was shaken by what she had just done. 'What sin must I have committed, that I have come to such a pass. How could I hit a young woman with a newly born baby!' Her eyes filled. Susila's anguish had driven her to this.

Susila had downright refused to remove her jacket. Arokkyam was breathless. She could not control the struggling woman. In the old days, however rough and tough a woman might be, she would quieten under Arokkyam's hands. That was in the past, she said to herself. Now she argued with Susila. She told her stories. She sang to her.

Gradually, as Arokkyam continued to sing, Susila forgot her pain and looked up. In an instant, Arokkyam pulled at the buttons and threw them away. Laughing gently, she removed the blouse. She knew what she would find. There was a discoloration that was turning green. Both Susila's breasts were hugely swollen, engorged and stiff. They felt as cold as an underground spring. But Susila would not stay still. Poor thing, Arokkyam thought, she is only a young girl. The fine green veins were all standing out stiffly. Under her arms, the lymph glands were swollen like marbles.

Susila shut her eyes and gritted her teeth. Her arms shot out and shoved Arokkyam away with a fierce brute force. But Arokkyam was a woman who never lost her patience at such times, even when a woman she was treating hit her or kicked her, hid from her or ran away. She only laughed as she would at a puppet's comical movements. She would gaze with the same steady interest that she might show towards a newly bought object.

And she did what she needed to do. First she held Susila against her chest and stroked her as gently as she would a baby, as if she were drawing lines all over her with her separated fingers. She pressed her gently with the palm of her hand, as if she were laying a poultice upon a bruise. Holding her close, she stroked her from her neck downwards. Slowly she began pressing down a little more firmly. Now she rose to her feet and applied pressure underneath each breast. She massaged them all over and on all sides with both hands. She smoothed them. She patted them. Gradually she increased the pressure, added more force. At last Susila loosened very slightly. Arokkyam continued to stroke and pat and massage, and every now and then she spoke to Susila, saying whatever occurred to her at that moment.

Nearly two days had elapsed since the baby had put its mouth to Susila's breast and suckled. It was exactly twenty-two days since the child was born. But not a single drop would come out now. Her nipples stood out stiff and dry, without showing the slightest wetness. Not even an ooze. As time wore on, her whole chest tightened up so that she could scarcely breathe. Leaving the baby howling constantly while Susila huddled helplessly in a corner, Chinnasaami had rushed to fetch Arokkyam. Susila had only just told him what was wrong. She had been too shy to tell him. But she could not go herself in search of Arokkyam.

Now Arokkyam made Susila stretch out on her back, and rolled a churning stick all over her and around each breast.

The tightness had slackened a little more. There was no further danger to her life. What use is it to be so shy? Another day and she might have stopped breathing. One should only be modest at certain times: she lost sight of that, Arokkyam thought to herself as she straightened up with a great sigh. She was gasping for breath. There was no strength left in her body. After all, she had recently suffered a fever. Besides, Susila's agonized mutterings had affected her in a strange way.

'Be patient. Look, it's nearly done, amma.'

'O God, O God, what will I do?'

'If you are like this, your baby will certainly die. You too might suffocate and die, my daughter.'

'O my God.'

'Here my love. It's done. Lie down a little. O Saint Anthony.'

As soon as the milk began to flow, Arokkyam rubbed her down, wiped her dry, and put her to bed. She tidied her sari at her waist. Susila lay there like a corpse. Then, because she was streaming with sweat, Arokkyam picked up a winnowing tray and fanned her. Susila was still in unbearable pain. Before this, the pain had been concentrated on her breasts. Now it seemed there was no part of her entire body that did not ache.

Arokkyam played with the baby for a little while. Then she placed her next to Susila. Susila picked her up and suckled her. She suckled soundlessly, her little hand squeezing her mother's other breast. She smoothed the fine hair with her hands. Tears stood in her eyes.

Susila asked after Mary, Josep and Peter. She wanted to know all about the family, and how business was going on. Arokkyam, who had been happy thus far, was troubled again, and began to weep. She brought out the letter that Peter had sent. Susila read it out to her. Arokkyam mourned aloud, 'If I had realized he would do this, I would have sent him to the priest after all.' Then she went on, 'It's not like it used to be any longer in these parts, amma. People do what they want. They won't even let us touch their grain, let alone handle it: No one is prepared to give us a morsel of food—they've got so miserly. How are we to survive, amma?' Arokkyam wailed aloud. All her former sorrow and resentment returned. Susila could only manage to speak a few comforting words. The pain all over her body stopped her from saying much.

Susila rose slowly and brought Arokkyam a bronze measuring-vessel full of varagu rice, along with tamarind, salt, a few chillies and some salt. Arokkyam told Susila to be very careful of her baby's health and her own. As if recollecting something, she called out suddenly, 'Ammadiyov, careful with the baby. Be careful; look after her. I'll come and see how you are tomorrow.'

Arokkyam's heart was troubled with unnameable thoughts. It struck her that she who looked after all the village women and their children, serving them at their good times and their bad times, washing their shit and urine away, could do nothing for her own children. She wept bitterly for Peter.

Savuri had come home ahead of her. He stared at her with a look that said, Where have you been all this time? What have you been doing? Then he turned his head away. Arokkyam understood perfectly. She strained the old rice, poured fresh water over it and placed it in front of him. She brought him four of the chillies that Susila had given her. He stared at them and began to eat. His expression was not pleasant. He was not the Savuri of old.

'Why didn't you come to the grove?'

'I didn't come. So what's it to you?'

'And what were you doing?'

'Hunh. I was playing with mud in the streets.'

'You think that the shit that's knocking in your backside is something else. You'll know soon enough what's what.'

'You corpse of a creature! Will you stay alive after this? Or will you go and destroy yourself? How can you speak to me like this? You'll lie down and die for it. O Saint Anthony, how can you listen to this and still keep your mouth shut? Haven't you got eyes to see what's going on?'

Early that morning, Savuri had called Arokkyam to go to the funeral grove with him.

'Get ready, come on, let's go.'

'Where is he asking me to go?'

'If we attend the last rites, we'll get two rupees and a piece of cloth.'

'So why should I come?'

'I'm not going on my own!'

'Why is there a moustache on your face? You go if you like; I'm not coming.'

For some reason she kept thinking of Harischandra's song:

I who once gave generous handfuls
To those who asked for silver coins
Now accept the funeral fee—such is my fate
Only the paltry funeral fee.

She was also furious at Savuri's silence when she told him, 'Peter has sent a letter, look!' She had only wanted to sit there, enjoying the sight of the letter. But Susila's husband had come and fetched her away. She had not wanted to go and beg for money at the funeral.

Savuri sat where he was, his face turned away.

'I was as well off as a paappaati. I lived like a landowner's daughter. You brought me down to this low paraya state, you wretch! I never had to do any work that required me to touch it with my left hand. What good have I seen since the day I came to you? Have I even had the joy of wearing four new saris? Have I gone anywhere, seen a new city or event, had any pleasure such as every female in the town enjoys? Because of you I've lost everything, money, goods and property. You've given me three children. You've shown me the thorapaadu. What else have you done for me, you traitor, you murderer. You'll die of a nasty disease.'

Arokkyam wept for a long time as she had not done for many days. Savuri simply sat there, his head bowed. Since the day that Periyaan died, he would either fly into a temper for no reason, or he would sit in silence, like this. Arokkyam wept, pouring out all her complaints. She felt a sudden urge to see Mary and Josep. She had never before found fault with Savuri quite in this way. But today, somehow, her heart was not at peace.

As if she were telling someone else, speaking her words into the wind, she recounted how, just as she was preparing to go to the funeral grove, Susila's husband had come for her. At last she finished weeping, dried her tears, wiped her face, drank a long draught of water to quench her thirst, sat down at the threshold of the house and spoke to Savuri.

'We've carried bundles of washing like donkeys all this time, but what good has it done us? I have just one beloved female chick, and she is living from hand to mouth. Can't I even go and see her? Even an aavaaram flower has its uses; can't a woman go and see her daughter?'

Arokkyam kept on lamenting. Savuri sat close by, but he gazed towards Ambaayiram's house as if he heard nothing.

'Well, shall I just go and make her a quick visit?'

'Don't ruin my life, woman.'

'O heavens, is your life so important?'

'Your life stinks of menstrual blood.'

'Your life! Look at your famous life!'

Arokkyam grimaced at Savuri and continued to mutter and whimper in her yearning for Mary. It was possible for her to carry on endlessly weeping, or talking, or working.

Having gone to announce the news of a death, recently, Savuri had returned with the news that Mary had conceived and was four months pregnant. From that day, Arokkyam had been trying to go to her. Uselessly. She had never so far. gone away, leaving Savuri to fend for himself. There was too much to do. It was Savuri who always went out of town when necessary. It was he who saw to all the business of weddings, deaths, mourning and last rites. Meanwhile there was the daily washing to do. So she was in a constant dilemma, whether she should go or not. Once Peter's letter arrived, she seemed to have no other topic of conversation. No other thought. Frustrated that she could not see them, she vented her anger on Josep, Mary and Peter. She would berate the one who came to mind first. Then she would weep for their sake.

Josep and Sahayam had taken the newly wedded couple, Mary and Diraviyaraj, to their home in Chinnasalem for two days, and then accompanied them to Diraviyaraj's home town. After that, Savuri had been to see them twice, on the Eighteenth day of Aadi, and at Deepavali. He had taken the bridal gifts: a bottle of groundnut oil; eight green plantains;

a large earthenware container decorated with kolam patterns and filled with paddy; and ten rupees in money. He had reported that Mary was well and happy.

Arokkyam would think of her, and then say the words aloud, 'Poor child, she is all alone! How do you pass the time, my daughter?' Then she would comfort herself. She had not so far been to visit Mary. Now she was angry that Savuri could not bring himself to tell her to go. He had never done something to please her specially. Nor had she asked him to do so. But she had never had a special wish before this.

Four months ago, Sahayam had delivered a baby boy. Apparently, Mary and Diraviyaraj had gone to visit them. Peter had been at home then. Savuri and he had seen Arokkyam to the thorapaadu, and then gone on to the free hospital in Chinnasalem to see the mother and baby. She longed to go herself, for the baby's sake even if not for Sahayam. Each time Savuri went on his own, he returned wearing a white veshti and upper cloth. They asked you to visit, he would report. But then, Savuri never made it possible for her to go. She would look questioningly at him. And he would promptly walk away. How long it was since she saw Josep!

'Have they asked us to move, as a family?'

'That's what I'm telling you.'

'Really?'

'Hmmm.'

'Honestly?'

'Mary also says the same thing.'

He repeated all this. Yet he refused to let her go and visit. She thought that Sahayam would be angry that she had not even been to see the new baby. She wanted desperately to see one of her children. Her heart was full of anguish. Once again she began to weep saying, 'I'm like an orphan with nobody to turn to, O God!'

Savuri was muttering to himself one of Periyaan's most frequently repeated songs:

Eight feet come towards you
Two feet lie stretched out
Within the pot comes a fire
Along come the family and kinsfolk
The drum comes with its heavy beat
A thousand, thousand follow on
Many come with stricken hearts
Wearing garlands of silence
Eight feet come towards you
Two feet lie stretched out.

✱

From the start of the month of Margazhi, there was a great deal of work to be done. It was just a week to Pongal. No one in the village fell over themselves this year to summon Arokkyam and Savuri for the winnowing of the harvest. Each family did their own, in a great hurry to finish it so that they could go on to the winnowing for the Gaunder and the Udaiyaar for whom they worked. Savuri alone went to help one or two families who did not have any menfolk. Even they complained that Savuri was no longer able to winnow properly and that he could not see very well these days. Not that Savuri took it to heart. There was a lot of washing because Pongal was near, and that kept him busy. Arokkyam, on the other hand, wept again and again. All her efforts came to nothing. She could neither understand nor accept the indifference that her own people showed towards her. Everything had turned upside down. Everyone behaved strangely.

The sun stood high in the sky when the two of them reached home. As soon as they returned, both of them drank some gruel. Savuri bit sharply into dried chillies, crunching four or five between his teeth. But it seemed to him that his tongue was numb and dead. Arokkyam too thought the same. If one's tongue were sensate, then the sharpness of the chillies would make it salivate, so that it hung out, dripping like a panting dog's.

'If things go on like this, what is to happen to us?'

'Nobody is going to snatch away the pot we hold in our hands. This much wealth is enough for us.'

'O Jesus, O Lord, people shrink even from looking us in the eye!'

Savuri lifted the vessel and poured the rest of gruel down his throat and gulped it down. Arokkyam kept stirring her portion with her hand. Without even being aware of it, she was deep in her thoughts. She was not in a normal frame of mind. For the first time she knew what it was to fear the future which would come the very next day. It pressed upon her mind like a ghost or demon which no one comprehends, but everyone speaks of with dread.

Savuri said to her, 'If you are searching for whole grains of rice, you'll stay hungry for most of the time, you know. You just have to shut your eyes and swallow whatever is in front of you, even if it's just earth. Otherwise you won't keep up your strength. Where are you going to get fine snacks now?' He was distressed too. Arokkyam's body wasn't even half what it used to be.

Savuri took the fine stick which he had stuck behind his ear and began picking his teeth. Arokkyam took out the grains which they had collected in two separate sacks, and put it all together. One bundle of varagu, and another, quarter of its size, of cholam. That was all. And there was only one street left. They would go there for their dues that evening. Nobody had given them much; very little, in fact. It had never been so bad, even in days of famine.

For the past four days, Savuri and Arokkyam had gone to every house and collected grain. People gave them their padi, their traditional allowance, according to what they had, either cholam or varagu. In the old days, when Arokkyam first went into the street to collect the padi, people would give eight marakkaal's worth if it were varagu, and six if it were cholam. Now, whatever it was, it only came to one marakkaal each. For all their winnowing, they had earned only one bundle of varagu altogether. They were not likely to receive much more from the one street that was left. Arokkyam was engrossed in working out how they were to survive that year on two bundles of varagu alone.

She had wanted to sell the padi they were paid that year and buy silver waist chains for Mary's baby and Josep's son. But now she realized that even if she sold all that she had accumulated, padi as well as payment for winnowing, she would not have enough even for a single chain. At this time, all the grain sold at half-price. It was only at famine time that there was a big demand. There wasn't even enough to keep themselves going until such a time. She was anxious about how they were going to survive. She had been sure that she would be given plenty of grain this year.

Even last year had been better than this. They had been asked to do a certain amount of winnowing. And the padi had not been too bad. This year, though, they would only survive for three or four months on what they had been given. And how would they manage for the rest of the time? People no longer gave them food. Only one or two families still cared for them. Only a few such as Susila and Minakshi bothered to stop and talk to her.

Why were people like this? When she was little, there was more grain in Arokkyam's house than in some of the big houses. Sometimes there was grain in the store that was two or three years old, still unused. People would buy it for seed. Matured grain, it was said, sprouted best. Even so, the granary was always full. Savuri's house never knew famine. There used to be bundles and bags everywhere, leaving hardly any space for people to sit or lie down. But everything was different now.

When Arokkyam first took over the responsibility for the family, they used to receive no less than ten kalams of grain for the winnowing. Along with the padi, they might accumulate fifty, sixty kalams. She would empty it all into the granary and seal its opening with wet earth. Arokkyam's family would survive on the food they were given every day. Anyway, they could never eat all the food they collected. Nowadays she would complain on their way to collect the evening meal, or on their return, 'Who cooks any longer in the style in which women of those days made their rice and curry?' Nowadays it was only Savuri who ate the town food. Arokkyam only collected it and brought it home. She boiled a little rice. Sometimes she didn't even do that. If people whom she cared about gave her something to eat, it was enough for her.

That morning, when they returned from collecting their padi, Arokkyam had got into a terrible wrangle with Anjalam of the west street. Anjalam had maintained that she was not prepared to go even a single grain above a marakkaal. Arokkyam could not understand why the woman had complained so much. Anjalam had shouted at her and abused her; her voice had followed her nonstop.

Savuri dozed off as he sat there. Arokkyam pushed her fingers through her hair, searching for lice and squashed them.

Whatever could they do with the grain they had received this time? Even if she were to sell the entire amount, she would not be able to buy two waist chains. She could only rise to one. What would she do with a single chain? Impossible to give it to one child and ignore the other. Arokkyam decided to buy anklets instead, for both children.

***

Periyaan's granddaughter, Kosalai, brought the goats back from the day's grazing and tied them up. After that she came straight away to sit by Arokkyam. She ran inside the house, drank some water and returned. Arokkyam laughed at this and said, 'Come on, di, why don't you drink the water in your own house? There isn't anyone here even to draw the water for us.'

'I'll draw the water for you hereafter.'

'O, my princess. Just say the words, that's enough for me, amma. You don't have to do anything else, di.'

'What are you cooking today, Aayaav?'

'Hunh. We have to put whatever we can find into our stomachs, that's all. Have we got fifty kaani of land in our home town and another ten elsewhere? Can we sit about idly and eat whatever we choose?'

'If you cook varagu and then mix it well with mashed sour greens and then leave it overnight, it's delicious to eat the next day, just like plantain stem.'

'So where am I to go for sour greens these days?'

'Mary-akka used to enjoy sour greens and varagu.'

'So what am I to do about it, di?'

'O, do something.'

Their voices broke into Savuri's sleep, and he roused himself to ask, 'Hei, little one, why are you suddenly longing for sour greens as if you are a pregnant woman?'

'Aayaav, look he's calling me a pregnant woman!'

'Here, is that the way to talk to a growing girl?'

'Come here, little one, don't act so haughty.'

'Aayaav, no, no.'

'Leave her alone now.'

Kosalai clung tightly to Arokkyam's neck, whining and pretending to cry. Savuri teased her mercilessly. For some reason, he was rather more lively today. He was very unpredictable these days, falling silent suddenly, and then being unexpectedly cheerful.

'Ei, little one, why don't you marry me? The ox might be old now, but it can still plough- a fine furrow.'

'Aayaav, no, no.'

'You be quiet, di. As if I don't know all about his ploughing. The old goat!'

'Ha, ha, ha. Do you know little one, I've fathered three times!'

'Yes, yes, we know all about it. Go on, pick up your sack, we've got to go.'

'All right then, woman.'

Arokkyam and Savuri picked up the two empty sacks, a fertilizer sack and a cement sack, tucked them under their arms, and set off, shutting the hanging gate behind them. Kosalai ran off home. Arokkyam heard and accepted her command that they should return soon.

It was the time when young and old were eager to go home, hastening to drive their cattle and their goats towards their stalls. Some women were standing in the middle of the street, putting out water for the pigs. Others were pounding something or other with their wooden pestles. Some were drawing water or carrying it home. In front of the temple, young boys were seated on a wooden bench, smoking bidis and swapping cinema stories. Some were washing, pouring water over themselves from the containers standing in front of them. Young women were bathing their babies with hot water. Small children attempted to seize the pigs by their tails as they wallowed in the dirty water gathering along the streets. Some were dredging out the gutters. Some were playing pari under the lampposts. Women were washing vessels in front of their houses, getting ready to cook the evening meal. The water flowed, pitch black. Everyone was engaged in some activity or other, which to them was their work.

As Arokkyam went on ahead, Savuri crept along behind. She had left out this one street this morning because it was late and there were few people left at home. Now she prayed all the time as she walked along. 'Saint Anthony, Jesus, God.'

'Saami, it's Arokkyam.'

'Well, vannaati woman, we haven't seen you in a long time.'

'I'm here all the time, saami. Where else would I go?'

'Ei, you there.'

'Ammov?'

'Saamiyov, your vannaati has come.'

'The man of the house has gone to town. He'll be back late. Why don't you come in the morning, di?'

'Tomorrow's Friday, saami.'

'So what, are we going to cut loose from the family and leave town or what? Come and take your dues the day after.'

'What you say is true enough, saami.'

Arokkyam and Savuri went and stood at the next house. The child was ill with smallpox, they were told. Come next week, they said. Arokkyam went inside and looked at the child; told them to nurse her with care. 'Male and female had best not mingle,' she said as she came out again. Walking on to the next house she called out, 'Give her a bath with plenty of neem leaves in it.'

'Saamiyov.'

'Who is it?'

'It's me, Arokkyam. The vannaati woman.'

'As time goes by, I can't even remember who is who.'

'We are all growing old, yejamaan.'

'So what do you want?'

'It's like this, saami. We have no way of feeding ourselves. We came to ask for our-padi.'

'True. And we too must do our part. Otherwise you will say that everything was lost because of a mere trifle. Ei, little one, woman from Chidambaram.'

As if she hadn't heard him call out, Annappu immediately began working the grindstone, grinding down chillies. Then, catching sight of Arokkyam she came out, her hands full of chilli paste, and asked, 'What is it, Arokkyam?'

'Saami, I came to ask for foodstuff.'

'Why do you say that, di? They used to say that in famine times, the burglar neglected to go to the farmer and raided the vannaan instead. Was that a lie, then, Arokkyam?'

'That was in the old days, saami.'

'Wait there, I'll be back.'

'Very good, saami.'

Annappu went off to finish grinding chillies. Arokkyam and Savuri sat at one end of the front steps, in the dark. Annappu came back after finishing all her chores. She brought some cholam. She asked after Mary, Josep and Peter.

When they went and stood at the door of the next house, Arokkyam overheard what Kuppan was saying. She shrank at the words. 'Do you think the vannaati woman washes clothes as she used to in the old days? She only comes to collect the washing at the New Year, and on festival days like Pongal, Deepavali and the Eighteenth. Even then, she never uses cleansing clay, just dips the clothes in cold water and wrings them out. But she never fails to come along for her food and for her padi. She'll wear out our streets with her feet.'

'Saami.'

'Wait a bit. I'll just pour some water for the pigs.'

'Very well, saami.'

'This year there's only paddy. Even that isn't very healthy looking. How is one to survive? As time goes by, the sky and the rain-clouds recede further and further away.'

In return Arokkyam asked with keen interest about the family, about the state of their crops, and about any wedding plans which were afoot.

'Saami,' she said at the next house.

'Ammov.'

The pig was battling with the dogs. The goat called out from the backyard. Then the baby started howling. There was no light at all. There were no faces discernible in the darkness. As if they were dumbfounded, people sat down in the street, and in the darkness, ready to eat.

This woman is a real virago. She'll pick a quarrel over a single word. Would we have refused her if she had come before the lamps were lit?'

'Saamiyov.

It's the vannaati, saami.

I've come for the padi, saami.

Saamiyov.

It's the vannaati woman.'

Arokkyam and Savuri walked on, stopping at each door and carrying away what they had collected. The next house, the next one, and the next one after that. The houses which stood opposite. Some said they had already lit their lamps. Arokkyam had lost all hope of the waist chains and was intent only upon the anklets. Even that might not be possible now, she thought, as she made her way home with the gathered grain. She hurried Savuri along. She insisted that he would have to go with her into the dark once again, to collect the evening's cooked meal. Savuri followed her, his hunched back hunching even further.

Arokkyam put away the bundles and hurried out again with the vessels. She could hear what Savuri was muttering. But she went out all the same.

'Here's this woman trying to drive an ox that's disabled; wanting what's impossible. As if there's anyone out there waiting to give us great big handouts. Why can't she leave it alone instead of rushing about like this! But how am I to knock sense into her? Are these ordinary times!'

Just as Savuri had warned, they received less than enough for a single serving. Even that was a mixture of four different sorts: freshly cooked rice and leftover soured rice, cooked varagu and cholam. She gave it all to Savuri. He told her to cook some fresh rice. She replied that what they had been given was enough for him; she did not need anything. Savuri ate his meal and went to sit in the spot where he and Periyaan used to spend their evenings conversing.

***

The advent of Pongal brought all sorts of thoughts crowding into Arokkyam's mind. All the women of the town had begun to whitewash their houses for the festival. Two Pongals ago, Peter at least had been with them; now, she lamented, there was no one at all left. Before Mary married and left home, she would bring home slaked lime, and whitewash their walls as all the other family women did. Every Pongal, her hands would be covered with blisters. She had learnt to do kolam designs from Susila. She would transform the house with whitewashed walls and kolam decorations on the floor. But the eastern wall, which had stood there even during the last Pongal, had fallen down at last in the storms of Kaartikai.

'My child isn't here for Pongal.'

Arokkyam wept. For the last four Pongals, Josep had not been home. But that year, he suddenly arrived for Deepavali. In fact, that year they had all come home for Deepavali. There had been unusual and heavy rains, though. It had not at all felt like a festival. It had started raining on the day before Deepavali and had continued for the following four days. Arokkyam had covered herself with a piece of coarse sacking and gone out on her own to the main street to collect all the festival foods such as idli, paniyaaram, kozhukkattai. Savuri ate four pieces of paniyaaram made of cholam. After that he only wanted rice and curry. Everything else was left as it was.

Mary only cared for rice paniyaaram. Sahayam would only touch savoury vadai. As for Josep, he craved for cholam paniyaaram. Mary would break up all the rest of the paniyaaram together and heat them over the fire in order to keep them from going stale. They would have enough paniyaaram and rice and curry to last them for two or three days. Who would share their paniyaaram and all the rest of the food this year? Arokkyam wept at the thought that there was no one. She longed to send word to all of them and bring them all home.

Mary had come home for the birth of her baby and had stayed for two months. At that time Josep and Sahayam had come with their child to visit Mary. Josep had fallen on Arokkyam's lap, and had wept loud and long like a bull roaring. He lamented that she had grown very thin. Sahayam said the same, handing her the child. Both Mary and Diraviyaraj agreed. Arokkyam wondered for the first time if she really had lost weight to that extent. She picked up her hair and looked at it closely. Yes, it lay in white clusters. She could not believe it though. More than anything else, she gazed at Josep. How changed he was, like a young chieftain with his moustache, and his veshti and shirt. Sahayam seemed just the same as she used to be. Mary, though, had grown as thin as a dusting pole. There was some sadness deep within her as if at some profound loss. She always thought a lot about Arokkyam.

When Arokkyam suggested that Josep should come back to his home town, they all banded together. They complained about trivial things. They said the vessels came back empty every evening. They pointed out that Arokkyam and Savuri went to the thorapaadu only once a week. There was no other income they could depend upon. They had difficulty getting enough to eat. 'I can spare a little now. Just come with us and stay with the baby,' Josep suggested. Mary immediately staked her claim. 'What about my child? No, no; you must come with me.' Even Sahayam argued that it was most appropriate that Arokkyam should make her home with Josep and her. But Arokkyam would not listen to any of them. She said she would decide later. She held the two babies on her lap, and played with them saying, 'I long to see the two of you married while there is still breath left in my body.' She would only talk to the two babies as they sat on her hip or lay on her lap. She wasn't even aware of the passing of time. She was completely happy; without a care.

***

It was just then that someone came to summon her. Immediately she forgot everything else, told Savuri she was off, shut the makeshift gate and set off at a run and panting for breath, towards the house where the birth would take place.

'Here she is at last; Arokkyam has arrived.'

'She knows all about it.'

'Is there anything the vannaati doesn't know? She has seen all the women of the town through their deliveries.'

'Yes, I tell you.'

'Everything will be all right if she gives a hand.'

'Yes, she has an auspicious hand.'

'What would happen to us without this woman? We would die, that's all.'

'True, akka.'

'Because this woman is in town, we can have some courage in our hearts.'

The women stood around or sat together in clusters along the streets, in front of the house, and on its front thinnai-ledge, as Chitra lay within. Arokkyam went straight into the house, saying, 'Move aside, move aside please.' All the women looked more hopeful. Of course the child would be all right now that Arokkyam was there to see to things, give a hand. All of them stood around, watching Arokkyam keenly. They all had a certain love and respect for her. And she too was not without love and respect towards them.

Chitra was clinging to the rope which hung down from the crossbeam of the house, screaming as if her very life was leaving her. None of the words of comfort that the women spoke fell upon her ears. Her screams were loud enough to be heard all along the street. She howled out in pain. She shrieked. She was only a young girl. She screamed out in helpless anguish.

'Give her some air, for God's sake give her some air, you wretches,' Arokkyam called out. The women moved off a little, allowing her some fresh air. Then they went on talking amongst themselves. Some husbands turned up to fetch their wives away. Susila was chasing away the smaller children, stopping them from coming any nearer. Minakshi alone stayed with Arokkyam, looking after Chitra. The women of the town were anxious. Chitra was a frail girl. Anything might happen.

Even in normal times, Chitra tended to have rather large breasts. For the last two months, she had not been able to fasten the two lowest buttons of her jacket. She was swollen and heavy with milk. With difficulty, Arokkyam pulled away her jacket and sari. She began to feel the same pain and exhaustion that she had endured at the birth of her own first child, Josep, as she stripped away Chitra's petticoat. During their first childbirth, all the townswomen tired her out similarly. At that time they never seemed to think of Arokkyam as another woman and a human being. They would hit out at her. Kick her. Push her away. But Arokkyam would only laugh.

Some of the women who had been there just for the sake of amusement, now rose up to go home and to bed; looked in on Chitra for a last time and left, still chattering amongst themselves about all the complications their daughters and daughters-in-law had suffered at childbirth. Those who still sat about, continued to chat, showing no signs of weariness. They were sharing and exchanging each other's troubles and concerns. Chitra's wild screams did not stop their conversation in the least, not at any stage.

'In the end they had to cut her open.'

'The second child as well?'

'Yes, I tell you.'

'What a fate!'

'Can it happen like that? It's amazing!'

'If things go on like this, what is to happen to this world?'

'It will be destroyed, for certain.'

'Why is there such a thing as a God?'

Arokkyam was bent over Chitra, looking down on her, one hand on her chest, the other massaging her hugely domed stomach. Now she looked out at the women. Karuppaayi and Anjalam suddenly realized that she was looking at them and ended their conversation abruptly. But those who were standing beyond the doorstep and talking in the darkness continued with their gossip. Their conversation continued to be lively. It was at such opportune moments that women could gather together and talk at length.

'It turned out well in the end.'

'Was it the vannaati who saw to all of it?'

'Who else? She herself.'

'When I saw her stomach, I thought she must be carrying twins, for certain. But just look at what happened. She lost it all like blighted grain.'

'Listen to this. She carries on like that at every delivery. The whole town will foregather to her yells.'

'True.'

'Of course it's true. Who can doubt it.'

'Ayyo, that woman! She'll drop her babies without even her neighbours knowing about it.'

'But she's got a well-built body, you know. Not skin and bone like us!

'Some women have strong bodies like that.'

'My daughter-in-law is due this month. God knows what is in store for her.'

'Everything will work out to her heart's content, don't worry.'

Arokkyam had only drunk some gruel at midday. Now she was exhausted from hunger. Her head felt as if it was spinning. She wiped her face firmly. Given the way Chitra was struggling with her, Arokkyam would not recover even if she ate a vat of rice later. She would ache all over for two days. She was trying every strategy she knew to quieten the screaming girl.

'Run, run...Hurry.'

'Bring me that, not this one...I said that, there.'

'Did you buy it? Why so much? Never mind, it will be a good thing to keep, any that's left over in the house.'

'Are you done? What kept you so long? We could have held a wedding in the time you were away.'

The cock crew. Susila had lost heart. Minakshi alone was left, agreeing firmly with Arokkyam that the baby would be born soon. They had not mistaken the dates. Nor were these false pains. Chitra was only fourteen years old. Arokkyam kept saying that it was the tightness of her flesh that delayed the birth so much. It was only a year since Chitra came of age. It was Arokkyam who had washed all the polluted cloths then. Now she reminded herself that Chitra was a very young girl.

At last, as the morning star rose in the east, it happened. Arokkyam pressed down hard on Chitra's upper belly. Only then did the baby's head appear. Covering her arms with castor oil up to the elbows, like one who is performing a conjuring trick, Arokkyam very gently thrust her hands inside. Minakshi and Susila were holding down Chitra's arms and legs, one on either side. Gently and smoothly Arokkyam drew out the baby. A girl child. The umbilical cord was tight about its neck. Chitra lay back on the straw bed, in a faint. Blood gushed down her thighs like water from a broken vessel, dark purple, in clots and lumps and as liquid.

As soon as she regained consciousness, Chitra clamoured for water. Arokkyam gave her pungent rasam to drink. Chitra flung the hot rasam at Arokkyam's face, then bent down and wept. Arokkyam was stunned for a moment, but recovered herself, laughed and comforted Chitra, 'A woman who has just given birth should never cry.' She poured out a couple of glasses of rasam. She herself drank a glass, too. Arokkyam's exhaustion did not end though. She ached all over, even more than the woman who had just given birth did.

Arokkyam walked Chitra to the backyard and made her stand there without clothes, shuddering, while she poured lukewarm water all over the girl, neck downwards. As Arokkyam poured a whole cauldron of water about Chitra's waist and hips, Chitra shouted, abusing Arokkyam with all the bad words she knew. Arokkyam washed her thighs, her stomach, her hands and hair until it was clean of clots of blood. Then she gave her a clean sari to wear. When Chitra asked for water once more, Arokkyam gave her hot rasam. Then she gave her healing herbs, ground into marble shaped balls, popping them into Chitra's mouth. Even though Chitra retched and resisted, Arokkyam would not let her off. She made her take it all. Then she made her lie down and sleep for a while. She asked her to suckle the baby. Until Chitra had suckled the baby and fallen asleep at last, Arokkyam would not leave her side.

She carried away the straw that was soaked through and through with blood and urine, and threw it all away in the thorny jungle which no one entered. She washed down the whole area with cowdung. When she had bundled up all the dirty clothing, said goodbye to Susila and Minakshi, and set off for home, it was broad daylight. Women who had already heard the news and were coming to visit Chitra met her on the way. They walked on, remarking that no one but Arokkyam could have managed the delivery with such confidence and ease.

For a moment Arokkyam forgot her lack of sleep and the pain spreading through her body.

It was ten days since Pongal. Savuri sat by himself, enfolded in his strange silence. They had received more than ten sheep-heads for Pongal. They were given paniyaaram, pongal rice, everything. But Arokkyam had not cared for any of it. She had prepared meat and sent it to Mary's and Josep's households through Savuri. All of them had been insistent that she should move house to Chinnasalem. Once again, Savuri had repeated their message. Arokkyam made no reply. Savuri kept nagging at her about going away. Finally Arokkyam argued that even if they didn't move house now, they could certainly go and visit their children. Savuri agreed that they should go in a couple of days' time. Overjoyed at the prospect, Arokkyam had set off in the morning to collect the washing.

'Ammov, put out your washing!'

'Just give her the cotton rug. Nothing else. It's all thin cotton clothing. If we give them to this woman, she'll beat them to shreds on the washing stone.'

'The vannaati woman has come.'

'I haven't got anything for you. What's the matter, di? Day by day you seem to forget this street altogether.'

'If I leave you, where else will I go, saami?'

Arokkyam went to the next street. She was given only coverlets and underskirts. She tied them together and walked on from street to street.

'It's the vannati, saamiyov.'

'Saamiyov, give me your washing.'

'Put out your clothes.'

She collected a small bundle. She slung it across her shoulder. Before she could return home, the sun was high in the sky, and Savuri was sitting there in exactly the same position, without even moving. She dropped her bundle at the entrance of the house, and picked up some earth to clean her teeth. Kosalai joined her and cleaned her teeth as well. Rinsing her mouth with water and then spitting it out, Arokkyam went inside. She put some rice in a container and sent it to Savuri through Kosalai. Savuri rubbed his hands against the coverlet which he had wrapped about himself and began to eat. Kosalai sat at the threshold of the house, receiving into her own hand the rice that Arokkyam gave her. At each meal-time, without fail, Kosalai would join Arokkyam and Savuri.

In a little while, five or six policemen went past Arokkyam's house and towards Ambaayiram's backyard.

Arokkyam went cold with terror. Had Josep or Peter done anything? In the next second she thought, Perhaps in Mary's house... O Saint Anthony, she prayed. Only after they had gone further, well into the thorn jungle, did she feel her life return to her. Savuri had run and huddled against the front thinnai-ledge. He was convinced that they had come to recruit men forcibly into the army. When Savuri was a small boy, they had dragged away boys who hadn't even sprouted moustaches, boys who could not read and write, saying, 'There's a war going on in the world.' He sat there, terrified that it was all happening once more, another war had begun. He had thought about that world war from time to time in the past.

There won't be anyone left in the town to do their washing, if they take me, he would think. Besides, how would he fight, and where? He felt no hostility towards anyone; he had no enemies, personally. So why should he fight?

Some time later, the policemen returned, frog marching Thangaraju, with a can of arrack on his head. They had caught four other men, as well. After they had all gone past, the crowd that had gathered in front of Arokkyam's house began to scatter. Until that day, to Arokkyam's knowledge, no policeman had entered the colony. This must be the very first time. After this, Arokkyam realized that they were actually building a police station in the main street. All sorts of things went on in the main street. How was she to know? Had Mary or Peter been at home, they would have brought her word.

Everybody said that this was all Ponnusaami's doing. Thangaraju was one of Ramasaami's labourers. He used to sell country arrack to Chinnayya Gaunder. Now that the government had intervened and auctioned off the liquor shop, it was Ponnusaami's contention that there should be no traffic at all in illicit liquor. In the last election too, Chinnayya Gaunder's party had lost. Ponnusaami's party had been in power for two, maybe three terms. Now he picked up all sorts of people who were making trouble; he started many new things. It was because of him that this place was changing into a proper town. People respected him a lot in these parts.

Arokkyam too belonged to Ponnusaami's party. At first, he had bought half a rupee's worth of idlis for Savuri, and asked him for his vote. After that, Arokkyam too had joined the same party. Now Savuri's entire family voted in the same way. Savuri always laughed as he told the story of how Ponnusaami had treated him to idlis. And when Savuri had cast his vote at the last election, Ponnusaami had given him a pamphlet about the party.

'I only belong to the stomach-Party,' Arokkyam would say.

'I'm on my father's side.' This was Josep.

'I, too,' Mary would add.

Then Peter would chip in, 'I've belonged to that party since my birth.'

'Each person has their own party, but each person has their own stomach too; don't forget that, da, Joseppu,' Arokkyam would say.

'You're on my side, aren't you?' Josep would emphasise.

'Of course I'm on your side, what else.'

Arokkyam had voted four times now. When she was about to vote for the very first time, three men from outside the town as well as Perumaal Konaar and Ganesan Udaiyaar from their own upper caste street had visited her at home. At the next elections, outsiders as well as their own townsmen had arrived by car. At the one after that, three carloads of men had come by. As for the last election, there had been vans, cars and autorickshaws; thirteen vehicles in all. The crowds had been like a festival procession.

At the last elections, Sahayam and Mary had dragged Arokkyam along and made her vote. Peter had stuck a paper banner on to a long broomstick, and run about with the other children, shouting slogans. And Minakshi would remind her every time Arokkyam went to her house for food or clothes, 'Don't forget, di, Arokkyam. We have to keep up our reputation.'

'Ever since I was born, I have voted as the yejamaans told me.'

Chinnayyan, Ramasaami and the rest had also made their plea. 'Watch out for the tree symbol. Don't you long for shade? Well then, keep that in mind, vannaati woman.'

'Can I do other than what the yejamaans tell me?'

'That's it. Don't forget.'

'Your wish, saami.'

Ponnusaami arrived with his crowd and dispensed his party's voting slips. He declared, 'This whole area is ours.'

'Is that so?'

'Believe me.'

'Anne, after you have said so, what doubt can there be?'

'And don't forget. They'll ask you your name. You must say it as clear as a bell.'

'Very good, saami.'

'You know that woman who died, the chettichi, Amaravati. You'll say her name is yours.'

'Yes, saami.'

'Now, Mary, if they ask your name, say Kokila. If they ask what street, say, quite softly, Konaar.'

'Very well, saami.'

'Come here, Chinnasalem child. You must say you are Vellachi Pushpavalli. Don't forget. Where are Savuri and Josep?'

'They've already gone, saami.'

'I've told them what to do. They'll do it. You be careful to cast your vote properly.'

Whatever caste Savuri's family claimed to be, nobody cross-questioned them. The reason was that each party assumed that Savuri's family was voting for them. Because every time a party solicited their votes, or handed out chits or gave them money, Savuri would promise them their votes.

That whole day Sahayam and Mary had teased Arokkyam and called her 'chettichi'. After they had cast their votes, they went to Ponnusaami's house. Minakshi gave them three makaani's worth of cholam. Savuri and Josep had cast their votes under the name of gaunders and had collected ten rupees from Ponnusaami. That night Savuri got drunk on arrack.

Later, Sahayam said they should make sure their names were on the electoral lists hereafter. The people who made up the census lists had so far left out the household of the chakkili community leader, Periyaan, and Arokkyam's household. Nobody had told them about these two houses, at a distance from the main and colony streets. The enumerators had come to the very edge of the colony, and then gone away.

***

Now Arokkyam sat at her doorstep, as if in a trance. Kosalai sat down beside her, clinging to the folds of her sari.

'I feel shocked, Aayaav.'

'Yes, I tell you.'

'Won't they sell arrack hereafter, Aayaav?'

'If they stop selling arrack, the whole world will come to an end, di.'

As they sat there, Arokkyam was grooming Kosalai's hair, searching for lice. Savuri sat and dozed upon the front thinnai.

'Aren't you going to the thorapaadu, Aayaav?'

'How am I to go, di? I've still got the jitters from this morning's business. Let it be. Anyway, have we got such heaps and heaps of washing lying about, or what? All I was given from the entire town was the washing from the new baby's house.'

'When will Mary-akka come?'

'She'll come, di.'

'I think she must be cross with me.'

As the day wore on, Arokkyam set off for the main street to fetch some water. Kosalai said, 'Aayaav, let me come, too,' picked up a small pot and got ready like a grown-up woman. Arokkyam looked at her, startled, and then smiled and said, 'My, my. How... smart she is. Pretty little thing. When she grows up she'll be the talk of all eight towns.'

'Go on, Aayaav.'

'It's true, my love. When Mary was little, she was just like you. My poor child.'

They walked on towards the well. Kosalai chattered away to Arokkyam, like an adult. Arokkyam looked at Kosalai with delight, stroked the child's face and then cracked her knuckles against her own temples, by way of warding off the evil eye.

My princess

My love

My precious.

She talks exactly like Mary would.

She's exactly like Mary. O Saint Anthony.

***

Because she was desperate to get some sleep, she would decide to eat rather more than her stomach could hold. She would even go so far as to pile the food on her plate. But having mixed it all as if she were kneading dough, she would then roll balls of it and give it away to Kosalai or Savuri.

Nowadays she woke suddenly and frequently at nights. She woke up at the sound of the mice scurrying, the mice fighting, the cat calling. If the wind blew hard, it was enough to wake her. If the trees in the nearby jungle shook more than usual, the rustling of the leaves startled her like thunder. Sleep did not claim her for any length of time. She sat there like cud-chewing cow, waiting until the sun crossed the thorn jungle and hit her doorstep.

She called up her memories, as if she were drawing them up from a well, and went over all of them, one by one and again and again. But it was like staring at the sun at midday and then turning one's gaze to the earth: everything dimmed and blurred to a blackish blue; nothing stood out clearly outlined.

***

My name is kanni, virgin
Mine is the flower-chariot of pain
Mine the mud-chariot that makes no journey

Arokkyam woke up at midnight and broke into a loud lament. First she wept for Josep, then for Mary, and then again for Peter. She sang her laments in turn. She castigated the laundryman and the tailor. She wept aloud saying it was because of them that her family had scattered and fallen upon evil days. She complained about the townsfolk. At last she railed against Savuri for not allowing her to go and see Sahayam's child nor even to visit Mary. She wept until it was morning at last.

No sooner had dawn broken than Kosalai's mother arrived, ready to quarrel.

'What good will it do you to cry throughout the night? Whatever sprouts wings must take flight one day. Let it go. Stop crying. What use is it for a woman to cry like this? What can we do on our own? There is a God to look after everything.'

Our family they said
Our life they said
Our relation they claimed
Our kin they claimed
And when he fell upon the bier
They wept for his mere corpse.

When Arokkyam finished her last tearful oppari, the sun's rays were falling upon her threshold. At last she rose to her feet, wiped her face and sprinkled the street with cowdung. Savuri sat warming himself at a small fire, well wrapped in his sheet, Kosalai by his side.

***

When she gathered up the clothes bundles, ready to go to the thorapaadu, a scorpion stung her.

Arokkyam was badly shaken. There was too much bile in her body, that was why it hurt so much, she thought. From the day she was born until now, no insect or small creature had caused her distress. Now this scorpion had stung her. Savuri went so far as to hit her, finding her screams unendurable. 'Murderous chandaala!' she yelled at him. Realizing that there was no other way out, he took her along to Datchinamurti Aiyar to have some mantrams said over her. Arokkyam went on wailing:

O Jesus O Lord
Saint Anthony save me
Which slut was it that cast an evil eye on me?
My life is coming to an end
O Jesus, God

Datchinamurti Aiyar was busy at his predictions. A Gaunder family had come for a consultation. They wanted to ask him about the loss of a cow, and what kind of an omen it was. The pujari of the main street in the town only officiated at the temple; he did not know any astrology. Neither the Gaunder, nor others from such communities, came into the colony without good reason. They might come to negotiate between the town and colony panchayats, to contract field labourers, or to call people to serve their families as coolies. Otherwise they only came for divinations and predictions. There were all of three astrologers in the colony. Neither Arokkyam nor anyone else in the town knew when these people learnt to tell the future. In the same way, nobody knew when or why these three had added the title 'Aiyar' to their names. Arokkyam had heard old men refer to them as 'Aandi' boys or mendicants. They were the ones who made the offerings at the Mariamman temple of the colony. In addition, they officiated at the marriages and all other important rites that took place within the colony. These three never, ever, went on coolie labour. Every family gave them a customary padi of grain in the month of Thai. In return, these three would cast the horoscopes for each family member. And although they were closely involved with the colony families at all their rituals, auspicious and otherwise, they never entered any home. They would not even drink water at their houses.

Arokkyam had often thought to herself that this Aiyar who told everyone of the good fortune they could expect, had never done the same for her. If ever she came across him when she went to collect the washing or evening meal, she would ask him something or the other, and he would always reply with a smile.

'Saamiyov, must my family go on diminishing and ruining itself?'

'What are you saying, child? Doesn't the food from every house and the grain from every field come to you? What can you lack then?'

'Yes, all that is mine. And you know that there is nothing I can call my own. So how am I to run my family, tell me?'

At this he would laugh for five minutes, showing his orange betel-stained teeth. Arokkyam would not be able to contain her laughter, either.

'Saamiyov, I relish your words, but our stomachs are not full. It is not like the old days, saami.'

'Why, how is it these days, amma?'

'It's as if I'm holding on to a dog's tail, saami.'

'True enough, amma.'

'So then, how am I to manage my family, saami?'

'Yours is the most important family in the town. Who can doubt it?'

'O, go on, saami. Well, tell me what are we to think of our times?'

'They are fine, di, my child.'

Aiyar would go off, still laughing. She would find she had forgotten to ask about the fortunes of her family members. Every time she saw him she would tell herself that she was busy just then, but that one day she would sit with him and ask at leisure. But later she would forget all about it.

Now he sent away the Gaunder family, having told them the direction in which the cow had gone, and turned to look at Arokkyam who was clutching her left hand and moaning.

Arokkyam sat down respectfully, some distance away, and extended only the middle finger of her left hand towards

Aiyar. The finger was stiff, slightly swollen, perspiring. It had reddened somewhat. He asked for a single stick to be brought from the coconut-palm broom used for sweeping the street. Then mumbling a mantram to himself, he passed it right over the scorpion bite and then tapped the floor with it. Again and again he stroked it over the scorpion bite mumbling his mantram, and again and again he tapped it against the floor. Arokkyam had tied Savuri's waist chain about her elbow. Aiyar told her to untie it. He smeared some sacred ash over the scorpion bite. He smeared some on her forehead. Savuri bent low, offering his forehead, too. Arokkyam felt the pain gradually lessen. She began to feel her strength return to her. She wiped away the gathering sweat.

'Where was the scorpion, then?'

'It's all because of this chandaalan,' she shouted in exasperation. Savuri was silent. Aiyar began preparing his betel leaf. He took his time to spread the lime over the leaf, and to put it into his mouth. At last he began to munch it, making loud slurping noises like a pig.

'Well, di, amma. How are things going on with you? Didn't you go to the thorapaadu today?'

'Don't ask me all that, saami, everything is upside down.'

'Why do you say that?'

'Nowadays, they never fill our rice vessel, saami. We get no good from winnowing in the fields or on the threshing floors as we used to. We are offered no charities at weddings or on good days. Who looks out for the vannaan either in their life or in their death? They see to their own rituals themselves. The way the townsfolk are behaving, it will be no surprise if we end up as beggars. Time passes by somehow. What use are we any more, saami.'

Arokkyam spoke of her fate and wept. In the old days she would say, 'A vannaan's life is a prince's life.' Now all that had been turned on its head. For an instant she thought of the laundryman and the tailor. She forgot utterly the pain of the scorpion's sting. Her whole body seemed to be on fire. Only at the spot where the scorpion had stung her, she felt a throbbing. Although Aiyar had spoken his charms and mantrams, the throbbing would continue until twenty-four hours had passed from the instant of the scorpion bite. She had seen with her own eyes the torment suffered by people after a scorpion bite. She herself had comforted them at such times.

Now she wondered about asking Datchinamurti Aiyar's advice. She thought to herself, O God, even if the whole family should be ruined, don't let it come to this! Josep, Sahayam and Mary had all asked them to wind up their affairs here and move to Chinnasalem. Now she wondered, in her anxiety about such a move, and how to do it, should she ask Datchinamurti to cast a spell on the village on her behalf? Then she herself decided against such a move.

If ever a woman from the colony was in distress, she would come to the Aiyar and ask for a prediction. Aiyar would not reject her in any way, but would ask her to name a month, a day of the week, a flower or a species of grain. Or he would ask her to extend any finger she chose. From such things he would make a divination. He would find out everything from his clients themselves, and then interpret these things in his own words. Most people then felt an overwhelming contentment and peace.

Tell me what you can see in the name of Josep.

How does the name Mary look to you, saami?

Just look at Sahayam as well, saami.

And while you are about it, just check Diraviyaraj as well, saami.

And what about Peter-lad, saami. Please have a look and tell me that.

'At least the elder one got himself a girl. But what is to happen to this small fellow who is wandering at will, no one knows where, having given up his father and mother? We have had no more news of him. If only we are granted Saint Anthony's grace, that will be enough.'

'Look at this woman, insisting on what she can't have!'

'Leave her alone, Savuri. Let it be. Peter has four more months to go. After that he will return by himself. If he had stayed here, there would have been funeral rites in your family. This way, the critical period will be over by the time he returns. Jupiter comes into the family position in six. That is, within sixty days.'

'O my God! Would it have come to a funeral? He is not in any danger of life, is he, saami?'

'No, no. He will be well.'

'Will he definitely come home?'

'Remember what I say. See if he doesn't turn up on the dot, exactly in two months.'

'Very good saami. Of course your words will come true, saami. It's enough if I see him once with my own eyes, saami.'

For some time Arokkyam sobbed quietly. Savuri kept pestering her to indicate that he wanted to go home. She would not turn to look at him, but stood bowed, staring at the ground and weeping. Aiyar began to feel embarrassed and chided her gently, trying to calm her down. Taking no notice of

Savuri's muttering, she asked once more, 'Just look at the name Anthonisaami, please saami.'

'Whose name is that?'

'That's your vannaan Josep's son, sir.'

'Oho, not bad! When was he born?'

'O, four or five years have passed now. And Mary has a baby girl now. Her name is Velangkanni. The baby stays with my daughter.'

'Both children will be well.'

'Will they be all right? Will they survive and stand firm on this earth, saami?'

'They will be well. I see no danger to them.'

Two other clients arrived to have their futures told. Aiyar told Arokkyam to come again when she was free, and turned his attention to the newcomers.

'Give us permission, saami.'

'Goodbye, Arokkyam, come again, amma. Don't lose heart. That's all I want to say to you.'

'You keep us in your mind. That way I will have courage. We can only trust you. If we leave this town, where can we go, saami?'

By the time Arokkyam and Savuri returned home, the sun was sinking and the shadows lengthening eastwards. Savuri was in a hurry. It was Amaavaasai, the night of the new moon. They would surely be cooking rice and vegetable curry in every house. They would observe fasts in every family until the evening's feasting. On days such as this, Arokkyam would set out twice to collect food. As soon as they reached home, Savuri asked her to go out with the vessels. When she refused to go, he went out himself. Even though they returned with empty vessels nearly every day, he thought that today, a special day, he would receive plenty. He picked up the vessels and rushed.

Sometimes Savuri would say, 'If I don't put a couple of mouthfuls of the town food in my mouth, my tongue tends to feel dead in my head.'

'Out of a hundred, it might be one hand that is stretched out to us. That is the hand for us. That is our God.'

It was only when he pushed past her, returning with his vessels full of rice and curry, that Arokkyam returned to herself. Her face was puffed up. Where she had lain down, the floor was soaked with tears and had risen up in a small circle, as wide as a rupee coin. It was a cowdung floor which swelled up even if slightly damp. Besides, it had not been paved recently, and was uneven.

'What is the matter, madam, had a good sleep in broad daylight, did you?'

'You can't bear the thought, can you? Your eyes should burn in the fire!'

'They've been burning long enough, di.'

'Look at his cheek, the old goat!'

Savuri gave Arokkyam's thigh a playful pinch as she sat there, her legs stretched out. She called out in feigned anger, and slapped his face with the back of her hand saying, 'You murderous chandaala, you wretch, look how you've drawn blood! Will you come to any good? May your hand become cancerous.'

'Oho, you fancy yourself as a young lass, do you?' Savuri burst out laughing.

✼

To Arokkyam it appears as if years have rolled past like a single day. Nowadays Arokkyam will doze a little in the early hours of the night. After that her eyes won't hold on to that sleep any more. She will sit at her darkened threshold, her legs outstretched. She will stare wide-eyed into the night, as if she herself were entering deeper and deeper into that darkness. Her eyes have grown accustomed to penetrating the dark. She will be aware of a strange sensation at the very thought of sinking her eyes into the night. She will hear the occasional beat of birds' wings in the night sky, like wind whistling through a pipe. The incessant sound of insects in the jungle and the lone cry of a woman from the colony will sound faintly in her ears, smudged out by the resonances of the wind. Arokkyam will begin to cry, letting the sound of her weeping mingle with the dark.

She will think of her birth, her childhood, her marriage to Savuri, and the large numbers of people in the house at that time. Gradually her thoughts will turn into a long chant of troubles and torment because of her children and all her relations. She will speak in turn of the townsfolk's changing behaviour over the years, of Josep going away with Sahayam, Mary's marriage, of Peter running away with Arumugam, of each one having chosen a different path, of the stars working against them as Aiyar had said. And she will weep. Hidden behind night's windows she will try to relive it all as song, as story and performance, in some inward voice unknown to anyone else.

She will try to separate and give voice to every single thing that happened in her life, right up to the previous day. But by daylight they will come out as formless and broken dreams, impossible to recount or even to contain within sound waves. In the morning her face will look swollen. Her throat will sound harsh and rasping. In the daylight she will clear her throat and spit again and again. Her anger will not be spent until the day darkens once again.

Everything good in my life has gone
My strength has left me
I have no possessions left
Everything has vanished like smoke, like magic
I had no complaints
I lacked for nothing
I was like a tamarind tree
Like a queen
Like a princess
I was as well off as a vellachi
I was as proud as the Maniyakkaaran's daughter
Now I'm only a shit-stained stone
What if the vannaan disappears in the shit pond?
Who cares if he is washed away by the river?
I followed like a shadow
I placed my feet in the footprints of the townsfolk
Now you have blinded me, God

Why did you create me as the downtrodden of the downtrodden, Saint Anthony?
I did not fear life I did not fear death I did not even fear the grave
But now I am frightened of people
Now I have no one to ask after me
There is no one to exchange a word with me
There is no shade where I can shelter
I have passed every hour of every day as if I were walking through fire
I was secure in the belief that where there are sheep, there must be a shepherd
Who is there today to belch after feasting
We all belch with fasting
As if we are yawning
How can one who is fasting shut her eyes at night?

Arokkyam usually looked forward to harvest time and counted the months and days until it happened. She would calculate the income that she could expect. She would reflect upon all the things she needed to do with the money.

As soon as one year ended, she would look forward to the next summer's income. She would think back upon the year that had passed, what she had received, and what she had not. It would all come out right in the following year; it must come out right, she would hope and believe. From the time she was carrying Mary, and had gone from street to street to collect their padi, every year she had calculated and hoped.

When will it rain?

When will they sow the seed?

Not many days now for the weeding to begin
How many months until the harvest?

Not many. They will go past like a single day. Arokkyam would begin to count the days and months as each summer came to an end, and wait like a pregnant woman. On a festival day, Arokkyam could never go home at a reasonable hour. At such times she was like a hired animal attached to the yoke. There was no accounting how long she would be. Even if she did not agree with everything the patrons wanted her to say, she would still go to each street and shout out the words enthusiastically, as if she were beating a drum. When she was sent again and again to invite important personages, she would move mechanically, like a creature who is no longer sensitive to the pain of living.

She would need to decorate the temple cart with banners. If they were torn anywhere, she would have to patch them up. As soon as people started tying on amulets in preparation for the festival, on that very day she would begin any repairs necessary to the cart's screen. Savuri's father had been sent by the town elders to fetch it from Kumbakonam. Arokkyam had patched it over the years; she had held it together. Gradually, as festivals came and went, year by year, the screen had grown longer and longer. Every year Arokkyam had brought different coloured materials and made human figures which she had attached on to the screen and draperies.

At festival times, Arokkyam could never refuse small children. Even the smallest ones, who had just gained enough strength to walk, would pester her. They would call out to her, demanding that she go to their house first. They would even quarrel with her about it. If those who summoned her were already quarrelling amongst themselves, then Arokkyam would be in a sorry state. Children from both families would then turn on her. If they had forgotten to give her their clothes in good time, they would bring them along and pursue her from street to street. They would even come to her house.

'Ei, vannaati woman, have you forgotten my clothes?'

'Wash them so that they are sparkling white.'

'Use plenty of cleansing clay.'

'Don't just dip them in water and rinse them out.'

'You must do my clothes first of all.'

'Ei, vannaati!'

'Arokkyam!'

'Vannaati woman!'

'Vannaati!'

When Arokkyam was young and healthy, as sprightly as a bird, her legs never stood still. She used to walk the furlong's length from the colony to her house in a single breath. Even if she had to walk it a hundred times a day, she would run like a child, never getting tired.

There were six streets altogether in the colony. Although they were called streets, they weren't streets as such. There was no neat order into which the houses fitted. Each house had its network of mazes.

The width of each street was barely six feet. Even that space was like the track of a snake. During the rainy season, walking along the streets was comparable to walking through muddy fields. One's foot would tingle at the very thought of setting out. There would be a smell of dampness and rot everywhere. The walls would be damp to the height of three feet at least, and would look pale grey with a faint green of mould spreading over that. In the narrow space, perhaps only a foot in depth, between the back walls of the houses, pigs would stand for days on end in the water, their bristles standing out as stiff as spears. And they would grunt together and at each other. Ammakkai plants would have sprouted greenly and spread all over the roofs so that they looked like groundnut fields.

If you had to go from one house to another, you had to lift your foot carefully each time you took a step, rather like labourers putting down sheaves of dry branches and leaves in order to step across wet fields. At each step, the mosquitos breeding there would rise up in a cloud, whining in chorus. In front of each house, a piece of sacking would have been laid for people to wipe their muddy feet.

During the monsoons, the walls of some of the houses would become waterlogged and start to lean over, or they might just collapse. If the cross rafts or the bamboo canes holding the sides of the house should have decayed, then they would break down with the weight of the wet thatched roof. The centre of the house would then lie open to the skies. People whose roofs or walls fell in, normally sought shelter in their own or in their neighbours' cowsheds. They would tether the cows and goats to the tree roots outside. The animals would shift from one leg to another in the wet earth, calling out, the hair upon their hides stiff with the cold.

People would go about covering themselves with pieces of sacking or plaited coconut-palm covers known as semmangkudu against the rain. If seen from a distance, they looked like some new and threatening beings of darkness.

The colony was built upon a hollow ground which leaned slightly to one side. Arokkyam's house was at an even lower level. But it sloped sufficiently to allow the water to drain away. The upper caste street was not on high ground as such, but certainly it was higher than the rest of the town. The water flowed down from the upper caste street to the distance of three or four furlongs before it reached the colony. The mingled water flowed past Arokkyam's house, coloured yellow and green, and finally reached the stream.

Whether it was the rainy season or the summer, gypsies, basket makers, snake catchers and anyone else who wished could seek shelter under the shade of the banyan tree which stood as boundary mark between the caste streets and the colony. And they could stay as long as they wished.

***

But now it was a long time since Arokkyam's eyes had seen anything in its natural state. Everything seemed to spread and spread like smoke. She stared rather more penetratingly than usual. Yet she could not see clearly. At the same time, whatever she wished most to forget would return to her mind, harder and, repeatedly, like a ball that bounces back with greater force when beaten into the ground.

To Arokkyam it seemed that time would hardly move. But then, she too had changed. In the old days she would go round and round the colony streets for no good reason. She had had a lot of work then. Now her legs itched and troubled her. Where could she go? And she did not have that much to do.

Certainly the town was no longer what it used to be. First of all there was the bus. Then they opened new schools, three different ones. Tea stalls began serving idlis, then whole meals. A tar road was laid. Gravel was heaped in the colony. A water tap and trough appeared at the crossroads. Some of the houses began to acquire running water and taps.

Suddenly, all along the streets there were posters in different colours; notices. Some of these were even pasted against the walls of houses. In the common ground in front of the temple were four or five flagpoles belonging to different parties. There were so many new things besides all this. She had only begun to be aware of these things when they had all become commonplace.

Just a week ago she had at last seen the man who kept the laundry shop. He looked strange to her, a dark, heavy man who looked like a slaughterer of goats. He sported a moustache which looked as if it would terrify even the owner of it. He walked at a rapid pace, as if he were taking part in a race. Arokkyam did not like him in the least. She said that his eyes bulged like hen's eggs. Later she saw the tailor as well. This fellow was light-complexioned. Everything about him—his figure, his bearing, his moustache, his manner—gave her the impression that he would bully and intimidate others.

Mary had already warned her. But she was able at last to confirm these things directly, to see it all with her own eyes. She described their appearance to everyone she knew, laughing about it again and again.

Yes, everything was upside down. In her youth, the fields were green even during the summer. The crops would continue to grow. Now, though, there was no greenness to be seen. There were only casuarina trees and cotton plants everywhere. People had stopped growing food crops and grains. Even the higher ground was given over to casuarina and cotton. Only those who had small holdings of a quarter or a half-acre were growing food grains.

It was those who lived on coolie labour whose position was worst of all. In the old days, in order to stave off starvation, they would go off towards Chidambaram to reap paddy. But nowadays, the men had gone off on their own as far as Madras and Bangalore. There were only old men and young children and women left in the town. The men came back only for important occasions. Some had left with their families.

In former times there would be famine only if the rains failed. There had been a severe famine the year that Mary was born. But although everyone in the town had left for different parts of the country in order to escape the famine, Arokkyam had not budged. She had enough in her store to tide the family over. She had even given some of it away, free of cost, to those in need. Some of it she had given on loan; some of it she had sold.

But now things were different. Although the jungle had been cleared and turned into cultivable land, there was no food to be had. Everywhere you looked, in all directions, there were only casuarina and eucalyptus trees to be seen. Meanwhile there was an everlasting famine in the town.

People left in the town always wandered about with a bidi or a cigarette in their hands. They looked stylish with their cropped hair and their shirts. Women nowadays wore fashionable saris and jackets. They sold the small quantity of grain left in the bottom of their jars and bought tickets for the cinema. They stood together, or sat, posing prettily, at the water-tap, or at street corners, or at each others' front doors, exchanging cinema stories. Some even showed off the songs they had picked up.

When Savuri came home after his second visit to Josep, he had cropped his hair. He said he didn't care any more to shake his hair loose, and to tie it back like a woman. At that time, Arokkyam could scarcely bear to look at him. But now, she had to admit, cropped hair certainly suited him.

As for Josep, as soon as he went to Chinnasalem, he cut his hair. Arokkyam had been shocked when she heard he had grown a moustache. At first she wept at the news, as if her whole family had been ruined. She railed against Sahayam, who, she believed, was behind everything that was changing and spoiling the family. What had she not instigated? Everything had changed because of her. When Arokkyam first entered this house as a daughter-in-law, all the vessels and jars were earthenware. Even the small dishes that were handled daily were earthenware. Just a slip of the hand and they smashed into fragments. All the vessels in which they cooked the curry or boiled the rice were made of clay. Four or five large jars were arranged in a corner, one on top of the other, all of clay, in which they stored different kinds of grain.

After Arokkyam took on the responsibilities of the household, she first bought a single aluminium vessel for collecting the evening meal. Then Savuri had made her buy another in which they could carry food to the thorapaadu. Some time later, if the earthenware platters broke, she started replacing them with aluminium ones. Soon neither Josep nor Mary would touch food that was served to them on earthenware plates. When Peter was born, she bought a brass drinking vessel. And it went from there to tumblers, chembus and so on.

Sahayam arrived. Everything changed. From plates, tumblers, chembus, serving spoons and strainers, everything in her possession was in stainless steel, even the pots for collecting water and cooking rice.

Was there a single house in the town these days, which used earthenware vessels? Everything was of brass or steel. And women's clothes had changed too. Their saris slid down from their waists, flowing like water. Their entire bodies were outlined. And their jackets were the same. Transparent, like muslin. Showing off their armpits. Arokkyam could no longer tie up anything into her sari. In the old days she would have five or six little bundles about her waist, containing dal, chillies, snacks, rice and other grains.

Nowadays the question frequently struck her, Have I actually arrived in a new town? There wasn't the old spirit here anymore. She would mourn that those feelings of affection and compassion had been lost forever.

This was certainly not the town it used to be. There was no special significance or love attached to its soil. In the old days, even the ashes in the cremation ground had a special flavour and aroma about it.

In those days, the barber who served the upper castes would not cut the hair of the paraya community. The paraya people were not allowed to enter the tea-stalls. They would sit under the tamarind or neem tree and cut their own hair. Then somehow or other, Kandan had taught himself that skill. He began to earn a good income, too. Nowadays, nobody took the blindest bit of notice of Kandan. Only old men and young children went to him. He used to bring all the hair clippings and dump them into the thorn jungle in front of Savuri's house. Now there were several barber shops in town run by newcomers who did not differentiate between their clients.

Nowadays, if Arokkyam had one of her headaches, she would send Kosalai to buy her some tea. Someone in the main street had suggested this to her one day, when she was suffering terribly from an unbearable headache. Since then, every time she had a headache, she would send for tea and drink it. In the old days, though, if ever she had a headache, she would make a hot pepper rasam and take an inhalation. Headache and fever would disappear, instantly.

All the firmness and strength in her body seemed to have disappeared somewhere suddenly. Nowadays her body was just bone, and loose wrinkled skin like an empty bag that had collapsed on itself. She had aged, it seemed, overnight—even her hair was as white as if it had been whitewashed. When she had no work to do, she would look at her own body. It had never— not even at famine times—been thin and weak and wrinkled. Her body had been as sturdy as a man's. She would stroke her own arms. She would stretch out her legs, touch them, run her fingers along them. It is as if this body is another person's, she would sigh to herself. Sometimes she would be confused, seized with doubt. How tightly-fleshed she used to be, firm as a kozhukattai. These very legs used to go round and about the colony many times a day, like a dog. They used to fly to the thorapaadu.

Arokkyam had begun to mutter to herself, these days. She had plenty of time to sit and think. There was no need for her to speak to anyone else. She did actually have the time now to hold long conversations. Only, nobody else seemed to have the time any longer, to talk to her. Old woman Arokkyam. Arokkyam kizhavi. Now she was known to everyone as kizhavi. First it was the children and youths who called her that. Now they all called out that name. When she first heard it, she wept for a whole week.

In those days, after she had washed the clothes at the thorapaadu, and laid them out to dry, she would never lie down and rest, however tired she might be. She would walk round the fields. How green the fields were, by the side of the river!

As she walked along the edge of a field she would be aware of a special kind of smell. It was a mixed smell, containing many things. There was a greenness as far as the eye could reach. All sorts of crops flourished there. They all gave out their different scents at the same time, when the wind blew over the fields. Then there was the scent of wild flowers. But the scent of the earth overwhelmed everything else.

As she came past each field, she would help herself fearlessly to brinjal, beans, lady's fingers and tomatoes. When she came back to the thorapaadu, she would sometimes have a week's supply of vegetables and greens in her lap. Nobody questioned her. If, by some chance, they did so, she knew exactly how to answer them. She would claim some kind of relationship with each of them. If a woman accosted her, she would speak lovingly to her, addressing her as akka, atthai, daughter. If it were a man, she would say, 'Whose fields did I go to, after all? If I can't help myself at my aandai's fields, who can?' If small children accosted her, she would be delighted. She would tell them how much their mothers had suffered at their birth. How she herself had washed out the dirtied clothes, most willingly. How their weddings should not take place without her assistance. How significant she was. She would persuade them to fetch her the vegetables and greens themselves.

***

Now she sat under the tree sometimes, drawing lines upon the earth with her fingers. Her fingers were not patient enough to create any clear shapes. They would go round and round the same few lines, deeper and deeper in the same places. Her tears would fall directly upon the earth. Her mouth would move quietly as she muttered to herself.

The time is evil, Kali kaalam
Fields are now just wasteland
What am I but a destitute
Not for me the bridal celebration.

Nowadays, Arokkyam dreamt a great deal. Last night, though, she had not been thinking about anything. She had not been weeping, either. In a state of numbness, she had spread out the end piece of her sari in the pathway in front of her house, and lain down.

...Two men walk past, carrying the corpse of a young child, in a hammock suspended between bamboo poles, which they bear on their shoulders. A single drum sounds ahead of them, but no sign of the drummer. From the hammock, drops of blood keep falling. It is broad daylight. The sound of weeping is heard. Many voices, male and female. Children raise their voices and wail loudly. But nobody can be seen. A drop of blood falling from the corpse splashes straight into her eye. Unable to bear its sting, she calls out aloud, and wakes up...

She could not tell what time it was. The entire town had disappeared into the darkness, like a corpse buried in its grave. Not even the morning star shone in the sky. She broke out in a sweat and began to tremble. She could not sleep again, after that. She thought about her dream. It was a bad omen. She believed something bad was about to happen, either to her family, or to the town. Perhaps the entire town would be ruined.

Only if a great famine were to come about would this town be entirely ruined. But if such a famine were to happen, what would people do? Would they roam the country in order to fill their stomachs? Was it only by wandering from place to place that one was able to fill one's belly? If that were the case, what would happen to her, Arokkyam wondered.

> From the time I dropped on this earth as a piece of flesh,
> until the day of my death, my stomach rules me like a God
> All my life's struggle is to fill the belly
> Like a donkey I carried bundle after bundle
> Night and day I carried my vessel and stood in front of every house
> It's all in aid of this stomach
> All the abuse and bad words thrown at me
> It's all for this belly
> It's like an ocean that can never be filled
> Even if I struggle all my life, I'll never fill it
> All that I have suffered was for its sake
> But my belly is never full
> For fifty years I've walked between thorapaadu and colony to earn my food
> What am I but my stomach
> The world is its stomach
> O Saint Anthony.

Arokkyam awoke and sat up. She felt as if she was going to faint. She went indoors to drink some water. Inside the house, just next to the broken-down granary, the sun's rays were falling in pools of light. Somehow she would need to repair the thatching, she thought to herself. She came out and stood in the pathway. There were no signs of people about. Once again she sat down at the front steps.

Suddenly she thought that although she had attended so many deaths, there might be no one at her side when she herself died. The people from the colony would not be there at her funeral. Her father-in-law, her mother-in-law, and so many of her relatives had died. Not a single person from the colony had attended. They might ask about it the next day, if they met her on the street. They might give her something towards the ritual expenses. That was all. Arokkyam suddenly began to fear her own death. Yes, it would be a forlorn death. The thought shook her that though she had a husband, though she had borne children, a woman who had spent her entire life in service of the whole village must die a lonely death. She took no heed of the passing of time, nor of the tears falling from her eyes.

It was evening. Savuri came home. Silently he sat down in the street, in front of the house. He made no reply to the questions that Arokkyam put to him. His eyes were fixed on the thorn jungle. In a little while, Kosalai drove home her goats, tethered them up, and then came directly to Arokkyam and sat on her lap. After a while, she went inside, looking for water, and began to cry. She complained that there wasn't any water there. It was only then that Arokkyam realized this. She pacified Kosalai, handed her a small aluminium pot, and set off with her, picking up the larger water pot.

Savuri stayed there, watching the darkness descend like a smoke screen.

Although it had just been a few years, for Arokkyam it was as if a long, long time had gone by, disappearing like a single day. But even the river waters, as they flow, will leave some imprints on both shores.

Arokkyam was playing 'five stones', with Kosalai sitting opposite her. Arokkyam caught the small round stones between her knuckles, palms turned downwards. She scattered the stones, flung one stone up, picked up another, and then caught the first between her knuckles as it came flying down. Kosalai watched eagerly and laughed as Arokkyam flung each stone in the air and caught it again between her knuckles.

Savuri scolded. 'The present famine is bad enough, tugging at one's loincloth. Is it necessary to invite even more starvation with your game of five stones?'

'So what? Leave it alone. There's nothing more to complain about that.'

The older men in the town would always scold women who played five stones. They would say that they were inviting a more severe famine. But young girls always played anyway, to pass the time during the less busy months of Thai, Purattaasi and Aippasi. Of course, nobody played during the sowing season. Savuri had just come back from a journey; he was irritable because he was tired, Arokkyam said to herself.

Kosalai set off with her goats. Arokkyam too prepared to go to the thorapaadu. Savuri grumbled. 'Where are the clothes? Why should we go?'

'Let's take the four or five pieces there are and go in good time. The goddess only blesses those who walk.' She dragged Savuri along with her and set off for the stream. It was several days since they had been to the thorapaadu. Suddenly she longed to see it again.

'What did Thambi say? How is that girl? And the little boy? Did you go to Mary's house? What is her news? How is the child keeping? How is the work going?'

Because there was no work just then, she had sent Savuri to visit all of them. All the way along now, she interrogated him mercilessly. He did answer to the best of his ability, but was irritated by the way she probed for every detail.

Arokkyam soaked the ten or twenty sheets that had collected during the week, in one of the containers which held the cleansing clay. The water was very low. They would have to dredge and deepen the water-hole. The little water that was left had begun to smell stale. Savuri deepened the hole by scooping out some of the earth with his hands, but left the earth there. He beat out the clothes, and then went to sit under the bushes. It was burning hot. It felt warm even in the shade.

Arokkyam rinsed out all the clothes, wrung them out, and laid them out to dry, one by one. She strewed some dry sand upon each, so that they would not fly away in the wind. The skin of her back felt as if it were peeling off in the sun, so she poured some water over herself and came to sit beside Savuri. The shadows from the plants lengthened steadily. She was sweating profusely when she came under the shade.

'What, sleeping again?'

'What else is one to do?'

'How can you sleep like this, as soon as you shut your eyes?'

'You too should put your head down for a while. You never seem to sleep, even at night.'

'How much can I sleep? The nights are too long these days.'

'Maybe.'

'This year people seem bent on growing such heavy loads of cotton; what will they do for food?'

'They are all going for cash crops. There's no rain, so they'll use the cotton money to buy food and eat good rice.'

'My God! Truly, is it cotton in every household?'

'Why don't you go and do the same, di, in the lands your father left you?'

'Yes, just wait for it. Keep on waiting for my father to fill your arms up to the elbow. You can't even tell the difference between good shit and bad shit. And you won't wash your mouth out after you've eaten shit. You'll go to ruin, you wait and see. Born in a stinking, low family! Do you think my father was a beggar in a loincloth? Do you know how I was cherished, like a rich man's child? It's after I came to your house that I lost it all. I live out my life like a widowed wretch. If my parents had seen me like this, they would have dropped dead where they stood.'

***

Arokkyam and Savuri talked anxiously about the sowing that was happening about them that year, and the noticeable lack of grains and food crops. This way, there would be no labour required for winnowing. Savuri, who usually found it hard to decide for himself, suggested they should go away to Josep.

'In a few days, you are going to burst your arse and die for lack of food, di.'

'So what do you think we should do?'

'There is no one to stop us from leaving. Do we have land, that we need worry about disposing of it? If there is no work here, there are other towns. Wherever it is, we still have to make a living by washing clothes.'

'What did the boy say?'

They've all been saying for a while that we should go to them.'

'So you think we should go away.'

'What else? Do you think we should stay here to starve and die?'

'You were always ready to be a wandering beggar. It's enough for you to hold out your hands at a couple of houses. You'll fill your stomach. As soon as you shut your eyes, you'll fall asleep. But what is my fate to be? O Saint Anthony!'

'As time goes on, I can't even see properly. In this, I won't listen to you. Even Sahayam agrees. We'll go there in a month or two. What have we got here, after all? A couple of carrying vessels, four or five pots, storage jars. That's all. And a few poles from the fallen roof. We should tell Ambaayiram to take that, and just go.'

Savuri had changed too. He no longer waited to hear what Arokkyam would say. He managed on his own. Sometimes he would stay silent. If he was irritated he would bark like a dog. In earlier times Arokkyam would take no account of Savuri.

She would do all her work by herself. But now, there was hardly any work that came to them. Savuri could not answer her endless questions. Some years ago, it was never possible for them to meet and converse quietly during the day. They were always too busy. But now, because they sat opposite each other and saw each other constantly, and talked, there were always quarrels. Even ordinary words turned into a battle. Savuri was not the old Savuri. He became angry over trivial things. He scolded Arokkyam. He even took his fist to her face.

'It's true. How can people like us who earn our living by wandering about belong to any one place? Who are our kinsfolk? We belong to all towns. All people are ours. Those who have land, property and inherited wealth stay rooted in one place. But is that our destiny? We live on what others give us. We are a humble people.'

Arokkyam buried her face in her knees and wept. Savuri was digging at the earth with his fingers, and pushing it about. But she continued to weep aloud as if she were dying. She thought to herself that everything Savuri had said was true. There was nothing that belonged to her. Those she had believed in had forsaken her. She lamented that even the children she had borne had gone their separate ways, taking care of their own needs with their own hands. She imagined crowds of people moving towards the tailor and the laundryman, clothes in hand, like shadows shifting and disappearing. At one time she had been useful in a crucial and significant way. But now, all the events of yesterday seemed like a game that is over. They remained only as memories of a dream. She was like a puppet that is relegated to the backyard.

'But this is my town. These are my people. This street, this temple, the trees and plants and creepers surrounding the town are all mine. The goats and cattle, this stream and this thorapaadu—everything belongs to me. Each child born here is my child. I thought that they were born in order to give me my life. All this time I believed that because they were born I had a reason to live.' She wept as she said this. Savuri sat by her side, silent. All about her, by the side of the stream, trees and bushes, the sand, the rocks and the sky were all burning in the sun.

The town and its stream without Arokkyam; the thorapaadu where she did not wash clothes; the empty pool surrounded by wild arali bushes and rocks. She could not even begin to imagine it.

Like a crazy woman, she pulled away the soft clay from the arali roots and ate it in lumps. How fine it tasted. It was cool and sweet-smelling, like fresh milk. As if she were gazing into the sun for the first time she looked about her with desire, bent over, until everything grew dim, filled with darkness, turned deep blue and disappeared at last. Am I really going to leave all this, she asked herself. She had become an old woman now. Her head was as white as if it had been covered with a white cloth. Her eyes were losing their ability to see. Their liveliness had faded. Even the thorapaadu had rejected her. The sides of the pool had fallen in, and it was half its former size. She had become like useless rubbish to everyone and everything. Were they all waiting for a new person with fresh blood and muscle and bone, another Arokkyam altogether?

'Even if this place becomes a garden overrun by dogs, a park full of ghosts, a town watched over by a demon, even if all these people leave it and go away, this stream is not going to abandon me and go away. Nobody is going to claim these rocks as theirs and carry them away. So why should I worry? Whose companionship do I need? Why should I leave my home to look after a handspan-sized stomach? We'll see who is more important, my stomach or myself. O Saint Anthony! Has it been just yesterday and today, just a couple of days? It is here in this thorapaadu that my corpse will lie.'

Arokkyam kept on lamenting. The sun was beginning to sink. She left the shade and went to sit in a more sunny spot. Her eyes swept over the entire stream. She looked at every tree and bush; she heard the buzzing and humming of the bees. A flight of birds went past, like a flag being lowered. Savuri came up and called to her, 'Why are you squatting there in the sun? Get up, let's go home.' He stood stock-still beside her. He seemed like a very old man. Even his voice was not the same any longer.

'My blood has gone numb. The warmth of the sun feels good to me. There isn't any healthy blood in my body. If there were, I wouldn't feel so cold. My body won't move. No strength in it. What are we going to do at home, after all? Are you dashing off to some foreign parts?

Just see how beautifully the sun glows as it sinks. It's disappearing into the mountains like liquid fire, look.

Half the people in this town fell into my hands the moment they were born.

Is there a single person in this town whose pollution I have not cleaned?

Is there a woman who has not had trouble suckling her child?

Is there a woman whose umbilical cord I have not cut and buried?

It was I who answered the summons of each person in this town; I worked for them all.'

Savuri went and collected all the clothes, folded them up, tied them into a bundle which he slung on to his back, and then returned to stand by her.

'Get up, get up. It's getting late. I've got a cold.'

'I have picked up after them. Urine, faeces and blood. I've washed all those clothes. I've carried them against my breast. Like a dog I've stood guard at their houses and worked for them. Is there a woman who has not tried to abort a child? I've known neither night nor day. Have I not decorated the marriage pandal? Have I not made the bier? The rat goes to its hole and the snake to its pit, as they say.

The girl who went to keep guard
Over the millet-field
Became the victim they sacrificed.

Everything has disappeared and gone, like smoke. When I look at the sun, I even forget that I'm alive. My mind and heart feel as if they have burnt out, like charcoal. They feel like stagnant water. But look, when night falls, it's as if the floods have just come. As if they have just sprouted wings. But then, I see the moon, and I can't remember any more that I'm alive. Then I'm terrified even by the croaking of a frog. I feel broken in mind and heart.'

Savuri scolded again. Arokkyam started, stood up and began to walk home with him. Savuri carried the bundle and hastened forward, moving in his own hunched fashion.

'I dreamt a dream last night. The night showed me something which it has never done before. At first it seemed that I was standing in the thorapaadu. After a while, I didn't know where I was. Then suddenly there was a huge banyan tree, full of flowers and fruit that were both raw and ripe. When I looked a second time, though, the tree was bare and withered. Again it looked green, covered with fruit and flowers. Once again it was as dry and bare as dried fish. And then, all of a sudden I woke up. I can't walk on. Shall we sit down a little?'

But Savuri would not listen to her pleas, and walked on until they reached home. As soon as they got there, Kosalai came running up to hug Arokkyam. She wanted to know if Arokkyam had been picking kilaa berries. Savuri went inside for a drink of water. Kosalai ran to fetch some for Arokkyam, too. Then Savuri said he would go and deliver the clean clothes, and was just about to set off. But he stopped at the sight of Paramasivam coming towards them.

'Yes, sir...' began Arokkyam.

'Saami?'

'Our Ponnamma has gone.'

'How did it happen, saami?'

'O Saint Anthony!'

Last night she had dreamed that dream. When she rose up from bed, there had been a lizard lying dead beside her pillow. When a crow had screamed along the right side of the thorapaadu, she had thought there would be news of a death somewhere. She was comforted that no relation of hers had died. She thanked Saint Anthony of Melnariappanur for it.

'The years caught up with her. So she is lost to us. I need to take the material for the shroud, and the vaaykkarisi. Look at all the expenses we'll have to bear.'

'How can you say such a thing, saami. It's you who have to do it. However highly we are born, it is only the two lengths of cloth that make our shroud that is important in the end.'

'Make a start, da, Savuri.'

'Saami.'

'Even if it is night time, we must make a start now, if we are to be there in time.'

'Very good, saami.'

'Be careful. Saint Anthony!' Arokkyam did not say anything further.

When she saw Savuri with his hunched back, setting off wearily, wrapped in his veshti, the tears came welling up. In a little while, the men disappeared as black shadows. The street was empty and dark. Darkness filled everything between the sky and the earth. Even as she stood watching, the darkness descended about her. There were no stars in the sky. When would the moon appear? Like a child sheltering at its mother's breast, the town was lost in the darkness.

After the corpse was carried out, Savuri would return home, bringing not less than ten rupees in money, and a couple of marakkaal of paddy. He would receive a veshti and sari for his services at the funeral rites. She thought to herself that she should send those things to Mary.

She took up the bundles and walked on to the street, empty of feeling, and delivered them. Then she went on to Minakshi's house. For some reason, that day, many people stopped in the street and asked after her. They remarked that she had lost weight. Some asked her whether she still lived there, and had not gone away to stay with her son or daughter. We see Savuri quite frequently, but never you, why is that, they chided her. You must come often, they insisted, you must wash our clothes well. Arokkyam replied to all this, and came home to find Susai sitting at the doorstep, waiting.

***

As soon as she heard the news, she fell on the floor again and again, like a ball that is being beaten back. She cried out in pain. She burst into laments. She seized hold of Susai and started running, fast as a snake.

> You were not of an age to die
> It was not yet time for you to fall
> You were not old enough to perish
> You should not have died this day.

Arokkyam sped like the wind, unmindful of the darkness, the thorns and stones. She hit herself on the chest. She slapped her own face. She beat her thighs. Her feet thrust forward and kicked the earth as she ran. She screamed out so loud that the darkness itself seemed to reverberate.

> The day I hoped you would tie a tali became the day of your fire.
> I should have made a kolam of turmeric
> And invited you to the bridal bed
> But I make instead this kolam of charcoal
> And send you away upon your bier.

Mary had washed the clothes in the thorapaadu and laid them out to dry, She sat in the shade of a tree nearby, lulling the child to sleep upon her outstretched legs. The sun stood high in the sky. It was very hot. Diraviyaraj came to sit by them and to play with the child. He loved Mary dearly. He would never raise his voice against her. After the child was born, he would never allow her to go out to work.

When the sun began to sink, they tied up the clothes in bundles. Mary picked up the child and stood up. Diraviyaraj climbed into the thorapaadu where they had just washed the clothes and began to bathe. Suddenly he felt a sharp sting in his leg. Thinking it might be a thorn, he put his hand down and searched in the water. He felt another sting in the thumb of his right hand. Then something long slithered past his foot. Instantly he pulled his hand out and looked at it. Everything became clear. He could see it now, sinking into the water, and then lifting its head nearer the shore.

He said nothing to Mary, picked up the bundles to hasten home, but began to feel faint along the way. He couldn't go on. It was then that he told Mary what had happened. Then he collapsed. Mary ran for help.

People hastened to carry him to the physician's house. Mary fainted there and could remember nothing.

'Had it been just the one bite, we might have seen to it. But he's been bitten twice!' exclaimed Pacchamuttu Servai. He was the one who dispensed medicines in these parts. He had medicines for snakebite as well as for insect, scorpion and bee stings. People were always healed. Now he ground up some leaves, poured the juice into Diraviyaraj's mouth and forced him to swallow it. He went in search of buttermilk, and made Diraviyaraj eat some rice mixed into it. He made him bite into green chillies. Diraviyaraj ate twenty chillies. Then he laid his head down and died.

***

After the eighth and the sixteenth day rituals and obsequies, Arokkyam brought Mary away, carrying the child herself. She had gone there the instant that she heard about Diraviyaraj's death, and she returned only after all the rites were over. However much Diraviyaraj's uncle pleaded, she would not leave Mary on her own, nor would she move to that town herself.

It seemed as if row after row of people came and went. They spoke endlessly to her. Yet nothing would stop Arokkyam's tears. Nobody could console her. Minakshi came. Susila spent half a day with her. Kosalai had not left them since Mary arrived. She took care of the little one.

Still death won't take me, what shall I do?
My child stands here, utterly ruined
Ruler of all things, Great Lord! O God, Saint Anthony!
His bright forehead has become dust now
His darkened brows are eaten by white ants
His shining eyes have gone to the termites.

'Nothing is in our own hands, Arokkyam.'

'Even he who rules the land is laid to rest and covered with earth.'

'You might cry for ever, but the dead never return.'

'How can we die along with them?'

'Just look, di. Because you are weeping, she is in tears too. The mother of a young child shouldn't cry. It's what you yourself have said to the whole town.' It was Minakshi who said this, taking Arokkyam's hands in her own.

'It is you who have always said, "A goat that is sold makes a profit, a goat that dies does not." Think that way, and let go.'

'It's the story of roasting a crab, and then leaving a fox to stand guard,' Arokkyam said, beating herself on head and chest. She kept pouring sand on her head. She looked almost as if she were possessed by a devil, her hair dishevelled and uncombed. She stopped her tears only when someone spoke to her really sharply, and let them flow again after the visitor had gone.

Saint Anthony has no eyes
Saint Anthony is dead, he is a corpse
With the yellow cord about your neck
Your lap full of flowers
You will walk in front of kings
In Vaikundam, amma
With your tali about your neck
Your hair covered in flowers
In front of Dhananjaya himself
You'll walk alone, amma
Oh, I was short of a small length of rope!
I thought you would carry me to my grave
I hoped you would bury me and cover me with earth
But instead you filled your own mouth with dust
My dear boy
How did your soul leave us? Why?
Yama's binding cord which attached your neck,
Should have summoned me instead
Now you cannot throw even a word to us
How you would call me Athai as if you were giving me
  your life
When will I hear that voice again
He was a mere child who had not forgotten his mother's
  milk
And I had to throw the earth upon him
How could you do this to me, Saint Anthony
In the heavy rains of Senji

Neither did my sari get wet
Nor did my small jewels grow dim
But with these endless tears
My clothes are soaked through
And my jewels lose their brightness.

Since Arokkyam brought Mary away, Ambaayiram and his wife talked to them at all times and tried to distract them. They did their best to speak words of comfort. But Arokkyam would listen to no one.

The blue-necked pigeon builds its nest for him
The peacock descends and calls out for him
The little dove will build her nest for him
The young peacock will call out to him
The money he gave the Dasi
Would build a golden palace
The money he gave the koothi
Would raise a whole gopuram.

'However close husband and wife are, is it possible for them to die together? Are we born together, after all?'

'Say it's all destiny, fate, and let it go.'

'Even when our parents die, after we have had a bath, we eat. We have to go on living our lives.'

'We can't all of us be performers, you used to say, there have to be spectators too. Have you forgotten that, amma?'

O Jesus, O God
Saint Anthony has no eyes
Saint Anthony is dead
Saint Anthony is a corpse. He has been dead a long time.

My one desire and dream has gone, burnt out like charcoal
You've disappeared like someone we dreamed about.
Now there is no laughter left in me.
Coriander, jasmine, alii
Should flower upon the climbing vine
There were no flowers upon the vine
For there were flowers inside you.
Had they not flowered in your entrails
But filled the pond with their blooms
Crores would have come to look at them
There were no flowers in the pond
For they flowered in your intestines.
And you left us, wrapped in your shroud.

Savuri tied the clothes which had arrived during the past week into a big bundle, slung it across his back and set off. He walked on with his bundle on his bent back, his eyes fixed to the ground. Arokkyam began to get ready.

'Amma, let me come too.'

'Listen to me. I don't want you to come. Aren't you like my own mother?'

'If I'm on my own, I feel as if I'm in a wasteland, Amma.'

'If you come with me, what will you do in all this heat in that wild place, saami? Hereafter, I only want to look after you. You give me faith. You are my whole life, child.'

'Let me just come and sit with you, Amma, and amuse myself. What will I do here without you? I must just lie here like a corpse.'

'Then lock the door behind you and come, child.'

'Yes, Amma.'

Arokkyam took the little one on her hip and set off, hiding her tears from Mary. She made haste, caught up with Savuri and walked with him. Mary came up and joined them. Because the earth was hard and firm, they made no footprints for the wind to destroy. As they walked on, further and further, they looked like dark shadows. Then those shadows too diminished. They appeared as mere dots. Gradually the dots merged. A single dot. Even that diminished, disappeared. Like the bare sky, the horizon stretched, endless. Then just space. Empty space.

Glossary

Aandai	: landlord and master of bonded labourers
Annan	: elder brother
Anne	: elder brother (vocative form, used when addressing him)
Athai	: mother's elder sister
Aayaav	: grandmother (vocative form, used when addressing her)
Ayya	: Sir; also father or (paternal) grandfather.
bhajanai	: devotional songs sung in chorus
chandaalan	: cruel person (term of abuse)
chembu	: small vessel used for carrying water, milk etc.
cheri	: slum
Chettiyar	: member of a community of shopkeepers
Chinnamma	: mother's younger sister
Chithappa	: father's younger brother, or husband of mother's younger sister
Dasi	: courtesan
Dhananjaya	: conqueror of riches: one of Arjuna's titles
dritti	: drishti, the evil eye
Durai	: lord; a word used formerly to refer to a European
etram	: a wooden structure, with a long pole and a device used to lift water from a well for irrigation

Gaunder	: member of a community of landowners
kaani	: a land measure
kaavadi	: wooden frame, decorated with peacock feathers, carried in a procession by devotees of the god Murugan
kalams	: measure of paddy
kali kaalam	: the last yuga, a time in which evil and atrocities abound
kamalai	: a device for lifting water from a well, using a large vessel with a bellows attached to the bottom
kanji	: starchy water, drained from cooking rice or millet; gruel
Kaarthikai	: the eighth month of the Tamil calendar, mid Nov-mid December
kazhividai	: an antidote to neutralize a spell
koil	: a small bird, well known for its sweet song
kolam	: decorative designs drawn on the floor
koothi	: dancer / actor
koothu	: folk play, based on puranic or epic episodes
kozhukattai	: steamed rice-flour balls, with savoury or sweet filling
Kubera	: a very wealthy man
kundaan	: a vessel with a wide mouth and a tapering bottom
Kuratti	: a woman of the kurava community, commonly called gypsies
kuzhambu	: a pungent sauce made of vegetables or meat
maakaani	: land measure
Maama	: uncle, mother's brother; also father-in-law
mai	: black pigment, applied to the edges of the eyes
Maniyakkaaran	: village official who collects revenues, etc.

mantrams	: sacred words and sounds; also charms and incantations
marakaal	: a measure of paddy or other grain
melam	: two-sided drum
Mount Meru	: fabled mountain containing the cities of the gods and celestial spirits
muram	: winnowing tray
Naataamai	: leader of the village community
oppari	: lament for the dead
paappaati	: colloquial name for a Brahmin woman
paavaadai	: long skirt, worn by young girls; also an underskirt worn under a sari
padi	: yearly allowance of grain paid to members of service castes
padinettu	: 18; festival on the eighteenth day of the month of Aadi
Paraya	: formerly 'untouchable' community of labourers
Pillayaar	: another name for Ganesha, the elephant-headed god
Pongal	: harvest festival, celebrated on the first day of the month of Thai
pottu	: auspicious mark made on the forehead
Prahalada	: son of Hiranyakasipu, well known for his devotion to Vishnu for whose sake he withstood the tortures inflicted on him by his father, until he was rescued by Vishnu himself, in the form of Narasimha
raachoru	: evening meal which was begged for by the washerman and his family, from the families they served

Rakshasi	: female rakshasa, a powerful, mischievous or evil spirit
Saami	: a form of address for holy men, priests, but also for God
Saamiyaar	: priest
Talayaari	: village watchman
tali	: gold chain or yellow cord with pendants, tied around a bride's neck; symbol of marriage
tavasam	: additional payment for specific pieces of work undertaken on occassions
Thambi	: younger brother
thamru-melam	: a kind of two-sided drum
thappattai	: small one-headed drum, hung from the shoulder and struck with a pair of sticks
thinnai	: raised platform at the entrance of a house, for resting, etc.
thomban	: basket weaver
thondi Kattai	: plank tied to the necks of cattle
vaaykkarisi	: the uncooked rice sprinkled on to a dead woman's mouth
Vaikundam	: heaven of Vishnu
Vannaan	: washerman (some washermen, but not others, belong to an untouchable community)
Vannaatti	: female vannaan
varagu	: a kind of millet
Vellachi	: a woman of the vellala (landowning) community
vetti	: cloth worn by men, wrapped around the waist
Yejamaan	: landowner, master

More from Tamil Literature:

D. Jayakanthan's short stories depict the life of common people in Tamil Nadu in the middle of the 20th century and reflect his progressive thinking. Selected and translated by the author's daughter, these stories sensitively explore situations in the lives of both the marginalized and the middle class and comprise some of the best of his writing.

Every story of this collection has its own beauty and each presents a different lesson for the world.

—Reviews

These stories – all of them written in the 1960s – reinforces Jayakanthan's relevance in Tamil literature, this time among a different readership.

—Scroll.in

Each story in this collection delves into the depths of the human psyche, revealing the hidden strengths ordinary people find within themselves when faced with extraordinary circumstances. Portraying courage, vulnerability and humanity in its many dimensions, The Heroine And Other Stories *reminds us of the richness of our regional literatures, presents highlights from the oeuvre of a master storyteller and holds up a mirror to ourselves.*

—The Statesman

More from Dalit Literature:

Samboli! means *echcharike* in Kannada—'*Be careful*!'

Samboli! This expression is not from yesterday or the day before; it is centuries old.

Manu, the ancient lawgiver, decreed that people belonging to any of the untouchable castes of this country had to hold a pole with jingling bells tied to one end and pound it on the ground at every step to make a sound—jal-jal. They had to call out, '*Samboli! Samboli!*' This is the Samboli pole warning others of their presence. They were to walk only on conservancy lanes and not on the main streets and only around noon when their shadow was tucked under their feet and would not pollute people of the upper castes by falling on them.

Samboli, by extension, could imply '*Beware!*' in the present context of Dalit uprisings. It could also be a clarion call for Dalits to fight for their humanity.

Samboli! *set in Kathriguppe village, Karnataka, goes beyond caste, and winding through resentments and humiliations, describes Dalit activist groups, where he (Lakshman) finds apartheid of a different kind and exploitation of Dalits by their own communities.*

—The Hindu